UNBREAKABLE

Books by Nancy Mehl

Inescapable
Unbreakable

UNBREAKABLE

NANCY MEHL

BETHANY HOUSE PUBLISHERS

a division of Baker Publishing Group
Minneapolis, Minnesota

© 2013 by Nancy Mehl

Published by Bethany House Publishers
11400 Hampshire Avenue South
Bloomington, Minnesota 55438
www.bethanyhouse.com

Bethany House Publishers is a division of
Baker Publishing Group, Grand Rapids, Michigan

Printed in the United States of America

Library of Congress Cataloging-in-Publication Data
Mehl, Nancy.
    Unbreakable / Nancy Mehl.
        p. cm. — (Road to kingdom ; bk. Two)
    Summary: "As her Mennonite town is shaken by strange incidents and outright attacks on its residents, Hope Kaufmann is forced to question all she knows and believes"—Provided by publisher.
        ISBN 978-0-7642-0928-4 (pbk.)
        1. Kansas—Fiction. 2. Mennonites—Fiction. 3. Violent crimes—Fiction. 4. Nonviolence—Fiction. 5. Ambivalence—Fiction. I. Title.
    PS3613.E4254U53 2013
    813'.6—dc23   2012035219

Scripture references are from the King James Version of the Bible.

Cover design by Paul Higdon

Cover photography by Mike Habermann Photography, LLC

Author represented by Benrey Literary, LLC

13 14 15 16 17 18 19   7 6 5 4 3 2 1

To my dear friend and second mother, Kay Curless. You were the embodiment of true friendship. I pray God will help me follow your incredible example. I love you, beautiful girl.

CHAPTER 1

"All I know, Hope, is that you folks in Kingdom need to be careful." Flo neatly folded the piece of fabric I'd just purchased, running her thin fingers along the edge to create a sharp crease. "Two nights ago a church near Haddam burned to the ground. Someone is targeting houses of worship in this part of Kansas, and they don't care about the denomination. They just hate Christians."

"But Kingdom is so remote. Besides, when anyone new comes around, we know it. There's only one road into town." My words sounded reassuring, but the rash of recent attacks left me feeling troubled. Was our small Mennonite town in danger? The idea that someone was harming people because of their love for God was hard for me to understand.

"Just yesterday someone tried to run a car off the road outside of town," Flo said. "Folks had a Christian bumper sticker. That was all it took to get them into trouble."

"Was anyone hurt?"

She shrugged. "No. I think they were just being hassled,

but the car was forced off the road. Something like that could do a lot of damage to anyone in a buggy."

"Well, no one's bothered us. Except for a few teenagers who drive past our buggies too fast and spook our horses, most people are very respectful."

Flo sighed. "I know you think Kingdom is special, that you have some kind of unique protection, but whoever is behind these acts of violence has shown nothing but ruthlessness. I'm afraid you're sitting ducks out there, without a way to get help if you need it."

She put my purchases into bags and handed them to me. "Please, even if you think I'm being paranoid, speak to your church leaders. Urge them to take precautions." Flo, usually a rather dour person, gave me a rare smile. "You're very special to me, Hope. I don't want anything to happen to you."

I smiled back, rattled by her words of caution yet appreciative of her concern. Flo and I were as different as night and day, but over the years we'd developed a deep friendship.

"What is your church doing to protect itself?" I asked.

She shook her head, causing the dyed red hair she'd piled on top to tilt to the side. "We don't take chances. Mixing faith with firearms doesn't bother us a bit. We've also added an armed security guard to watch the building at night when it's empty."

"I guess we'll just have to trust in God's ability to keep us safe. We don't believe in using violence for any reason."

Flo's right eyebrow shot up. "Not even if you have to defend your lives?"

I stared at her, not quite certain how to answer. "As far as I know," I said finally, "we've never had to face a situation like that. But our leaders would never bend our beliefs to suit our circumstances."

"Forgive me for saying this," Flo said, shaking her head, "but that sounds pretty stubborn."

"We're not trying to be stubborn," I said slowly, "but we are firm in our convictions. Changing our faith isn't an option."

"I'm trying to understand," Flo insisted, "but what if the life of someone you loved was at stake? Would you alter your doctrine to protect them?"

I shook my head and picked up my bags. "All I can do is hope I never have to find out."

She frowned. "Look, I realize you're trying to live by your teachings, but I can't accept the notion that God wants you to stand by and let evil men do whatever they want." She reached out and grabbed my arm, her eyes bright with worry. "Please don't blow this off, Hope. The Methodist church on the other side of town was vandalized one night while a young man was inside cleaning the carpet. He was beaten up pretty badly."

I patted her hand. "All right, Flo. I'll talk to one of our elders when I return."

"Do you swear?" Her grip on my arm tightened.

I laughed. "Now you've asked me to do something else I can't do. Mennonites aren't supposed take oaths."

Flo's eyes narrowed as she stared at me. "Following a bunch of rules doesn't make you any closer to God, Hope. You know that, right?"

"Yes, I do. But at the same time, why should I swear to something when I've already told you I will do as you asked? Isn't my word good enough?"

Her expression relaxed as she thought this over. "Yes, your word is good enough." She finally let me go. "But next time you come in, I'm going to make sure you followed through."

She came around the side of the counter, and I put my packages down to give her a hug. "You're such a blessing to me. Thank you for caring so much."

Most people would probably think we looked odd. An older woman with bright red hair and overdone makeup hugging a plain Mennonite girl wearing a long dress covered with a white apron and a white prayer cap on her head. But Flo and I had moved beyond seeing our differences.

She let me go and swiped at her eyes with the back of her hand. "You take care of yourself, and I'll see you next month."

"I will. Do you think that royal blue fabric I ordered will be in by then?"

She snapped her fingers. "Well, for pity's sake, I forgot all about that. It came in yesterday. You wait here a minute, and I'll fetch it."

I smiled. "Thank you. My friend Lizzie and her new husband are fixing up a house they bought on the edge of town. I want to present them with a quilt before they're completely moved in."

Flo chuckled. "Well, if anyone can put it together quickly, it's you. You're the fastest quilter I've ever known."

"I suppose it's a good talent to possess, since I run a quilt shop." We laughed, and Flo went into her back room to get the material. She'd just left when I heard the bell over the front door ring.

I turned around and stared at the young woman who'd walked into the store. She was beautiful, with long blond hair that fell softly over her shoulders. She wore jeans and a white cotton blouse with stitching around the neck. Bright red toenails peeked out from her sandals. The color on her toes matched her long fingernails. A little makeup accented her thick, dark lashes and large blue eyes. I'd seen beautiful women before, but there was something about this girl that caught my attention. I couldn't put my finger on exactly what it was.

I glanced down at my ordinary dress and my hands with short, unadorned nails. Quilting and sewing forced me to keep my fingernails trimmed, and none of the women in my church ever painted their nails. For just a moment, I found myself wondering what it would feel like to be the attractive girl who seemed so happy and carefree.

The fleeting thought left me feeling confused. I grabbed my packages and hurried toward the door. As I passed the young woman, we locked eyes. Hers widened with surprise as she took in my dress and prayer covering. For a brief second I felt a flush of embarrassment, but it quickly turned to remorse. I wasn't ashamed of God, nor was I ashamed of my Mennonite heritage. I made sure my packages were secure and nearly ran from the store.

As the door closed behind me, I looked back and saw the girl watching me. At the same time I saw my reflection in the glass door. A girl from the world and a girl from a small Mennonite town both stared back at me. The reason for my overreaction became clear. We could have been twins. The look on her face told me she'd seen the same thing.

I turned and walked quickly toward my buggy. Daisy, my horse, waited patiently outside, tied to a post near the door.

I put my sacks in the storage box under the buggy seat and then unhitched her. "You are such a good girl," I said, rubbing her velvety muzzle with my hand. She whinnied softly, and I climbed up into the carriage. "It's time to go home, Daisy." I wanted to glance back toward the store to see if the blond woman was still watching me, but instead I kept my eyes focused on my beloved horse. Lightly flicking the reins, we headed into the street.

As Daisy and I turned toward Kingdom, the odd reaction I'd had to the woman in the store dissipated quickly. I had no interest in living a different life. Although several of my friends had left Kingdom at one time or another, I'd never had the urge. I'd been born and raised in the small town, and I loved it. Papa and Mama settled there not long before she became pregnant with me. Then Mama died after a severe asthma attack when I was only seven, and Papa had become both mother and father to me. I loved him with my whole heart. He would spend the rest of his life in Kingdom, and unless God told me to leave, I would do the same.

I loosened my hold on the reins and relaxed back into the seat. I could nod off to sleep and Daisy would deliver us safely home without any direction from me. We'd been making this monthly trip for a long time, and I was confident she knew the way as well as I did.

The main road toward Kingdom was never very busy. The few vehicles that used the road stayed pretty close to Washington, and after a few miles away from the city, I might not see any cars or trucks at all before taking the turnoff to our town. Most of the traffic I dealt with was in Washington itself. Although a lot of the people who lived there were accustomed to their Mennonite neighbors, some liked to drive slowly by us, gawking and sometimes even taking pictures.

I took a deep breath, filling myself with the sweetness of spring air and deep, rich earth. The wheat in the field was tall enough to wave in the gentle wind, and I was struck once again by the beauty of Kansas.

From the other direction, I saw a buggy coming my way. As it approached, I recognized John Lapp, one of the elders who'd left our church over a disagreement with our pastor and some of the other elders. Kingdom was moving away from a works-based culture. Our pastor taught lessons about the importance of grace and reminded us that Christ had set us free from works of the law. This didn't sit well with some of our members, John Lapp being one of the most vocal opponents.

I nodded to him as he drove past, and he returned my gesture with a barely discernible tip of his head. John's wife, Frances, had been ill for quite some time, and John was constantly driving to Washington for medicines and supplies she needed.

As Daisy's hooves clip-clopped down the dirt road that led home, the buggy swaying gently in time with her gait, I thought back to my conversation with Flo. I couldn't help but wonder who could be behind these vicious attacks. Perhaps I should take her warning seriously, but this kind of hate was beyond my experience. Kingdom was a special place, safe and protected from the outside world. The idea that we were in danger seemed extremely unlikely. However, since I'd told Flo I'd mention something to our leaders about the situation, I began to rehearse exactly what I would say.

Suddenly, the roar of an engine shook me from my contemplation. I automatically pulled Daisy as far to the edge of the road as I could. Glancing in my side mirror, I saw a bright red truck barreling down the dirt road, a wave of dust behind it. Only seconds before it reached us, I realized with horror that it was aimed straight for the back of my buggy. Not knowing what else to do, I pulled tightly on the reins, guiding Daisy into the ditch.

The truck roared past us, spraying us with gravel. The buggy teetered for a moment and then began to tip over on its side. Before it fell, I was able to jump into the ditch, landing hard on my hands and knees. Daisy staggered under the weight of the stricken buggy.

I forced myself to my feet even though my right arm hurt and my knee burned where it had been badly scraped. I stumbled over as quickly as I could to unhook Daisy from her harness, pushing against the weight of the buggy so she wouldn't topple. Breaking a leg could put her life in jeopardy, and I had no intention of losing her. I cried out as I struggled to release her from her restraints, holding tightly on to the reins. Fear caused her to fight me. She whinnied and tried to rear up, and I held on for dear life while trying to calm her. Once I finally got the harness off and she was freed from the buggy, she began to quiet down.

I took the reins and started to lead her back up to the road. Over her soft, frightened nickering I heard the sound of an idling engine.

Surely the driver of the pickup was coming back to help me, regretting his carelessness. Thankfully, his lack of judgment hadn't cost us more than a damaged buggy, a nervous horse, and a few cuts and scrapes. I hoped he was aware that the situation could have been much worse and that he would be more careful when approaching any other buggies he might encounter on this road.

Although it was difficult to make anything out through all the dust, I could see the red truck had turned around and was parked about fifty yards down the road with its motor racing. As Daisy and I strained to make it up the incline, I waved at him. I hoped he would help me get the buggy out of the ditch and back to Kingdom. One wheel had come completely off, and the axle was bent. There was no way I could drive it home.

It wasn't until he put his vehicle into gear again and stepped on the accelerator that I became aware that he wasn't concerned about my condition. This man had another interest entirely. Whoever was driving that truck was purposely trying to scare me!

I pulled hard on the reins and attempted to lead a terrified and confused Daisy as far back into the ditch as possible before the truck reached us. I prayed as loudly as I could, calling on God for help. The truck's engine seemed to grow louder. Was he already upon us? I turned quickly to look and saw another truck racing down the road, coming from the other direction. It was headed straight for the red truck. A few feet before they would have collided, the red truck slowed to a stop and the blue truck slammed on its brakes. Then it sat in front of the other vehicle as if trying to provoke a confrontation. The driver of the red truck gunned his motor several times, challenging his adversary to respond. I watched this frightening encounter, unable to do anything to protect myself and Daisy. There was nowhere to run. Nowhere to hide.

Finally, the driver of the red truck threw it into reverse and, with engine whining, sped down the road backwards. Then it spun around and drove away, leaving a huge trail of dust and gravel in its wake. The blue truck waited a few moments and then began to back up slowly toward Daisy and me. I trembled with fear, putting my hand to my chest as my heart pounded wildly. Was this driver a threat as well? Flo's warning about a car being forced off the road near Washington rang loudly in my head.

The only thing I could think of to protect myself was to kneel down in the ditch, put my hands over my head, and plead for God's intervention. It was a desperate prayer borne out of terror. I held Daisy's reins tightly in my trembling hands, wondering if I should let her go. Perhaps she could run away to safety. She whinnied and stomped as the sound of the truck's engine grew closer. Then everything became quiet. Afraid to look up, I simply waited with my eyes closed.

A man's voice cut through the silence. "Hope, are you all right?"

I raised my head and found myself staring into Jonathon Wiese's bright blue eyes. Jonathon, a fairly new resident of Kingdom, wasn't trying to hurt me. He'd just rescued me. His face was pinched with concern.

"Oh, Jonathon. That . . . that truck . . ."

"Was out to get you." He held out his hand and I stood up, almost losing my balance. He reached out to catch me. "Hold on tight," he said as he lifted me out of the ditch and onto the road. He took the reins from my hands and led Daisy up, talking gently to her, trying to calm her rattled nerves.

"You . . . you may have just saved my life," I said, attempting to catch my breath. "I was so frightened." Without any warning, I suddenly felt dizzy and cried out. Jonathon grabbed me before I fell. Then he picked me up in his arms and carried me toward his truck. I laid my head against his muscular chest, feeling safe and protected. He held me as if I weighed almost nothing.

"You stay here and rest," he said as he gently put me onto his passenger seat. "I'm going back to get Daisy."

Jonathon was a young man who had moved to our community with his family almost a year ago. He'd immediately started sharing his ideas about reforming Kingdom Mennonite Church. His opinions excited me as much as they upset my father. Right now, that argument didn't seem the least bit important. I was just grateful God had sent him to help me.

Realizing that something felt amiss, I put my hand on the top of my head and discovered that I'd not only lost my prayer covering, most of my hair had been tugged out of its bun. Since my hair is usually anchored in place by a ribbon and several pins, it takes a lot to pull it out of place. I tried to gather my disheveled locks back together, but it was useless. My ribbon was gone, and the few pins I had left weren't enough to hold my long hair. Not knowing what else to do, I yanked out the rest of the remaining pins and stuck them in my pocket. Then I ran my hands through my hair to make it less unkempt. Having Jonathon see me like this made me want to cry.

A few minutes later, Jonathon stuck his head inside the cab. His eyes widened as he gazed at me.

"I . . . I'm sorry," I said, trying to push the thick tresses back from my face. "My hair must have gotten snagged on a branch or something. My prayer covering is gone . . . and my ribbon . . ."

Jonathon reached over and took my hand. I winced in pain. "Oh, Hope. I'm so sorry. You've been injured."

I shook my head, trying not to cry. "I'm fine, really. I was just so scared." Compassion shone in his eyes. "I'm sorry you have to see me like this." I touched my hair with my other hand. "I must look just . . . awful."

Jonathon didn't say anything for a moment, and I realized with surprise that he was blushing. "Hope, you look like an angel. You're so beautiful. . . ." He cleared his throat and the red in his cheeks deepened. "I'm sorry. I have no right to say something like that."

I wiped my eyes with my apron, which probably wasn't a good idea since it was torn and dirty. I wanted to act like a proper Mennonite lady, but something inside me jumped for joy to know that he thought I was beautiful. Of course, acknowledging his compliment wasn't appropriate, so I quickly changed the subject.

"Is . . . is Daisy all right?"

"She's fine, but your carriage is in bad shape. There's no way you'll be able to drive it back to town. I'm afraid we'll have to leave both the buggy and Daisy here for a while because my truck is full of lumber. I can't carry anything."

The idea of deserting Daisy filled me with despair. What if the man in the red truck returned? What would happen to her? Even if he didn't come back, she was frightened. I couldn't just drive away and leave her alone. The tears I'd been fighting reappeared, and I shook my head. "No. I'll ride her home."

Jonathon looked at me with concern. "I don't think that's a good idea. You seem pretty shaken."

He was right, but I had no choice. Daisy was my friend and she needed me. I dabbed at my eyes again and forced myself to laugh lightly. "I'm sorry. I was a little rattled at first, but I'm calm now. Daisy and I will be fine." I climbed out of the truck and stood in the road, trying to put on a brave face. Unfortunately, the dust stirred up by the dueling trucks was still swirling in the air. A spasm of coughing hit me. The warmth of the afternoon added to my discomfort.

"Are you okay?" he asked as he patted me on the back.

All I could do was hold up my hand to signal I was fine. I must not have been clear enough because Jonathon continued slapping me lightly. Finally I caught my breath.

"I really should be getting back," I said in a raspy voice. "Papa is probably wondering where I am."

He stopped thumping me. "If you insist on riding Daisy home, I'm going to follow behind you."

I felt myself flush, embarrassed by his attention.

I shook my head. "You don't need to do that."

"I don't want to hear another word about it, Hope. Some of the things I've heard in Clay Center chilled me to the bone. Maybe the person driving that truck was just trying to annoy you, but what if it was more than that? What if he was purposely trying to hit you? I won't leave you on this road alone."

"All right. I appreciate it." I put my hand over my eyes, trying to shield them from the sun, which was shining brightly, nearly blinding me. "My friend in Washington believes everyone in Kingdom needs to be very careful right now. Until this happened, I have to admit I thought her warning didn't really apply to us. But now . . ."

Jonathon's expression was grim. "A lot of folks in town are aware of the problem, but like you, I guess we've felt it wasn't a direct threat to us. I have to wonder if what just happened proves we were wrong." He ran his hand through his thick, dark hair. "If I hadn't offered to pick up supplies for Noah, I wouldn't have been here and . . ."

Even though we were standing in the sun, a shiver ran down my spine. Neither one of us needed to finish his thought. We both knew that the results could have been more serious.

"I-I guess we'd better head home." I started to walk toward Daisy, who was standing nearby.

"Are you sure about this, Sister Kauffman? You still look a little pale."

I smiled. "I'm afraid you can't use my skin tone as a way to measure my condition. I'm always pale."

He chuckled, helping to break a little of the tension. I felt warm at the sound of his laughter. It was deep and genuine. He reached up and pushed a lock of hair from his forehead. I felt my pulse race as he looked at me. The color of his eyes reminded me of the forget-me-nots that grew wild on the side of the road leading into Kingdom.

Jonathon stirred up emotions inside me that were hard to comprehend, especially in light of my engagement to Ebenezer Miller, the young man I planned to marry at the end of June.

"It feels strange for you to call me Sister Kauffman." I

wondered if he realized he hadn't used the formal greeting until now. "It seems rather decorous for a man who is so opposed to tradition."

He grinned. "I'm not opposed to all traditions, just the ones that don't make sense. Conventions that don't bring us any closer to God."

"And does calling me Sister bring you closer to God?"

He chuckled and shook his head. "Point taken, Hope. I'll work on it, but if I slip once in a while, I'll trust you to remind me."

"Don't worry, I will. Jonathon, you mentioned Clay Center. What happened there?"

"A pastor's house was set on fire, and two local churches were bombed."

I gulped. "Did you say *bombed*?"

"Yes, homemade bombs called Molotov cocktails."

"I don't believe I've ever heard the term before. What does it mean?"

"Molotov cocktails are bottles filled with gasoline or some other flammable substance. Then something else, like a piece of cloth, is soaked in the same liquid and stuffed into the bottle. After it's lighted, it's thrown at a target. It explodes just like a bomb."

I shuddered. "What an evil thing to do. Someone could be seriously injured or killed."

"The house and the churches were vacant when they were struck, so it's hard to tell if the bomber was trying to hurt people or just destroy property. But it's obvious someone could have been hurt . . . or worse." The sun shone right in Jonathon's face, and he squinted at me. "That's precisely why I'm following you home. Until whoever is behind these attacks is caught, I think it might be best if you stay in town. I'll grab a couple of men, and we'll come back for your buggy."

"We have to pray that this was an isolated incident and that Kingdom is still safe. Quite a few of us have been out on this road, and no one has been attacked before today. Maybe it had nothing to do with what's going on in neighboring towns. Perhaps it was a teenager who thought it would be fun to run a Mennonite woman off the road."

Jonathon frowned. "I guess it's possible, but even if that's true, we need to be careful. I think it would be best if our people stay close to home for a while."

I still wasn't convinced it was necessary, but I had to agree that it might be wise to use caution. "I'll certainly heed your advice," I said, trying once again to push my hair back from my face. "But I have to wonder how long we'll have to cower in Kingdom, afraid to leave."

"I don't think it's cowering. We just need to be cautious. You could have been killed, Hope. If anything ever happened to you . . ."

I was so surprised by his words that I swung my eyes downward, afraid my expression would betray my emotions. For some reason my hair suddenly felt like it weighed too much for my head. I wanted desperately to put it back in its bun so I'd feel better. Safer. "What else can we do besides hide? We're taught not to resist violence."

He was quiet for a moment, and I looked up so I could see his face. He was staring at me with an odd expression. "Well, we're instructed not to resist evil with violence, but the Scriptures are clear that we are to resist the enemy. The

question is, how do we do that?" He shook his head. "Some
in our community believe we're not to do anything but pray.
I don't know if I can accept that, and I think there are others
who agree with me. In light of what's happening, it seems
prudent to find a way to keep our town safe. When I get back,
I'm going to talk to a few people. See if we can come up with
a plan to protect our borders."

Before I had a chance to think it through, I blurted out,
"I'll help you, Jonathon." I immediately felt foolish. Why
had I said that? "I-I mean . . . Well, you probably don't want
women . . ."

His easy laughter embarrassed me. Did he think I was silly?
He reached out and briefly touched the side of my face, but
then he quickly jerked his hand away as if my cheek were
hot to the touch. "I would be honored to include you, but I'd
rather you didn't tell your father. I'm afraid his opposition
would make things . . . difficult."

I tossed my head back. "I'm twenty-six years old. Old
enough to make my own decisions. My father doesn't need
to know every single thing I do."

He looked up at the sun beating down on us. "Let's talk
about this later. Right now we need to get you home."

I nodded. "All right. Thank you, Jonathon."

First he got my packages out of the storage box and put
them in his truck. Then he led Daisy over to me. He stood
next to her, putting his fingers together like a stirrup. I hoisted
my skirt up, put my left foot in his hands, and jumped up
onto Daisy's back.

"You sure you can ride her without a saddle?" he asked
once I was seated.

"I grew up on horses. Riding bareback is second nature to me." I didn't tell him that riding bareback was something I'd done as a child, not as a grown woman.

Daisy was still skittish from our narrow escape, and I could feel her tremble beneath me. I reached down and ran my hand along her neck trying to calm her.

"It's okay, girl," I said softly. "Everything's all right. We're going home now." As I talked, she became quieter. When she was ready, I sat up straight, my skirt pulled up and tucked under me. It wasn't very dignified, but unless I wanted to ride sidesaddle, something I wasn't used to, it was my only choice. I couldn't imagine what I looked like, dirty and scraped up, my hair undone, sitting on top of a horse.

"Are you ready?" Jonathon asked, his tone hesitant.

"I'm fine. It might be a good idea to keep some distance between us though. I don't want the sound of your engine to frighten Daisy. She's never minded it before, but I'm not sure how she'll react now."

Instead of going straight to his truck, he stood there a moment as if he wanted to say something else. Finally, he just shook his head and smiled. "You're quite a woman, Hope. I've never known anyone like you. You seem so quiet and meek, but you have such great inner strength. I wish . . ."

I quickly looked away, fearing we might be headed to a place we shouldn't go. "We . . . we'd better get going."

After hesitating a few more seconds, he turned and walked to his truck while I began to urge Daisy forward. She faltered some and then began to walk slowly. Before long, her stride became more confident, her gait steady.

Jonathon's words echoed through my mind. *"You're quite*

a woman, Hope. I've never known anyone like you." What did that mean? Could he have feelings for me? All along, I believed there was nothing between us except a silly schoolgirl crush I'd tried hard to ignore. Was I wrong? And what was he going to say after *"I wish . . ."*?

My heart was beating so hard in my chest, I felt slightly faint.

CHAPTER /2

As I rode, I took several deep breaths, trying to calm myself. I had no business even thinking about Jonathon's Wiese's intentions, and he had no business stating them. I was engaged to Ebbie Miller, and I loved him with all my heart. In two months, we would be married. It still seemed a little unreal. I'd never been that interested in marriage, unlike some other girls in Kingdom. I loved working in the quilt shop and spending time with my best friend, Lizzie Housler. Getting married had always been . . . unimportant. But in the last couple of years, my feelings for Ebbie, who had been a close friend since we were children, had started to grow into something more. Something stronger. We were both slow to admit our feelings, so our fathers, pleased by our potential union, made wedding plans for us. Ebbie and I didn't try to dissuade them. We were both excited and looking forward to our upcoming marriage. That's why these odd feelings for Jonathon confused me.

True to his word, Jonathon drove slowly behind Daisy and me, keeping enough distance so as not to spook my skittish horse. It took almost an hour and a half for us to reach Kingdom. I was very relieved to enter the safety of my hometown.

We passed the large white church building that sat on the edge of town. A few houses dotted both sides of the street, and then our small business area came into view. I loved the wooden walkways that lined the street. Some of the town's women had planted flowers along the sidewalk. Marigolds, zinnias, and petunias bloomed with vibrant colors, decorating the town with red, yellow, purple, orange, and blue. We rode past Eberly's Hardware and Menninger's Saddle and Tack Store. A large sign had been painted and mounted for our newest enterprise, Metcalf's General Store.

By the time I rode up in front of Kingdom Quilts, I was hot, tired, and thirsty. Jonathon's presence had certainly made me feel safer. The fear that felt like a tight band around my chest had relaxed, and I'd begun to feel like my old self again.

Jonathon waited until I dismounted and tied up Daisy before getting my packages from his truck. Then he followed me inside the quilt shop, still holding the supplies I'd bought from Flo.

As I entered the store, Papa came from behind the corner. His eyes took in my hair and disheveled condition. "Hope! What has happened to you? Are you all right?" He glared at Jonathon. "Did you have something to do with this?"

"No, Papa," I said quickly, embarrassed by his outburst. "Jonathon may have just saved my life."

Jonathon, who had come in behind me, quickly explained what had occurred on the road.

Papa's face went white, and he rushed up to me. "Were you hurt? Are you injured?"

I shook my head. "A few cuts and scrapes. That's it. But our buggy will have to be repaired."

My father hugged me tightly and then frowned at Jonathon. "I am grateful, Brother Wiese, but how is it you happened to be on the road at the same time as my daughter?"

"Papa!" I said. "What a question. I thank God he *was* there."

My father let me go. "I do thank God, but I am concerned about the coincidence."

Jonathon took a step back and stared at Papa through narrowed eyes. "Although I don't believe I need to explain myself to you, Brother Samuel, I was coming back from Washington after picking up lumber for Noah Housler. I just happened to come upon Hope. Perhaps it was God who arranged for me to be there."

"Perhaps," Papa said slowly.

I wished I could sink into the floor and disappear. Feeling I had to say something, I turned my back on Papa and addressed Jonathon, hoping my face wasn't bright red with humiliation. "I'm very grateful, Jonathon. If it wasn't for you, I might have been seriously injured today. Thank you so much for your bravery."

"You're very welcome." After giving me a warm smile that made my toes tingle, he left. But first he shot my father a penetrating look that should have made him feel ashamed for his unchristian attitude.

"Papa," I said forcefully after the door closed behind Jonathon, "what were you thinking? That man risked himself for my safety. How could you talk to him like that?"

He stared down at me. The look on his face was one I

knew well, and it meant we weren't going to talk about this any further. Trying to discuss his attitude toward Jonathon would get us nowhere. If it had been anyone else, my father would have gone out of his way to show his appreciation. Papa and I were so close, yet there were times when he seemed like a complete stranger.

"I saw Aaron Metcalf over at the old feed store building," Papa said, his tone confirming that our discussion about Jonathon Wiese was at an end. "I am certain he will help me fetch the buggy. Tell me exactly where you left it."

I quickly described the spot, and Papa nodded. "I know the place you mean." He went over to the coatrack by the door and grabbed his hat. The light filtering in through the window glinted off his reddish-blond hair and beard. Papa was still a handsome man, but since my mother died, he'd never shown any interest in another woman. I noticed that the arthritis in his legs made his steps slow today, and I wondered if self-consciousness about his condition was the reason he had no interest in female companionship.

After he left, I started putting my supplies away and realized I'd forgotten the new blue fabric for Lizzie and Noah's quilt. I'd been so distracted by the young woman who'd come into Flo's shop that I'd left without it. I felt so stupid and ridiculous. My silly reaction had cost me the chance to accomplish something that was very important to me. If I tried to produce the quilt without the right colored fabric, it wouldn't look right. What could I possibly do now? I ran different scenarios through my head as I worked at putting the rest of the supplies away.

I still hadn't come up with an acceptable plan by the time

Papa returned with Aaron in tow. Aaron had arrived in town almost four years ago, asking permission to buy a house and live here. He met with the elders, who'd approved his request to become one of us, but whatever personal information he'd given them had stayed private. He refused to talk about his past, no matter how innocent the questions posed to him. His standard answer was always, "The past is the past, and I have no interest in talking about it." I was extremely curious about him, but so far I hadn't been able to discover anything even remotely interesting.

"Hello, Brother Metcalf," I said when he stepped inside. "Thank you for agreeing to help Papa bring our buggy home. We appreciate it." When Papa looked at me strangely, I realized my hair was still down. I'd been so distracted by my failure to bring back the fabric from Washington, I'd forgotten all about it. I tried to pull my wild locks back, feeling mortified that Aaron had seen me appearing in such an unseemly manner. I picked up a stray ribbon under the counter and quickly tied my hair back from my face. A twinge of pain gripped my arm, and I tried not to wince. No point in drawing more attention to myself than I already had today.

Aaron looked me over with surprise. "I'm glad to help, Sister Hope. Your father says you weren't badly hurt, but I must admit that you look a little worse for wear."

I smiled at him. "To be honest, I feel somewhat bruised and beaten up. I'll be glad to clean up and tend to my scratches."

"Well, I think we should get going," Papa said. "And like my daughter, I am grateful you can find time away from your projects to help us."

Before leaving, Papa came over and kissed me on the

forehead. "Why don't we have supper at Lizzie's tonight? You must be weary after your experience."

"I'd like that. Thank you." I tried to keep my tone light, but I was still upset with the way he'd treated Jonathon. Bribing me with a trip to the restaurant wasn't going to change my feelings.

He put his hand on my cheek and looked into my eyes. "I am so thankful you are safe. God is good. I could not bear to lose you."

My heart melted a little, and I put my hand over his. "You won't lose me, Papa. Please don't worry."

He squeezed my fingers and blinked away tears. "I am trying, Daughter, but sometimes casting my care on the Lord is more difficult than it should be."

"I know." I forced a smile. "But I'm perfectly fine. Shall we leave for Lizzie's as soon as you return?"

He glanced at the small battery-operated clock we kept on the counter. "Yes. Why don't you clean up and close the store a little early? You may want to rest some."

I nodded. "Will you give Daisy some water before you leave? I'm sure she's thirsty after our long trip."

"Yes, I will do that." He hugged me again, which surprised me, since Papa wasn't usually very demonstrative in front of other people. I said good-bye to Aaron, and they left.

I watched Aaron gently help my father up into the cab of his truck, obviously aware that he was having some trouble with his joints. Several townspeople who passed by greeted Aaron with enthusiasm. The whole town was excited about the new store. Of course, Lizzie was thrilled at the prospect of buying more of her restaurant supplies in town. Although she bought a lot of food items from local farmers, there were some things that could only be found in larger cities like Washington. Having a general store would cut down on weekly treks out of town for the supplies she needed to keep her business running.

After Papa and Aaron drove away, I headed to the back room to fix my hair and try to make myself more presentable. I caught a glimpse of my reflection in a piece of polished tin Papa had purchased for the roof of our chicken coop. Horrified by how disheveled I looked, I untied the ribbon holding back my hair and shook it out. Jonathon had said that I looked like an angel, but I doubted seriously that angels were this dirty and messy. I got some water from the pump out back and washed myself off the best I could. Then I treated my scratches with Mercurochrome and put bandages on the larger cuts. Thankfully, I had an extra apron in the closet. I brushed the dirt and leaves out of my hair, pulled it into a bun, and put on a fresh prayer covering. One final glance in my makeshift tin mirror revealed the Hope Kauffman I was used to seeing. Gone was the wild-looking girl with the long, unkempt hair.

I was just starting my chores when the front door opened and Ebbie stepped inside. "Hope, I heard you were assaulted on the road. Are you all right?"

I smiled at him. "I'm fine, and I'm not sure I was *assaulted*. Someone in a truck thought it would be funny to force me into the ditch."

Seeing Ebbie made me feel better. I loved his ginger-colored hair that seemed to have no idea where it wanted to lie on his head and his deep brown eyes that reminded me of turned-over earth before planting begins.

"Still, it sounds like you could have been hurt." He came around the counter and put his hand on my cheek. "If anything had happened to you . . ."

I was startled to hear him use the same words Jonathon had used earlier and stumbled over my reply. "I-I'm all right, Ebbie. Honestly."

He reached down and kissed me lightly on the cheek, and then he smiled at me. "I would give my life to protect you, Hope. I love you so much."

I felt my eyes mist. "And I love you too."

He looked me over and frowned. "You do look a little banged up. Maybe you should sit down. I can help you in the shop if you want."

I laughed. "No, really. I'm not incapacitated. Just bruised, scratched, and a little humiliated."

"You're sure?"

I nodded. "I'm so grateful to Brother Wiese. If he hadn't been there, I don't know what would have happened."

Ebbie took a few steps back. "Jonathon Wiese? He was there?"

My face suddenly felt warm, and I hoped I wasn't blushing. "Yes. He was on his way back from Washington and drove up just as the man in the truck was getting ready to take another run at me. Jonathon chased him away."

Ebbie's eyes widened. "Oh, I had no idea. I'll have to thank him when I see him."

I nodded, wondering why I suddenly felt so uncomfortable. "That would be nice."

"Are you sure you don't want me to stay with you?"

I shook my head. "It's not necessary. I'm sure you have things to do."

"As a matter of fact, I did tell Ruth Fisher I'd come by and check her roof."

I grinned. "The trials of an elder."

He smiled. "It may not sound very spiritual, but God tells us that true religion is caring for the widows and the orphans."

"I'm sure Ruth is very appreciative of your help."

He patted his lean stomach. "She knows I love her peach cobbler, so there is always some waiting for me. Payment in full as far as I'm concerned."

"So I should ask for her recipe and make peach cobbler for you after we're married?"

He laughed. "And here I didn't think you could be any more perfect than you already are." Ebbie glanced at the clock sitting on the counter. "I'd better get going. Do you have plans this evening?"

"Papa mentioned going to the restaurant for dinner."

"Good. I'll try to meet you. I'm not sure how long I'll be at Ruth's. If I'm not there by the time you're ready to order, go ahead. Don't wait for me."

"All right. But I hope you make it."

"Me too."

He brought his other hand around from behind his back and held out a bouquet of forget-me-nots. "Do you remember the first time I gave you flowers?" he asked softly.

I smiled at him and took the flowers. "We were only twelve, and you left them on my desk at school."

He nodded. "But I was too shy to tell you they were from me."

"And I had no idea who put them there. I didn't think of you. We were just friends."

He gazed deeply into my eyes. "*You* thought we were just friends. I've loved you ever since you were seven. Your mother died and you needed a shoulder to cry on. You sat next to me on the front porch and leaned your head against me. I put my arm around you while you sobbed. I knew then that we were meant to be together."

"Every time you tell that story I find myself wishing I'd known how you felt. Maybe I would have wanted to get married a long time ago."

He laughed warmly and kissed me on the nose. "That's all right. You've made up for any slight from our childhood."

"I'm glad."

Ebbie smiled at me once more and then walked out the door.

After it closed behind him, I found myself comparing him to Jonathon. Ebbie was thin and lacked Jonathon's muscular physique. The two men were opposites in most other ways as well. Jonathon was confident and personable, whereas Ebbie was quiet and reserved, a deep thinker. Yet sometimes, when he got excited about something, he reminded me of an overenthusiastic child. The simplest things fascinated him. His zest for life wasn't something most people got to see, but I'd been blessed to know the real Ebbie. Although I couldn't say I'd fallen in love when we were young, I'd always felt comfortable around him. Perhaps that was one of the reasons it was so easy to love him now.

Even though Papa suggested I close early, I knew there were still chores to be done, so I got busy. Being alone in the quilt shop made me feel peaceful and happy. I carefully polished the wooden table and four chairs that Papa had crafted. I'd spent many happy hours sitting there, giving lessons in quilting to some of the young women in Kingdom. The pleasant scent of lemon oil filled the room. Then I got a feather duster and dusted the display window next to the door, carefully removing the quilts I'd made and shaking them out. Once they were back in place, I dusted all the shelves that held quilt patterns, colorful spools of thread, embroidery floss, quilting pins, and needles.

I found the quilting and embroidery loops in disorder and wondered if Sophie Wittenbauer had left them in a mess. I usually had to straighten up after one of her visits. Sophie, the daughter of Elmer and Dorcas Wittenbauer, was a young woman with a bad attitude. It was hard to get angry at her though. Her parents showed very little interest in their daughter. Elmer had once been an elder in the church but had withdrawn when Lizzie's father and John Lapp resigned. In my opinion, Elmer should never have been elected in the first place.

I sighed as I dusted the shelf, and then I neatly restacked the hoops. When I was done, I gazed around the large room and sighed contentedly. Kingdom Quilts was like my second home, and I couldn't imagine not having it in my life.

After I put the duster away, I carefully wiped down the large cutting table that sat in the middle of the room. I'd just cleaned the large quilting frame in the back room yesterday and knew it didn't need attention today. It was almost time to schedule another group quilting party. I so enjoyed those times when some of our women gathered to sew quilts, to fellowship and laugh together. Lizzie always provided cookies and coffee for these unique social events, especially since her mother usually joined our group. Most of the time the quilts we made went to a new mother in our community or to someone in the hospital.

As I went through and sorted out the week's receipts, I struggled to put the terrifying confrontation on the road out of my mind, but it was impossible. How could someone who didn't even know me be so careless with God's precious gift of life? Could a fellow human being's heart really be that dark? It didn't make sense. Nor did Papa's attitude toward Jonathon. Basically, Papa agreed with almost all the changes going on in our church. He'd even painted the outside of our store a beautiful cornflower blue after Pastor Mendenhall pointed out that God must like colors since he used so many of them in nature. That was all it took for Papa. Once he had a clear picture of something, he had no trouble following his heart. Jonathon was exactly the same way. As far as I could remember, he had never said anything that didn't agree with Papa's views. The situation on the road and Papa's attitude toward Jonathon bothered me the rest of the afternoon.

Avery Menninger, who owned the saddle and tack store, stopped by around three thirty. "How are you this afternoon, Sister Kauffman?" he said as he came in the door.

"I'm fine. And you?" This was the same greeting we exchanged every afternoon. It never varied. A kind man who'd lost his wife many years ago and whose daughter had moved away to get married, Avery spent quite a bit of time visiting folks in town before going home to his lonely house.

"Well, fair to middlin'. Just fair to middlin'. Bursitis is kickin' up a bit, but that's to be expected, I guess. Gettin' old ain't a lotta fun."

"I'll keep you in my prayers, Brother Menninger." Sometimes his personality seemed a little gruff, but when you got to know him, you could clearly see his soft heart. Whenever anyone needed help, Avery was the first person on the scene.

"I appreciate that, Sister." He cleared his throat and held out a paper bag. "Sister Hobson dropped off a whole load of oatmeal cookies this morning. I thought you might like a few."

Sister Hobson had set her cap for Avery years ago, believing the way to his heart was through his stomach. So far it hadn't worked, but she persisted and Avery allowed it, probably because she was an incredible cook. Her oatmeal cookies almost melted in your mouth. Someone might have pointed out to Avery that stringing her along wasn't completely ethical, but they both seemed happy. Sister Hobson had hope, and Avery had lots of home cooking. We shared a couple of cookies together, visited for a while, and then he left.

I decided to take Papa's advice and close the shop a little early. I'd finished all the chores I'd set out to do, and I wanted nothing more than to take a quick nap on the cot in the back room. But before I could lock the door, it swung open and Sophie Wittenbauer sauntered in.

"Hello, Hope," she said loudly. Even her voice was irritating. Nasal, whiny, and impudent all at the same time.

"Hello, Sophie," I said evenly. "I'm about to close. . . ."

She didn't appear to hear me, or if she did, she ignored me. "I need this order filled." She shoved a crumpled dirty sheet of paper across the counter toward me. "My mother says you need to take this fabric back and exchange it for what's on that list." She reached into the filthy bag she held in her hands and pulled out a wrinkled piece of fabric, dumping it in front of me. I immediately recognized it. I'd sold it to Sophie several weeks ago. Or what was left of it anyway. It was now about half the size of the original piece, and it was stained with something that looked like grape juice. This wasn't the first time Dorcas had tried to return supplies she'd either ruined or had left over and didn't need. At first I'd refused to refund her money or give her a replacement, but Papa intervened, explaining that the Wittenbauers had little money and needed our help. That might be true, but since their circumstances were caused by their own carelessness and refusal to work, I felt they should reap what they sowed.

The church had helped them out many times, yet when work was offered or they were asked to help others in our town, the Wittenbauers always had an excuse. Their lack of community spirit wasn't viewed with much patience. A sense of kinship and willingness to help others was the foundation of life for a Mennonite. Eventually the church's eagerness to extend charity had dwindled. Except for Papa's. With his voice ringing in my head, I silently took the ruined cloth and filled Sophie's order.

Even though she exasperated me, it was hard not to feel sorry for her. The girl was nearsighted and needed glasses but was forced to wear her father's castoffs. The large black-framed spectacles looked ridiculous and did nothing to help her appearance. Her lifeless dishwater-blond hair was twisted into a messy bun, and loose strands stuck out from underneath a dirty black prayer covering. Sophie wore only black dresses, and it seemed as if she only owned one. It was usually soiled and always wrinkled.

Yet underneath her messy exterior, I recognized a distinct

beauty that had little chance of being noticed. Her large amber eyes appeared almost golden in the light and were framed by thick, dark lashes. Her full lips and cheeks were naturally rosy. Since her overall demeanor didn't convey a sense of good health, the flawlessness of her skin and the color in her cheeks were surprising. I couldn't help but wonder what Sophie would look like if she cleaned up, got glasses that fit her, and wore a light-colored dress.

Of course, saying something to her about her looks was out of the question. Sophie wasn't the kind of person who welcomed personal comments or even attempts at kindness. Somehow she managed to look pitiful and still come across as proud and independent. I couldn't figure out how she managed it, but every time I started to feel sorry for her, as I did now, she'd do something to infuriate me. Today was no different.

"Have you seen Jonathon Wiese around anywhere?" she asked, her voice like fingernails on a chalkboard.

I shrugged as I handed her the brand-new fabric and threads. "I saw him earlier, but I have no idea where he is now. Sorry." I had no intention of telling her about my encounter on the road. In a town the size of Kingdom she'd find out about it soon enough. She'd probably be sorry the driver of the red truck had missed his mark.

She turned her head sideways and peered up at me. "Jonathon told me I'm his best friend." She gave me an odd grin and waited for my reaction. She smelled unwashed, and I fought an urge to gag.

"That's wonderful, Sophie. I'm glad." I looked at our clock. "I've got to close now, but it was nice to see you."

Liar! I heard my own voice in my head, accusing me of being dishonest. I silently repented.

"Jonathon tells me things he doesn't tell anyone else, you know."

I smiled at her, willing her to go away. It didn't work.

Finally, after a strange staring contest that I lost, she grabbed her bag. "Some people need to leave him alone. He doesn't like girls who chase him." With that, she flounced out of the store, leaving me standing behind the counter with my mouth open. What in the world was wrong with that girl? As soon as the thought crossed my mind, I felt ashamed. It was pretty obvious what her problem was: parents who didn't care about her and only used her to fulfill their own selfish purposes.

Well, at least thinking about Sophie had gotten my mind off other things. I looked at the clock again and realized that Papa could be back anytime. I hurried to the back room, washed my hands, and checked out my image one last time. Sighing at my washed-out complexion, I pinched my cheeks, hoping for some color. Lizzie had remarked more than once about my "flawless alabaster skin," but the truth was, I looked ghostly and pale compared to her. Lizzie had coal-black hair, and mine was colorless, almost white. The only feature of mine that stood out was my eyes. Ebbie said they reminded him of the purple tulips his mother grew in front of their house. And Papa said I have my mother's eyes. I can barely remember her face now, but I do recall her incredible violet eyes.

I removed my prayer covering so I could tuck in stray strands of hair that had already escaped from my quickly formed bun. Once my hair felt in place, I put the covering back on. Quite a few of the younger women had stopped wearing them during the day, saving them for church. I couldn't help but envy them. It would be so nice to go without it sometimes, but keeping my prayer covering was one thing my father insisted on. Most of our older members felt the same way. So for now, the covering would stay. At least I'd been able to switch to a white cap instead of the black one I'd worn all my life. And Papa had allowed me to start wearing dresses with colors and designs. The dress I'd changed into was light blue with small violet flowers. It looked very pretty with a crisp white apron over it. I sighed, adjusted the ribbons that hung on each side of my cap, and made my way back into the main room in our store. Papa was just coming in the front door.

"Our buggy is in Brother Matthew's building across the street. It will need a lot of repair." He shook his head. "You could have been badly hurt, Daughter."

"But thanks to Jonathon, I wasn't," I reminded him.

He shot me a look of reproach but didn't say anything.

"Maybe we should forget about what happened this afternoon," I said quickly. "Are you ready for supper? I'm starving."

Papa frowned at me. "I understand your need to get your mind off today's incident, but we cannot dismiss it completely. There are other Kingdom residents who ride to town on that road. Their safety concerns me."

His words reminded me of something that had completely slipped my mind. "Papa, I saw John Lapp headed toward Washington before that truck showed up. Until this moment, I'd forgotten about it."

Papa nodded. "He's fine. He drove past us while we were

retrieving the buggy. But I think we should let everyone in town know what happened to you. Until we are certain it is safe, no one should be out on the main road alone, especially in a buggy."

"Do you think the men on the road are the same people who've been attacking churches in the county, Papa?" I asked softly. "I'm really not convinced the incidents are connected."

"I don't know, Daughter," Papa said slowly, "but I have to admit that I have a bad feeling about this."

"I'd hate to see our town overreact because of some careless teenager who thought his antics were funny."

"I understand that, Hope. But what if it was more than that? I think we will all need to be very careful for a while."

I wanted to bring up Jonathon's idea to gather some people together to try to set up plans to protect Kingdom, but I didn't dare. Papa would never understand, and Jonathon might pay a price for my indiscretion.

"It is nothing for you to worry about," Papa said firmly. "This is something Pastor Mendenhall and the elders will have to address. I do not have the solution."

"Papa," I said slowly, "Flo asked me a question I couldn't answer, and I want to ask how you would have responded."

"And what is the question, Daughter?"

"If . . . if someone you loved was in danger, would you resort to violence to protect them if there was no other choice?"

His eyes widened before he looked away. I waited in silence for his reply. Finally he cleared his throat. "In truth, Hope, I cannot answer you. I have been brought up to believe we are to live in peace with every man, and when assaulted, we should turn the other cheek. There is nothing wrong with resisting evil, but to use physical force against another human being?" He shook his head. "You are my daughter. I would lay down my life for you. That is all I can say."

"Thank you, Papa." He hadn't really answered my question, and it bothered me.

As we stepped out onto the wooden sidewalk outside our shop, we greeted quite a few friends who were already making their way to Cora's Corner Café. When it first opened, many in our town had shunned the small restaurant. Our former elders hadn't approved of a female selling food, stating that it was a woman's duty to stay home and prepare all the meals her family required. But its original owner, Cora Menlo, had seen a need for the many single men and women in our community. And although business had begun slowly, eventually most of the town embraced Cora's. It even took the place of some of our church suppers, becoming a popular gathering spot where residents could spend time fellowshiping without all the work a large supper entailed.

After taking over the restaurant from Cora, Lizzie kept the name, even though several of us had suggested she change it. But her love and appreciation for her old employer prevented her from removing Cora's name. Last month, Cora came for a visit and chided Lizzie for not repainting the large wooden sign that hung outside the red and white building. Secretly, I believe she was touched by Lizzie's devotion. Cora, who had given Lizzie and her daughter, Charity, a place to live when they needed help, left Kingdom when her sister in Oregon became ill. She sold the restaurant to Lizzie for much less than it was worth and went to care for her sister. Now Lizzie and Noah were able to make a good living because of her generosity.

As Papa and I walked through the front door, Lizzie saw us and hurried over. "Hope and Samuel, I'm so glad to see you both!" She put her arms around me, hugging me fiercely. "Aaron told Noah what happened on the road, Hope. I'm so grateful you're all right." She let me go and peered into my eyes. "What if you'd been really hurt?"

Touched by her concern, I smiled. "I'm fine, Lizzie. Really. Just a little rattled. It's still hard to believe there are people out there who care so little for other human beings."

She nodded. "I was saying the same thing to Noah." Her dark eyes were wide with concern. "I saw so much violence when I lived in Kansas City, but Kingdom seems so far away. So remote. It makes us feel this kind of evil can't touch us."

"Well, it almost touched us today," Papa said. "We will all have to be much more careful."

"There's an elders' meeting tonight at the church," Lizzie said. "They intend to talk about the situation and try to figure out what to do. Noah suggests that we keep our people off the main road. Maybe those of us with trucks can run any necessary errands for a while."

"I agree," Papa said. "I will be praying that God will guide our pastor and our elders as they search for wisdom."

Lizzie patted Papa on the shoulder. "Thank you, Samuel. I know they'll appreciate your prayers. Now, let's get you both some supper." She pushed a strand of hair behind her ear. "You look hungry, Hope."

I laughed. "Actually, I'm starving, and the aromas from your kitchen aren't helping a bit."

She grinned. "Good. That means maybe you'll clean your plate for once. You eat so little, sometimes I get concerned."

"As do I," Papa said. "Hope has the appetite of a small bird."

I shook my head. "You two worry too much. If you had your way, I'd have to let out all my dresses."

"Wouldn't hurt you a bit," Lizzie said, smiling. She finally took her attention off me and looked up at Papa. "Samuel, it's been a little over a week since you joined us for a meal."

"Now, Lizzie," he said, "does that mean you have missed me?"

She chuckled. "Now that you mention it, what was I thinking? How could I miss a feisty old codger like you?"

Papa shook his head and sighed. "I wonder why I keep coming here when all I get is abuse."

I couldn't hold back a giggle. Normally my father was not a joker, but Lizzie seemed to bring out a side of him I rarely saw. They had a very special relationship, and I was grateful for it, since Lizzie was the closest thing to a sister I've ever had.

"If you two are finished, I'm ready to order dinner," I said.

Lizzie took my father's arm and led him over to his favorite table in the corner. "Why don't you two sit here." She crossed her arms and frowned at Papa. "Now, let me see. I suspect you came for my incredible meatloaf, didn't you, Samuel? Or my beef stew?" She gazed up at the ceiling. "Yes, that's it. Beef stew. I'll get it right away."

"Very funny," he said, taking off his wide-brimmed straw hat and putting it on the empty chair next to him. "You have been frying chicken all day just to tempt me. Your efforts have been successful. Bring me a fried chicken dinner, woman. And be quick about it!"

Lizzie was aware that Papa loved her fried chicken, yet she

teased him the same way every time he came in. I laughed at the both of them.

"I suppose you want the same thing?" Lizzie asked me.

"Oh yes. Please. I can't watch Papa enjoy your chicken and not have some myself. The spirit is willing—"

"But the flesh is weak? I'd hate to think I'm corrupting you, but you have no need to worry about your waistline."

"Then I will enjoy my meal without concern," I said with a smile.

Lizzie leaned over and lowered her voice. "You should both know that everyone's talking about Hope's narrow escape. Jonathon Wiese is getting together some men to guard the town. He feels Kingdom needs to be prepared in case we're attacked. Noah's asked him to wait until after the elders' meeting, but Jonathon doesn't seem willing to do that."

Papa's right eyebrow arched. Not a good sign. "And how does he plan to protect us?" he snapped. "Surely not with weapons of violence."

Lizzie shrugged. "I really have no idea, Samuel. But if we become targets, we have to defend ourselves."

Papa's eyes narrowed as he stared back at her. "Mennonites do not condone violence, Elizabeth. You were brought up here. You know that."

Lizzie put one hand on her hip and matched Papa's stare. "I know what I was taught, Samuel, but that doesn't necessarily mean I agree with everything. Having a relationship with God means you should be led and guided by His Holy Spirit. Not by men. I know what the Mennonite church in this town teaches, but when it comes to defending the life of my daughter, I'll do whatever I think is best." She glanced at me. "Are you trying to tell me that if someone tried to hurt Hope, you'd stand by and do nothing?"

Papa's face began to flush, and I cast a warning look toward Lizzie. She saw it and quickly gave him a forced smile. "I'm sorry, Samuel. That's not a fair question. I know you're a good man and that you work hard to honor your beliefs. I guess all I'm trying to say is that the issue isn't settled in everyone's mind like it is in yours."

Papa's color started to fade, and I breathed a sigh of relief, although I was bothered that this was the second time he'd been asked the same question, and he still hadn't answered it. Children look to their parents to keep them safe, even when they become adults. Would my father actually allow someone to harm me in defense of his convictions?

"I understand your confusion," he said after taking a deep breath, "but I must choose peace and forgiveness. It is the way I was raised and the way I brought Hope up. We believe it is the way God would have us respond."

Lizzie frowned at him but didn't challenge his statement. Papa included me as if he knew my thoughts, but I certainly had questions. However, I had no intention of telling him that. For now, I'd bide my time and pray about it. At least Papa knew about Jonathon's group, and I wouldn't have to be the one to tell him. I wondered how many others there were in Kingdom who didn't agree with Papa. We had just weathered one huge storm of controversy, and we didn't need another one with the power to cause an even deeper divide.

"Is Noah here tonight?" I asked, trying to change the subject.

"He was for a while, but Jonathon was kind enough to

pick up lumber for us while he was in Clay Center. Noah's trying to get some work done before the meeting."

Noah had been really busy lately. Besides helping his wife in the restaurant from time to time, most of his attention was geared toward fixing up the old Strauss farm outside of town. Deserted by the Strauss family after the death of their daughter, Ava, it sat abandoned for twenty years, falling into disrepair. Lizzie had fallen in love with it, so they bought it, determined to renovate it and make it their home.

"I'd better get you two some fried chicken before it's all gone," Lizzie said, wisely letting the previous debate drop.

I gave her a small nod, signaling my appreciation for her willingness to appease Papa. I knew it wasn't easy for her to walk away when she clearly believed she was right and Papa was wrong. She did it more for me than for Papa, and I loved her for it.

"Where's Charity this evening?" I asked before she had a chance to leave.

Lizzie's seven-year-old daughter, Charity, was usually in the dining room when we visited. Charity was almost a carbon copy of her mother, with blue-black hair and dark eyes. But her widow's peak and turned-up nose came from her father. She sometimes stopped by the quilt shop after school so I could help her with homework, and we'd become fast friends. I loved her unbridled eagerness, even though she seemed to have an unending list of questions. Many times her curiosity focused on our faith. I tried to answer her inquires the best I could, but lately I'd noticed she'd been rather quiet and introspective. I sensed that something was bothering her but decided to wait for her to bring it up. I wasn't willing to overstep our friendship and hurt the easy trust we'd built between us.

Charity's biological father was currently incarcerated in a state prison. Lizzie had chosen not to tell her daughter the truth about him, but I'd begun to wonder if Charity knew more than her mother suspected. People talk. Could Charity have overheard something? Her behavior made me wonder if she was dealing with feelings she didn't know how to handle. She seemed to be growing up so quickly, but in truth, she was still just a child.

"She's with her grandparents tonight," Lizzie said. "She has some worksheets to do, and it's just too noisy here for studying."

"She's really an exceptional student."

Lizzie nodded. "Charity's made great progress this year. You and Leah have really helped her." Although her words were delivered lightly, there was a look in her eyes that concerned me. "Well, I'd better get going," she said. "It's going to be a busy night."

With that, she turned and left, stopping by two other tables to take orders before heading into the kitchen. I gazed around the cozy dining room. The dark wood floors shone, as did the wood paneling that went halfway up the walls. The upper walls were covered with brightly colored red-checked wallpaper, although not much of it was visible, since almost every space was adorned with gorgeous quilts, hand-stitched samplers, and beautifully painted plates. The tables and booths were covered with red-checked tablecloths that matched the walls. In the winter, a fire crackled in the fireplace, but even without the inviting flames, the room exuded warmth. A large ceiling fan moved slowly overhead, circulating the crisp spring air throughout the dining room. I loved this place almost as much as I adored my quilt shop.

As a few other people filtered in for supper, I was relieved to see Callie Hoffman hurry in, going straight for the kitchen. A few minutes later she emerged, wearing an apron and holding an order pad. Besides caring for her sick father, she worked as Lizzie's right-hand girl at the restaurant. In her spare time, she assisted Leah in Kingdom's one-room school.

"I do not like this talk of guns and vengeance," Papa said suddenly. I was so deep into my thoughts that the sound of his voice made me jump.

"I know, Papa," I said, "but unfortunately, these incidents throughout the county appear to be getting worse. I'm praying that the police will apprehend the people responsible before anyone else gets hurt."

Papa reached over and took my hand. "I pray the same thing, Daughter. I have to admit that I am angry you were put in danger today, but we must find a way to forgive. We must also pray that the hearts of these men are changed. Obviously they are very unhappy people who need the love of God in their lives."

I immediately felt ashamed that the same idea hadn't occurred to me. "You're so good to think of that, Papa. I'll certainly pray for them."

He nodded absentmindedly. "There is something else I need to talk to you about, Hope. It is about all the time you spend with Jonathon Wiese."

I felt my face get hot, and I withdrew my hand from his. "I don't spend an inordinate amount of time speaking to

Brother Wiese," I said a little too quickly. "We are friends, Papa. Nothing more."

His eyebrows knit together, making them look like one long, hairy caterpillar. "You are betrothed to Elder Miller. I am concerned that you may be developing inappropriate feelings for Brother Wiese."

"Papa!" My shock at his charge was matched only by my dismay at the truth behind his words. "Is that why you were so rude to Jonathon? Because you think I have feelings for him? I'm completely aware of my betrothal, and I look forward to becoming Ebbie's wife."

Papa stroked his beard, a sure sign he was worried. I wanted to say something to make him feel better, but my heart betrayed me. My attraction to Jonathon was much stronger than was proper, and try as I might, I couldn't seem to control it. Before I could speak again, Callie brought coffee to our table. We thanked her, and Papa asked about her father.

"Some days he does quite well, Brother Kauffman," she replied, "but other days he is barely able to get out of bed." I could see the sadness in her huge blue eyes.

"I am so sorry to hear that," Papa said gently. "It has been too long since I have been to visit. May I come by sometime in the next few days?"

Callie's expression immediately brightened. "Oh yes. Please do. Seeing you would make him so happy."

Papa nodded. "I will stop by one afternoon this week."

"That would be wonderful," she said with a smile. "When I get home tonight, I'll tell him you're coming. Thank you so much."

"I look forward to talking with him. James has been a

longtime friend. Forgive me for not calling on him sooner. I will do much better in the future."

"I understand that you're busy, and Father understands it too." She glanced toward the kitchen. "Your meals should be ready shortly. I'll keep an eye open for them." She patted me lightly on the shoulder and left to check on a nearby table.

I saw Levi Housler, Noah's brother, sitting alone. I waved to him, and he nodded toward me. Levi looked a lot like Noah, but he was taller and his hair was blonder. They weren't much alike in personality though. Noah was extremely social and made friends easily, while most of the time Levi was very quiet and thoughtful. Callie shared with me once that she had set her cap for the gentle, reverential man. I'd been watching them for months, but Levi didn't seem to notice Callie except as the woman who waited on him whenever he came into the restaurant.

I focused my attention back to Papa and started to make a comment about Callie's father when Papa suddenly interrupted.

"I have not forgotten our topic of conversation, Daughter. I must insist that you stop spending time with Jonathon Weise. He is stirring up division in the church with his ideas. His beliefs about meeting violence with violence are against our core Mennonite doctrine. I have brought his actions to the attention of our elder board."

My mouth dropped open. "But you haven't even heard his suggestions. How can you judge what you don't know? And approaching the elders about him will surely cause dissension, Papa. How can you accuse Jonathon of divisive behavior and then turn around and do the same thing? I don't understand—"

"Hope," Papa said sharply, "we will not have this discussion. You obviously care about this young man, and I believe he also has an unhealthy interest in you. Even though I am in his debt for aiding you this afternoon, I want this relationship nipped in the bud. Now. I will not allow it to continue."

I felt tears spring to my eyes. Although Papa could be a very severe man, he was usually gentle with me. I felt scolded, yet I hadn't done anything wrong. Or had I? Indignation rose within me, along with a feeling of shame. Together they made me feel sick inside.

Without warning, Jonathon's face drifted into my mind. Thick dark hair, blue eyes the color of a cloudless sky, and dark eyelashes that any woman would be proud to own. Emotions boiled that an engaged woman shouldn't feel toward another man. I tried to push them down, but they wouldn't be so easily controlled.

As Father quietly sipped his coffee, once again I found myself comparing my fiancé to the man I had such a strong reaction to. Jonathon was a firebrand. Passionate. Intelligent. Interesting. I could listen to him talk for hours. He spoke with enthusiasm, and his ideas sparked excitement in me.

And Ebbie? Once while on a walk, he found an anthill and spent the rest of the afternoon explaining to me the exciting world of ants. How they could lift several times their own weight and how intricately they set up their colonies. I enjoyed his enthusiasm, but would our lives be filled with long stories about bugs? Someday would I find him boring? It hurt to even consider the possibility. I loved Ebbie. But no matter how hard I tried to forget about Jonathon, I just couldn't seem to do it.

"Hope, I would like to know that you understand me. Your silence does not assure me that you have taken my concerns to heart."

My father's curt comment snapped me out of my contemplation.

"Yes, Papa," I said slowly. "I hear you, but I don't agree. Jonathon and I haven't done anything to be ashamed of, and I don't want to lose his friendship."

"I do not care what you want," he said harshly. "I believe I know what is best in this situation and would appreciate it if you would not question my authority. You will not speak to this man again, and that is the end of it."

I glanced around, looking to see if anyone was paying attention to us. Thankfully, all the other customers seemed to be more interested in their own conversations than they were in the drama unfolding at our table.

"Papa," I said quietly, "will you please lower your voice? You're embarrassing me."

"Your discomfort is not my concern. My concern is for your soul. Jonathon Weise is dangerous and not just because I do not agree with his views. The way he looks at you is . . . sinful."

"Papa," I hissed, "I am twenty-six years old—not a little girl anymore. I manage the quilt shop—"

He started to protest, but I held up my hand to stop him. "Yes, I know you own the store, but you don't spend much time there. You have to admit that I actually carry out our day-to-day operations. My point is that I am a grown woman, responsible, and level-headed. When will you trust me? When will you allow me to make my own choices?"

Without warning, Papa jumped to his feet. "I will not have a daughter of mine running around with a man like Jonathon Wiese. Either you will stop seeing him or you will move out of my home. You are engaged to be married, but your interest in this man is obvious. You are humiliating yourself and causing me shame. I will not have it!"

Papa stormed out of the restaurant, slamming the door behind him. I didn't need to look around me this time. The silence in the dining room made it clear that everyone had heard. I was so embarrassed I could barely raise my head. And when I finally did, I saw Ebbie standing a few feet from our table. The look on his face made my heart sink.

CHAPTER /3

I pushed my chair back and stood up, not sure what to do. I could feel my cheeks burn with humiliation. Callie, who had been pouring coffee at a nearby table, hurried over to me.

"If you need to leave," she said softly, putting her arm around me, "I'll give your dinners to someone else. Abner Witsman and his wife just ordered the same thing." She squeezed my shoulders.

Too mortified to speak, I just nodded and fled from the dining room. Even though I was too afraid to look at any of the other diners, I could almost feel the stares. When I reached the steps outside, I slumped down to a sitting position and hid my face in my hands. I wanted to run to the safety of the quilt shop, but Papa was probably there, and I couldn't face his anger.

"Are you all right?"

I looked up to see Ebbie standing over me. The last person I wanted to see. "I-I'm sorry, Ebbie. I didn't mean . . ."

He sat down next to me, his deep brown eyes searching mine. "You know, Hope, I've suspected for a while that you

59

had feelings for Jonathon. I just kept hoping they would pass. But they haven't, have they?" He reached into his shirt pocket and pulled out a handkerchief. "Here, you should wipe your face."

I took it gratefully and dried my cheeks. "I don't know, Ebbie. I love you. Very much." I sighed heavily. "But I have to be honest. My father was right. I'm having inappropriate feelings for Jonathon." I looked into his eyes and saw the deep hurt there. Fresh tears spilled down my cheeks. "I-I'm so sorry, but you deserve the truth. If you'll just be patient with me, I know this will pass. I wish I could explain it, but I can't. It's as if I don't know myself anymore." I wiped my face again and handed the handkerchief back to him. "I still want to marry you. If you'll have me."

He studied me for several moments. As I looked back at him, I realized how cute he really was. His reddish-brown hair glowed in the late afternoon sun, and his eyes held depths I could get lost in. Perhaps his face wasn't as manly as Jonathon's, but his long aquiline nose and perfect cheekbones gave him an appealing, romantic look.

He clasped his hands together and stared out at the street, the pain of my words still etched in his face. "I don't know, Hope. I think you owe it to us . . . No, you owe it to me to explore the feelings you have for Jonathon. If you are meant to be together, it wouldn't be right for me to stand in your way."

"Jonathon isn't attracted to me, Ebbie. As far as he's concerned, we're just friends. Nothing more." Although I wasn't sure that was true, in that moment I had to face the fact that Jonathon had never expressed any romantic interest in me.

Ebbie took my hand and peered deeply into my eyes. "I'm

not worried about Jonathon's intentions. I only care about your heart, Hope." He let go of my hand and stared down at his boots for a moment. Then he slowly stood up, refusing to meet my gaze. "I'd like to marry a woman who has eyes only for me. Who never compares me to anyone else because I'm the only man she will ever love. I want a wife who looks at me the way my mother still looks at my father. Maybe I'll never have that, but I'd like to hold out hope that someday I will. I think I'll regret it if I don't." He paused and took a deep breath. "So I'm ending our engagement. I know our plans have already been announced in church, but I'll talk to Pastor Mendenhall."

"Oh my." I blinked away the hot tears that filled my eyes again. "It . . . it will be quite a scandal."

I could remember only one other time when an engagement in Kingdom had been broken. Even though most people had no idea why the marriage was canceled, speculation ran rampant. It was several years before the young woman finally married someone else, and to this day her would-be groom was still single.

"Don't worry," Ebbie said gently. "I'll tell Pastor Mendenhall the truth. That it was my decision, and I'll refuse to explain my reasons. You'll be able to hold your head high." His voice broke, and he paused to clear his throat. "If you need a friend, I'll be here for you." He finally looked at me with shiny narrowed eyes. "I'll always love you, Hope. I pray you'll find what you're looking for."

I wanted to cry out, to beg him to change his mind. Was it my own embarrassment at having a broken engagement? Or did he mean even more to me than I'd realized? Perhaps my feelings for him weren't the swooning kind I felt for Jonathon, but they were strong. I loved him, and I couldn't believe what was happening. But instead of protesting, I sat quietly and watched him walk back into the café.

I grabbed the handrail and pulled myself up. Several people came out of the restaurant and walked past me. A couple of them said hello, but the rest were silent, probably uncomfortable after the scene between Papa and me. I had decided to go back inside and ask Lizzie what to do when someone gently took my arm. I turned to find Papa standing next to me.

"Please forgive me, Daughter," he said softly. "I behaved like a fool, and I am shamed by my actions. You are my child, and I love you. Even though it does not seem like it, I am aware that you are too old to have your father make every decision in your life. I cannot understand why I reacted so abruptly. "

His kindness started my tears again. "Thank you, Papa. I don't know where I'd go if I couldn't come home to you."

"My darling daughter," he said, his voice catching, "you can always come home." He struggled for a moment to control his emotions. "Are you too ashamed of me to go back into the restaurant and have supper?" he asked finally.

I sighed. "I'm not ashamed of you, Papa, but I don't think I'm quite ready to face everyone."

He nodded. "I understand. You go to the shop and wait for me. I will have Lizzie wrap up our meals, and I'll carry our plates back to the store. We can talk there while we eat. My harsh words have created a poor harvest. Let me pull up the bad seed I have sown." He touched my cheek. "You are the most important person in my life, and I think my desire for your happiness has made me careless. Instead of reacting with anger, let us share our hearts with each other and find healing."

I smiled for the first time since leaving Lizzie's. "That sounds wonderful, Papa. Thank you."

He patted my shoulder and then headed toward the restaurant. I felt proud of him, knowing that going back there now was very difficult.

As I walked toward the store, my mind kept running over my conversation with Ebbie. Had I done the right thing when I admitted my feelings for Jonathon? Ebbie was a good man, and I'd just lost him. I truly believed we could have been content together. Why had I thrown away our chance at happiness? Because Jonathon *might* like me? Ebbie's words kept coming back to me. *"I'd like to marry a woman who has eyes only for me. Who never compares me to anyone else because I'm the only man she will ever love. I want a wife who looks at me the way my mother still looks at my father."* My own heart convicted me. I couldn't give Ebbie the kind of love he wanted until I found out if Jonathon and I had a future together.

Telling Papa about my broken engagement wasn't something I was looking forward to. He wouldn't be pleased. Perhaps it was cowardly, but I decided to wait until tomorrow to share this news. Revealing too soon that Ebbie had called off the wedding might make it difficult to mend my relationship with Papa.

"Hey, I think you need to watch where you're going."

I glanced up, startled. I'd been staring down at the sidewalk, lost in thought. Noah Housler was standing in front of me with a big grin on his face.

"Oh, Noah. I'm sorry. I was just thinking."

He laughed. "Thinking that hard can get you into trouble. I hope it's nothing too bad."

I smiled at him. "Bad enough, but that still doesn't give me the right to run into people."

"Can I help?"

Putting the situation with Ebbie aside for now, I quickly told him about the truck on the road. His expression grew solemn. "I'm fine," I assured him, "but Papa and Lizzie think we should alert our people about the possible danger that exists outside of Kingdom."

"I agree. We need to ask everyone to stay in town for now. Just in case." He shook his head. "Hopefully, they'll heed the warning. We have some rather independent thinkers in Kingdom."

His words made me smile. I certainly would consider him to be one of those "independent thinkers." For example, he was always getting teased about his beard, or lack thereof. In Kingdom church, married men wore beards while single men stayed clean-shaven. However, Lizzie had made it clear to her husband that she wasn't partial to facial hair. So Noah, trying to follow tradition yet keep his wife happy, grew what my father referred to as "dirty stubble." Frankly, I found Noah's concern about his wife's wishes refreshing.

"I'm sure you'll be able to convince them," I said. "But I must admit that I'm troubled by these events. I can't understand the motive behind this persecution."

"We don't war against flesh and blood, Hope. It's important to remember that the people behind these attacks are fueled by a hate that doesn't come from God. I'll bet if you asked any of them to explain themselves, they'd have a hard time doing so. They're just blindly following orders from the enemy."

"Well, maybe. But how can they not understand that setting churches on fire and hurting innocent people is wrong? What if someone dies?"

"I know. I think about that too." He rubbed his hands together as if cold, but actually it was a rather warm afternoon. "Is your carriage still out on the road? I'd be happy to get it."

"No, it's back. Papa and Aaron picked it up. It's in Brother Engel's blacksmith shop."

Noah looked down the street toward the building that would soon be our general store. "Aaron's a great guy," he said. "I'm glad he was available to help you."

"How are things going with his plans for the store? I see him working there almost every day, and it seems to be shaping up fast."

"He plans to open by the end of the month," Noah said. "Several of the men from church have been helping him, including me." He sighed. "Sure could save me a lot of trips out of town."

"Papa gave him a list of things our shop could use, but there's no way he'll be able to carry everything we need."

"I'm sure your father would feel better if you didn't have to ride to Washington for your supplies."

I nodded but didn't respond. Noah would have understood my desire to spend at least one day away from Kingdom every month, but I didn't want Papa to discover how important those trips were to me. Maybe it was silly, but I had a nagging fear that if he knew, he might try to stop me from going. Papa's not a mean-spirited man, but he has definite ideas about things that are "frivolous" and things that are "important." I couldn't take the chance that my expeditions to Washington would fall into the "frivolous" category.

"Well, I'd better get inside and let Lizzie know I'm back." Noah smiled at me. "It was nice to talk to you, Hope. We don't get a lot of chances to—"

The sound of a siren cut off the rest of his sentence. We both turned and looked as a car from the sheriff's department barreled down the street, raising lots of dust. Several of the horses tied to hitching posts bolted out of fear, and Noah raced over to calm them. Harold Eberly ran out of his hardware store and started waving his arms at the car, trying to get the driver to reduce his speed and turn off his siren before one of the animals injured itself. Thankfully, the driver appeared to get the message. He cut off the terrible noise and slowed down, finally stopping right in front of the restaurant.

I suspected the driver was Sheriff Saul Ford, and my guess was confirmed when he stepped out of his vehicle. Sheriff Ford served as the county sheriff, but why he was here was a mystery. No one in Kingdom would have called him. The sheriff had made it clear that he considered Kingdom a strange town full of religious zealots. His lack of respect for us wasn't any deeper than our lack of trust in him. Without any apology for the commotion his entrance into Kingdom had provoked, he strode into the restaurant, a young man trailing behind him.

I hurried after them, wondering what would cause the sheriff to darken the borders of our town, let alone come with his siren wailing. Noah followed me, obviously also wanting to know the reason for the sheriff's visit. He held the door open for me, and we both stepped inside to find the sheriff standing at the front of the crowded dining room. We walked past him and stopped next to Lizzie, who was staring at the sheriff with surprise. Before Ford had the chance to say anything, the young man who'd ridden into town with him walked around from behind the large lawman and stood by his side. Where the sheriff was large and rotund, this man was thin and small with slumped shoulders. Covered in acne, his face was frozen in a sneer.

"I wanna wait in the car," he said in a whiny voice. "It's too hot in here."

"You stay where I can keep an eye on you," the sheriff snarled. "I grounded you to the house, and then found you hangin' around in a bar with your no-good friends. If I have to tie you up and drag you along with me for a month, that's what I'll do until you start listenin' to me."

The young man stuck his hands in his pockets and hung his head. I felt rather sorry for him.

"This is my son, Tom," Ford said, addressing us. I had to look closely to see the resemblance, but it was there.

Ebbie nodded at the young man. "Nice to meet you."

Tom didn't respond. His eyes swung around the room, staring at us as if we were oddities in a sideshow. When he got to me, he stopped. The look on his face made me uncomfortable. His slow gaze traveled from my face down and back up again. He gave me a mocking smile that made me shiver.

"Hi, Tom."

I looked around and saw Sophie sitting at a table on the other side of the room, a rather coy expression on her face. Tom looked close to Sophie's age, so I assumed they knew each other from the school in Washington where Kingdom children had gone before we'd gotten our own school.

Tom only glanced at her and then turned his attention back to me. Sophie glared first at him and then at me. I tried to focus on the sheriff while ignoring his son.

Then I noticed that my father was standing near the door with two covered plates in his hands. Our supper. His eyes were fastened on Ford just like everyone else's in the room. All conversation had ground to a halt.

"I'm right sorry, folks," Ford began, "but I . . . I have some bad news for you." He pulled off his hat. His balding pate was stark white, yet the skin on his forehead and face was red with sunburn. Obviously the sheriff wore his hat a lot. He began to twirl that hat around in his big beefy hands. With every turn, my heart skipped a beat. "It . . . it's Avery Menninger," he said finally. "I'm afraid he's dead."

CHAPTER 4

There were several seconds of complete silence until finally someone cried out. It was Lizzie. She slumped down into a chair and began to cry softly. Papa set our plates down on a nearby table.

"What happened, Sheriff?" Noah's expression was grim.

"Someone ran him off the road. His horse must have bolted, and his buggy flipped. Threw him out. Poor old guy never had a chance."

The news hit me like a ton of bricks, and I sank down to the floor without even realizing it. It had to have been the man in the red truck. Whether it was on purpose or not, he'd finally killed someone. Avery.

Papa hurried over to me, kneeling down and wrapping his arms around my shoulders. He didn't say a word, just held me.

"I-I didn't mean to upset the young lady so much," Ford said. The distress on his face seemed real. He didn't know many people in Kingdom personally, but he'd met Avery a few months ago when a body was discovered on the road that led to Kingdom. It was difficult not to like Avery Menninger. Even for the sheriff.

"Hope was almost run over this afternoon on that same road, Sheriff," Noah said, pointing at me. "I'll bet it's the same man."

Ford scratched his head. "Well, it coulda been an accident. Those buggies aren't fit for the road. Just a little bump and they fold up like a cheap lawn chair."

I flushed with anger. "This was no accident, Sheriff. That's too much of a coincidence."

He folded his hefty arms across his massive chest. "Young lady, if you was almost struck by a vehicle, why didn't you call the Sheriff's Department? That don't make much sense, now does it?"

Tom sniggered as if Ford's statement were humorous. The sheriff swung around and slapped his son on the face. Several people in the room jumped at the sound. Tom put his hand on his cheek, his features locked in a grimace of rage and humiliation.

"You shut your mouth, boy," Ford growled. "There's nothin' funny about this. A man's dead. A good man."

Tom's eyes locked on mine, his eyes burning with anger. I felt as if he somehow blamed me for his father's actions.

The sheriff stuck his finger in his son's face. "You get yourself out to my car, Tom. Right now. And you wait there until I'm done here."

With one last hateful look, Tom spun on his heels and walked out the front door, slamming it so hard the windows rattled. Out of the corner of my eye, I saw Sophie sneak out behind him.

I struggled to my feet, Papa helping me up. An unusual boldness, fueled by exasperation, filled me. "Whether I should have called you to report what happened has nothing to do with anything," I said forcefully. "I'm telling you that someone tried to run me over on the very same road. And on the same day. You need to look for the driver of a red truck. It's obvious he's the person who killed our friend."

Ford scowled at me. "I don't need you to tell me my job. I'll be lookin' into it. If we've got some idiot out there playin' cat and mouse with anyone, even you people, I'll get to the bottom of it." He snorted. "But I'm gonna need a little more to go on than just tellin' me it was a red truck. We got lots and lots of red trucks in this county, miss."

"It was a Ford, Sheriff. Red, like Hope said."

Everyone turned and looked toward the front of the room. Jonathon had come in unnoticed. His face was pale. "Tinted windows on the sides. Caught a glimpse of the driver through the windshield, but I couldn't see his face. He was wearing a cap, some kind of ball cap, pulled down low. Nothing really unusual about the truck that I can remember. Pretty standard. Except the driver's door might have been dented. I'm not sure if it was the sun's reflection or if there was an actual dent. I was busy trying to get his attention off Hope."

"And just who are you, young man?" Ford said, looking displeased. If he really wanted more information, he should have been happy to find someone who could offer it.

"I'm Jonathon Wiese, and I was there this afternoon when this man tried to kill Hope."

"Now, wait a minute," Ford snapped. "Just because some yahoo decides to have a little fun with a lady in a buggy don't mean he was trying to kill her. And it also don't mean he's the same one who caused Mr. Menninger's accident."

Jonathon took a deep breath and let it out slowly. "Look, Sheriff. One of our residents has been threatened. Another one is dead. This is serious. For once, why don't you put out a little effort and find out who's behind this? You're supposed to protect the people in this county. Even us."

His reference to the sheriff's previous comment seemed to send Ford over the edge. His already red face darkened. "I don't need no sissy boy Mennie tellin' me what my job is. I'll thank you to keep your opinions to yourself." He slapped his hat back on his head. "I'm gonna look into this, but you all better think about this long and hard. I know you like your privacy. If this really was done on purpose, the news will spread like wildfire. You'll be in the paper, and the media will swarm all over here. Kingdom won't be a secret no more. Trust me."

His remark seemed to hit home. Even Jonathon took a step back. I knew the sheriff didn't like us, but I got the feeling his statement was sincere. Then he pointed at Jonathon. "Just for your information, boy, I liked Avery Menninger very much. If I find out someone ran him off the road on purpose, I won't rest until they're brought to justice."

Once again, I heard a note of sincerity in his voice.

Jonathon opened his mouth to say something else, but Papa held up his hand. "We thank you for your assistance, Sheriff. Anything you can do to help will be appreciated. We will need to contact his daughter, Berlene, and let her know what has happened. Where is . . . Avery now?"

Ford was still staring at Jonathon, sizing him up as if debating whether to let him off the hook or dress him down a little more. Luckily for Jonathon, he turned his attention to my father. "Mr. Menninger is at Doc McDaniels' in Washington. His family should call the doc to arrange for burial."

"Wait a minute, Sheriff," Noah said. "If Avery's death turns out to be more than an accident, won't his body need to go to the coroner's office?"

Ford's right eyebrow shot up. "You tellin' me my job, son?"

Noah frowned. "No. I'm just asking."

"According to Doc, Mr. Menninger was killed by blunt force trauma due to the accident. There ain't no clues anyone can get from his body at this point. Besides, Doc McDaniels serves as the coroner in this area." He frowned at Noah. "You don't need to worry about autopsies and clues, boy. This ain't CSI, you know."

I'm sure the puzzled looks on our faces caught the sheriff by surprise. He snorted. "Oh, sorry. Guess you people don't watch TV. I'm just tryin' to tell you that the injuries to your friend don't need no further investigation. They won't tell us anything that would help us catch the guy who did this."

Papa shot Noah and Jonathon a warning look. "Again, thank you, Sheriff. We do not wish to take any more of your time."

Jonathon's expression turned stormy as he glared at Papa.

The lawman nodded. "I understand. You're wise to keep this to yourselves. Won't do nobody no good to get the Feds pokin' around in here. And with the recent harassment of churches and church folks, makin' a big noise will only drop a big red target right in the middle of this town." He nodded at Papa. "Good thing these people have someone like you lookin' after them. Somebody reasonable." With that, he turned and walked out, the door slamming behind him. I looked outside and saw Sophie leaning in the sheriff's car, talking to Tom. When the sheriff approached his car, he said something, and Sophie jumped back as if he'd hit her.

Suddenly Jonathon exploded at Papa. "How could you let him get away with that? We can't trust him to really investigate Avery's murder. What if he lets the killer walk free?"

"I do not believe the sheriff will do that," Papa said. "His advice about opening ourselves up to the world's scrutiny was wise and for our benefit. We cannot allow ourselves to lose what we have fought so hard to protect. A safe place where our people are not forced to accept the sin and violence in the world. We'll have to leave this in the Lord's hands. Vengeance does not belong to us."

"The violence in the world?" Noah said, a note of incredulity in his tone. "Violence has touched Kingdom, Samuel. Avery is dead. Our dear friend is dead."

"Noah's right," Jonathon interjected. "We need to protect ourselves. We can't sit around and let men with wicked intentions pick us off one by one."

"Yes, Avery is dead," Papa exclaimed, "and you want to start a war with the men who killed him? How many more of us will end up like our brother? And what will we lose if we pursue this?" He stared at Jonathon, his expression stony. "What would Avery want us to do, Jonathon? He loved this town, and he loved our people. Do you not realize that he would tell us to respond with love and forgiveness? To turn the other cheek? I can assure you that Avery is with God now. He is not looking for any kind of revenge."

Jonathon started to respond but before he could get a word out, the front door swung open, and Sheriff Ford came in again.

"I forgot somethin'," he said. "Mr. Menninger had this with him when we found him." He pulled the door open, and a small border collie slunk into the dining room.

"Beau!" Papa said. "I didn't even think to ask about him."

Avery's best friend lay on the floor, trembling and frightened.

"I can take him to the pound, but that'll probably be the last place he'll ever see," Ford said. "If none of you wants him . . ."

Everyone in the room was silent as we stared at the small black and white dog. I felt as if my already tattered heart were being torn into little pieces as he looked back at our assembled group, the terror of losing his beloved master evident in his eyes.

"I will take the dog," Papa said suddenly. "It is the least I can do for Avery."

I stared at my father in surprise. I'd been pleading for a dog ever since I was six, and Papa had always said no. *"Dogs are too much trouble,"* he'd say. *"They are dirty, and they tear things up. We don't need one."* Ruth Fisher, one of Kingdom's oldest residents, told me once that when she was a girl, most Mennonite people she knew viewed all animals as livestock. Hardly anyone had pets. But down through the years, things had shifted. Some of it had to do with hard-hearted people dumping unwanted animals off in the country. Many of them wandered into Kingdom, and every one of them found a home. Now there were all kinds of dogs and cats running around town. Regardless, my father had held firm to his old viewpoint. Until today.

"That's fine then," Ford said. He turned and walked out the door. I watched him trod down the steps to his car. Sophie stood on the sidewalk and stared at the vehicle as it drove away.

"Now, before you two start arguing again," Noah said to Jonathon and Papa, "I've called for an elders' meeting. We'll decide what needs to be done"—he frowned at Papa— "or not done about this situation. But for now, someone needs to contact Berlene and tell her about Avery." He looked at Lizzie, who was much more composed now. "Do you have her number?"

She nodded. "It's in Cora's phonebook."

"Good. If you'll show me where it is, I'll make the call."

They got up and left the room. Papa stood up and walked over to where Beau lay cowering on the floor. "Come here, Beau," he said in a gentle but firm voice.

The anxious dog stood slowly to his feet and took a few tentative steps toward Papa. Then he sat down next to his right leg.

"Avery would be grateful to know you took Beau," Jonathon said. "You're a decent man, Samuel. I'm sorry you don't like me. I wish you did." It was obvious he was still upset, but it was to his credit that he was able to hold his tongue. He nodded at me and left the restaurant.

Papa didn't say anything, just stood looking down at Beau.

Callie came up next to me and put her arm around my waist. "What about your food? Do you still want it?"

"Oh, I'd forgotten."

"I am sorry, Daughter," Papa said. "In all the confusion I forgot that you still haven't had your supper."

"I'm not really hungry anymore, Papa."

"If you do not eat, you will be weak, Hope." He walked over to our plates and took the tin foil off the top of each one. "It's still warm." He gave me a small smile. "I realize supper is the last thing on your mind now, but I would feel much better if you had some food in you. Will you try to eat something? For me?"

I did feel rather faint, and even though I wasn't hungry, I realized it was probably wise to put something in my body. "Yes, Papa."

"Good." He put one of the plates in front of me, and Callie went to get me a glass of water.

Papa started to sit down at the table, but suddenly stopped as he stared down at Beau, who remained where he was. "Oh, I suppose I must tie Beau up outside."

"Nonsense."

Lizzie had come back into the dining room. The color was back in her cheeks, and she looked much more composed. "Beau will stay right where he is. He's welcome in here any-time. Since the health department doesn't even know about this place, I doubt we'll get in trouble over it."

"Thank you, Lizzie," Papa said. "I would hate for him to be alone right now. I expect he will need some time to settle down after what he has been through."

Beau's large brown eyes held so much sorrow I felt my own eyes well up. "I remember how happy he always was to see people," I said, trying not to choke up. "That tail of his had a mind its own, always wagging. Whenever he was around, you could hear it thumping against the floor." Beau's tail lay still, almost as if it were broken. Would it ever wag again?

"Come, Beau," Papa said gently. Beau got to his feet and came over to the table, but instead of sitting next to Papa, he walked slowly over to me and laid his head on my lap. I stroked his soft fur, not caring about the tears that ran down my cheeks. As I gazed into Beau's soft brown eyes, I felt something stir inside me, and I knew the small dog and I would be more than dog and owner. We would be lifelong friends.

I finished eating my meal with one hand while keeping the other one on Beau's furry head. Every once in a while, when Papa wasn't looking, I snuck Beau a piece of chicken. He took it willingly. I was grateful he was able to eat.

I wanted desperately to discuss Avery's death with Papa and to appeal to him to reconsider Jonathon and Noah's concerns. But no one knew my father better than I did, and this was the time to be quiet. His emotions were raging, and when that happened, it took him some time to listen to reason. Setting him off now wouldn't help anyone.

After finishing our dinners, Papa, Beau, and I prepared to go home. Papa led Daisy back behind the quilt shop so he could harness her to our other buggy. I waited for him on the steps in front of the shop, Beau by my side.

Before I saw a horse, I heard hoofbeats pounding hard on the street. I turned just in time to see Ebbie pull his horse, Micah, up to the hitching post in front of the restaurant. He jumped off the horse before he came to a full stop, and quickly tied Micah up. Even from where I sat I could see that Ebbie was as white as a bleached sheet. His body trembled as he started toward the front door of the restaurant.

"Ebbie?" I called out. "Ebbie, what's wrong?"

He froze in his steps and turned slowly toward me. When he saw me, he sank down to his knees. Alarmed, I got up and ran to him, Beau right behind me.

"Are you all right?" I knelt down next to him. "Ebbie? Ebbie, what's the matter? Are you feeling ill?" I was shocked to see tears on his cheeks.

"I was at home and John Lapp came over to buy milk. My father talked with him for a moment and then came running into the house. He said you were run over on the road to Kingdom, and that you . . . that you had died."

"Oh, Ebbie. I *was* almost hit by a truck earlier today, but I'm fine." I put my hands on his cheeks. "Ebbie, it was Avery Menninger who was killed."

Fresh tears filled his eyes. "Avery? Avery's dead?"

I nodded. He put his head against my shoulder, and I held him as he composed himself. Ebbie's display of emotion was foreign to me. Papa believed that men should keep their feelings private and never lose control in public. I'd never seen a grown man act this way, and although it moved me, I felt confused.

"I'm all right now," he said finally, pushing himself away from me. He stood to his feet and put his hand down so I could pull myself up. "I'm sorry. I was afraid I'd never see you again. I-I wanted to tell you . . ." He shook his head and wiped his face with his sleeve. "Never mind. I'm just glad you're okay."

The look in his brown eyes seemed so familiar. It took a moment for me to realize that it was the same expression I'd seen in Beau's eyes. Fear and sadness. The realization startled me. Was I responsible for creating those emotions?

I placed my hand on his arm. "Thank you for caring so much. It means a lot to me."

He didn't say anything, but his breath caught. He took a step back, as if he wanted me to remove my hand, so I did.

"This violence," he said, his voice low, "reminds me of the Scripture about the thief who comes to steal, kill, and destroy. Satan is working through these men." He shook his head. "Avery was a good person who had the right to live his life without someone deciding to take it from him." He leaned over and picked his hat up from the street, where it had fallen when he collapsed.

"Jonathon is getting a group of men together, Ebbie. They're going to find a way to protect us."

He looked at me intently. "The elders are meeting tonight to decide what to do. We don't need a group of vigilantes taking matters into their own hands."

I put my hands on my hips and scowled at him. "You know, I'm really getting a little tired of hearing that we have no right to defend ourselves. Avery is dead, Ebbie. Dead. If Kingdom is attacked, are we going to simply stand by and watch our friends and neighbors get hurt? Maybe even killed?"

He frowned at me. "Hope, you know what we believe. You've grown up in the teachings of the church. Are you questioning them?"

"Yes, Ebbie, I'm questioning them. Shouldn't my faith be something more than parroting what I've been instructed to think? Shouldn't it be what I actually believe?"

He considered what I'd said for a moment. "Yes, you're right," he said slowly. "It should be what you really believe."

I folded my arms across my chest. "Then convince me.

Make me believe what you believe. Explain to me why we're supposed to stand by and let violent men get away with murder."

Ebbie looked up at the sky as if he thought God might send down a message to help him with this crazy girl who had the audacity to question the long-held doctrines of her church. I was surprised to see the corners of his mouth twitch in a smile.

"Hope, you are one of a kind. An amazing person." He took a slow breath. "I'll pray about it, but if you truly are seeking counsel in this area, you may need to approach a different elder."

"Why? Because you can't give me an answer that makes any sense?"

"No. Because I think I need some time away from you. The feelings I have for you are too strong, and I don't trust myself to remain silent about them. If you don't mind, I think I've humbled myself enough for a while."

"Forget that," I insisted. "Counsel me like you would anyone else in the church. I want to understand why you think God wants us to be picked off like birds sitting on a fence."

His eyebrows shot up. "You've been shooting birds?"

I glared at him. "Are you taking this seriously?"

"Yes. I'm taking it very seriously. Trust me."

He started to say something else, but at that moment, Papa came around the side of the building with the buggy.

"I've got to go," I said.

"All right." He cleared his throat. "And again, I'm sorry if I embarrassed you with my display of emotion."

I shook my head. "I understand. Avery was your friend. He was mine too." I was aware that most of the grief Ebbie had demonstrated was because he thought I'd been killed, but I thought it best not to address it. What could I say that would help anything? Mourning Avery had to take precedence now.

Ebbie stared at me for several seconds, and then I turned to go. I called for Beau to follow me, but instead of obeying, he walked over to Ebbie and licked his hand. Ebbie squatted down and put his arms around the small border collie. I had the strangest feeling that dog and man were exchanging something silently between them.

"Let's go, Beau," I said again, but the dog just looked at me. "Come on, boy."

"He's afraid to get in the buggy," Ebbie said. "After what happened, can you blame him?"

"Oh, I hadn't thought . . ." I could feel tears sting my eyes, but I blinked them away. My whole body felt weak and washed out from crying. "What should I do?"

"Why don't you get in," Ebbie said. "Let me see if I can help."

I shrugged and went to the buggy, quickly explaining the situation to Papa.

He shook his head. "Poor dog. No one can understand how terrifying this day has been for him."

"Well, apparently someone can. Look." I pointed to Ebbie, who was walking slowly toward the carriage with Beau following tentatively behind him. When they reached us, Ebbie motioned for Beau to get in. The collie sat down, seemingly unable to master his fear. Ebbie knelt down beside him again and spoke gently in his ear. This went on for several minutes, while Papa and I waited silently, sensing we shouldn't interrupt. Suddenly Beau stood up and jumped into the buggy seat, plopping himself on my lap.

"He should get in the back," Papa said hesitantly.

"It's all right," I said. "He feels safer with me. Let's go home."

Papa didn't argue, just flicked the reins and told Daisy to get going. As she began to trot down the street, I looked back at Ebbie standing in the road, watching us. I waved good-bye, but he didn't respond. I stared at him in the side mirror until we turned toward home and I couldn't see him anymore.

CHAPTER 5

I woke up early Friday morning. Beau had slept next to my bed all night. Papa had planned to put him out in the barn, but when it came right down to it, he didn't have the heart.

"Beau is an animal, Hope," he'd warned me. "If you treat him like a person, it will confuse him. He can sleep in the house for a few days, but after that, he will have to stay outside."

I nodded to let him know I understood, not voicing my belief that Beau would never spend one night in the barn. Maybe my father didn't wear his feelings on his sleeve like Ebbie, but underneath his bluster beat a heart too tender to turn the little dog out.

Every morning after cooking breakfast and packing our lunches, I liked to take a cup of coffee outside with me and sit on the front steps of our house. Papa always fed and watered Daisy, checked the chicken coop for eggs, milked our cows, and tended his garden before we left for town. My time alone on the front porch had always been a peaceful time for me. Sometimes I read my Bible or prayed quietly, and other times I just meditated on different things.

However, this morning the world felt different. Avery's death had changed our town, and a pall of something dark and sinister seemed to hover over us. Someone full of hate had brought destruction to this special place, even though our forefathers settled here in the belief we would be safe from the influence of sin. Ebbie's words about Satan working through malicious men drifted into my head, and something rose up inside of me. I had no intention of allowing anyone to destroy Kingdom. Our spirit would never be broken if I had anything to say about it.

The morning air was warm, but a shiver ran through me, and I cut my coffee time short. I wrapped up a large loaf of friendship bread for Berlene and her husband, Herman, as I expected they would arrive at Avery's house from Summerfield today, tomorrow at the latest. Though I wasn't allowed to travel on the main road outside of town, I was certain someone would be going that way and could deliver it to them. Our community was very supportive, and when one of us died, everyone took the loss personally. We delivered food and helped in any way we could.

As Papa and I prepared to leave for the shop, Beau came running and jumped right into the carriage seat. His routine of riding with Avery seemed stronger than his fear of our buggy. I don't think Papa planned to take him with us, but once again, he didn't protest. As he had yesterday, Beau climbed up on my lap, and I stroked his head as we rode into town. We were confident about our safety because our house sat near town, and we didn't have to use the main road to reach the quilt shop. I couldn't help but wonder about those who lived on farms outside our borders. Would we get to town only to discover someone else had been assaulted?

When we reached the shop, Papa jumped out of the buggy and tied Daisy up. "You go in and open the store, Hope," he said. "I want to talk to Noah and find out what happened at the meeting last night."

Beau and I got out and went inside the shop. I found an old blanket in the back room and made a place for him to lie down behind the front counter. I also put some water in a bowl and placed it near him. Last night Papa had filled a dish full of rice mixed with ground beef and carrots for Beau's dinner.

"Chicken will be better for him than beef," Papa said. "I'll buy some tomorrow from Brother Anderson and grind it up. And when I pick the peas, we can add them to his food."

"How do you know how to feed him, Papa?" I'd asked.

"We had a dog when I was a child, Daughter. My father used him to herd livestock. One day he was attacked by coyotes and killed. I learned then that becoming attached to an animal can have grave consequences. I have no desire for you to feel that kind of pain, but I could not turn Beau away. All I can do is pray that you will not allow yourself to care more for this dog than you should."

And that was all he said about it. Strange how you think you know everything about a parent only to suddenly discover something new. Lizzie once said, *"Parents are a gift that keeps unwrapping itself. You never know what you'll find under the next layer."* That was certainly true of my father.

While Beau investigated the store, I put change in the cash register and tidied up. Then I sat down on my stool behind the counter, picked up my own quilt, and began to work. Beau, who seemed to have satisfied his curiosity, discovered the blanket and plopped down on it.

"Good dog," I said. He gave me back a doggy smile, but his tail remained limp. At this point, I was just grateful he was doing as well as he was after going through such a terrible ordeal. I was certain he missed Avery terribly.

I ran my hands over the quilt I was working on. I'd started it as a wedding quilt, something to adorn our bed after Ebbie and I were married. Even though it looked as if that wasn't going to happen, I decided to finish it anyway. I loved the pattern and the deep blue and yellow colors. I'd planned to embroider our names in the final square, but now I'd just leave it empty. Funny, that's how I felt. Empty. Before, when I thought about my wedding to Ebbie, I'd been excited about the future and having my own home. I tried to console myself with the knowledge that Ebbie and I weren't really meant to be together. Odd how much I missed him.

I worked for about thirty minutes. Then Isabelle Martin came in for some fabric and threads. A tall red-haired girl with a smattering of freckles across her nose, Belle had a sweetness about her that was infectious. We visited for a little while. Not long after she left, Papa returned from his meeting with Noah.

"So what did the elders decide?" I asked as he entered the shop.

"Goodness, Daughter. Let me at least close the door behind me." His sharp tone made it clear he was upset.

I waited patiently until he joined me behind the counter. He noticed Beau lying on the blanket I'd put on the floor. He frowned and started to say something but stopped and shook his head. Then he pulled up another stool and sat down.

"The elders have concluded that it might be wise to keep a closer eye on the road into Kingdom. Watch for strangers but only as the opportunity presents itself. However, Noah expressed his belief that the elders' decision did not go far enough. He suggested regular patrols. Although the other elders did not agree to sanction this idea, it was decided that should anyone wish to guard the road on a more structured schedule, they will not oppose it." He rubbed his beard and sighed. "I am afraid Noah is being influenced too much by Jonathon Wiese."

"Protecting our citizens isn't a bad thing, Papa."

"I understand how you feel, but we must be careful that our emotions do not stir us up to react in a way contrary to God's Word."

I cleared my throat and tried to look as if I were concentrating on my quilt. "So where does Ebbie stand?"

Papa was silent for a moment. "I think you know the answer to that, Hope. He will not sway from his belief that we should spend our time in prayer rather than trying to find ways to defend ourselves. He says that God should be our only protection."

That made my head snap up. "Well, God didn't do a very good job of protecting Avery, did He?" I was sorry as soon as the words popped out of my mouth. Usually Papa would be upset with something I said that sounded rebellious, but he didn't seem angry at all. Just sad.

"I know it seems like that, but I still believe in the goodness of God. Sometimes things happen we do not understand, yet I will still trust God's promises of protection. We are in a war against a cruel and heartless enemy, and although we may not pick up carnal weapons, we must certainly fight with spiritual ones." He shook his head. "I have seen my share of death, and more than once I have found myself wondering why a particular person, a good person, has died before their time." He gave me a small smile. "But I will trust God's Word over mortal circumstances until the day I draw my last breath. My father brought me up like that, and I believe he was right."

"I heard Miriam Zook say that God took Avery home. It hurts me to hear people blame our loving heavenly Father for the violent death of one of His children."

"It hurts me too. God is the bringer of life, Hope. It is our enemy who steals, kills, and destroys."

I almost dropped my needle. Ebbie had quoted the very same Scripture. I guess I shouldn't have been surprised. He and Papa were a lot alike.

"Well, I'm glad Grandfather brought you up the way he did. And I'm grateful you brought me up the same way."

He smiled at me. "Thank you. That means more to me than you can imagine." He crossed his arms over his chest and frowned. "Now, just when were you going to tell me about Ebbie breaking your engagement?"

This time I didn't drop my needle. Instead, I jammed it firmly into my finger. "Ouch!" I stuck my throbbing append-age into my mouth, which was fine since it gave me a little time to think. Grabbing a nearby tissue with my other hand, I finally took it out. "I was going to tell you, Papa. I just didn't know how. I knew you'd be upset."

He let out a deep sigh. "I was upset at first, Daughter, but Ebbie talked to me for quite a while about it. He reminded me that I was in love with your mother, and that I should want the same thing for you. Somehow I ended up feeling as if I should apologize to both of you. I have no idea how he did that. He is a very persuasive young man."

I shook my head slowly. "But I do love Ebbie, Papa. If it matters, I told him I didn't want to break our engagement. He wouldn't listen to me."

"He doesn't believe your love for him is strong enough to make a good marriage, Hope. No man wants to spend his life wondering if he was his wife's second choice."

I started to respond to Papa's comment when he held his hand up, signaling me to be quiet. "It doesn't matter now. The engagement is ended." He pointed at me. "I want to make one thing perfectly clear. I do not intend to get into another argument about Jonathon Wiese, but I vehemently oppose a marriage to him. I will not change my mind."

I sighed with exasperation. "Why do you keep implying that Jonathon and I have a serious relationship? We don't. He has never expressed a desire to marry me, Papa. Not once."

"Good. I will pray it stays that way."

"You're wrong about Jonathon, you know."

Before he had a chance to say anything else, the front door opened and Lizzie came in. I greeted her, thankful to escape any further conversation about Jonathon with my father.

"I thought you'd like to know that Berlene and her husband have arrived at Avery's house. The funeral will be Monday morning."

"Thank you, Lizzie," Papa said.

"We're preparing food for everyone after the service, but if you want to bring a salad, that would be helpful."

"We'll be glad to," I said. "How did Berlene receive the news?"

She shook her head. "She hadn't been back to see Avery for a while. I'm sure she's regretting it now."

"I feel bad for her."

Lizzie nodded. "I do too. Father is having a hard time of it. He and Avery were very close. I will always remember his kindness to Charity and me when we first came to Kingdom. He gave us most of our furniture."

"Avery was a very giving person," Papa said sadly. "He will be missed."

"Berlene asked me to pass a message to you, Samuel. She would appreciate it if you would come by Avery's house this afternoon. She has something she wants to talk over with you. I have no idea what it's about."

He looked puzzled. "Of course I will go, but I cannot imagine what she has to say to me."

I felt my stomach clench as I looked at Beau. "Maybe she wants Beau back."

Papa shrugged. "Perhaps that is it. I should probably take him with me."

I put my head down and stared at my quilt, but the tears that filled my eyes made it impossible to see.

"I'm certain that's not it," Lizzie said. "She asked about Beau, and when we told her he was with you, she was pleased."

My heart leapt with relief. I quickly wiped my eyes but not before a tear splashed down on the quilt.

"Then I won't take him," Papa said. "I will go to Avery's house right after lunch."

"You must drive on the main road to get to Avery's house, Papa. I don't want you out there alone."

"Noah and the elders have asked that we let them know if we need to travel out of town," Lizzie said. "Someone will go with you. I know Noah would be happy to drive you in his truck."

"I would appreciate that," Papa said. "Are you sure it is not too much trouble?"

"No, not at all." Lizzie smiled at me. "We haven't had much time together lately, Hope. Do you think this crotchety father of yours would let you come over and have a piece of pie with me this afternoon while he and Noah are gone?"

Papa chuckled. "I think that could be arranged."

"Thank you, Papa," I said with a smile. "About two, Lizzie?"

"That would be perfect. See you then."

I waved good-bye to her. My heart soared knowing we would have some time to visit. Lizzie liked to call it "girl time."

"I wonder why Berlene would want to see me," Papa mused, stroking his beard again.

I shook my head. "I have no idea, but I'm glad we can do something to help her."

Papa agreed. A few minutes later Bethany Mendenhall, the pastor's wife, came in with one of their daughters, and I spent some time helping them pick out fabric for a new quilt they wanted to make together. Bethany wasn't an experienced seamstress, so teaching her daughter to quilt would be a bit of a challenge. We talked for almost an hour about how to choose the right fabrics and notions, along with what quilt pattern might be the easiest for a beginner. By the time they left, I felt confident they were equipped to create the kind of quilt they would be proud of.

The rest of the morning passed quickly. We'd just finished lunch when Noah came by to pick up Papa and drive him to Avery's house. I cautioned them to be careful.

"I doubt anyone would suspect we were Mennonite by my truck," Noah said with a grin.

"Oh, right. And your hats won't tip them off at all," I said wryly.

"Oh, I forgot." He looked at Papa. "Maybe we should take our hats off and put them in the back seat."

My father's face took on an expression I was familiar with. Steadfast and resolute. "I will not remove my hat for fear of any man." He peered intently at Noah. "I know it is nothing more than a hat, but for me to take it off would mean I am hiding who I am and what I believe. I will not do that."

Noah looked embarrassed. "Of course. You're right, Samuel. My apologies for suggesting it."

Papa patted him on the shoulder, his humor restored. "I am too quick to react sometimes, Noah. You are a good man, and I am happy to call you my friend."

"I'm only sorry your response wasn't mine," Noah replied. "You always seem to find the right path faster than I can."

I sighed heavily. "If you two are finished congratulating each other on your finer qualities, perhaps you could get going? I need to get ready for some serious girl time with Lizzie."

Papa looked stunned for a moment, but then both men began to laugh. I couldn't help but join in.

"My daughter has a way of making me look ridiculous

sometimes," Papa said, still chuckling. "I must agree with her. We can express our admiration for each other later. Let's get over to Avery's and see what Berlene needs."

"I have several casseroles from some of the women in town as well as a basket of Lizzie's fried chicken and a bowl of potato salad in the truck," Noah said. "I'm sure Berlene and her husband have been visited by other residents delivering food and assistance."

"Oh my," I said. "I almost forgot. I have a loaf of bread for them. Let me get it." I hurried to the back room, where I removed the bread from our propane icebox. I wrote a quick note of condolence and slid it between the layers of cloth I'd used to cover the loaf. "Here it is," I said as I came back into the main shop room. Taking a sack from under the counter I slid the loaf inside so it would be easier to carry.

"Thank you for thinking of this, Daughter," Papa said. He leaned over and kissed my forehead. "We will be back later this afternoon. Have a pleasant visit with Lizzie."

"I will, Papa. Please be careful." I smiled at Noah. "Hats or no hats, don't take any chances, okay?"

"I won't, Hope. We'll be fine." Noah picked his hat up from the counter where he'd put it when he came in and planted it firmly on his head. I saw him cast a quick glance toward Papa, and I found it touching that he cared so much what my father thought.

After they left, I put all the supplies away that were lying on the counter and prepared for my appointment with Lizzie. It had been too long since our last visit, and I needed to unburden myself to her about my broken engagement to Ebbie. Leaning down to put some thread on the bottom shelf of the front counter, I heard the front door open. I hoped desperately it wasn't Maybelle Crabb. She was a nice woman who lost her husband several years ago and craved company. Her visits could go on and on, and I wanted to get to the restaurant.

I straightened up, praying I'd see anyone but Maybelle. My prayer was answered. Instead, I found myself looking up into the intense eyes of Jonathon Wiese.

CHAPTER 6

"Oh my, Jonathon," I said, my voice a little too squeaky. "Wh-what are you doing here?"

He gave me a quick smile. "That's a good question, Hope. You've probably guessed I don't quilt much."

I laughed, but his humorous statement did nothing to quell the nervous butterflies in my stomach. We'd had many conversations, but they usually occurred in the presence of other people. Except for our time out on the road, which didn't really count, we'd spoken alone only a few times. All of those instances had happened in public places, like in the restaurant or on the street. Once we'd talked after church while Papa was having a long conversation with Pastor Mendenhall in his office.

"Are you busy?" he asked.

"No. I mean, yes. I mean . . ." I cleared my throat and tried to get control of myself. It wasn't easy with his eyes fastened on me. He'd removed his hat, and his dark, longish hair framed his face, making him look so handsome I found it hard to catch my breath. Of course, Mennonites weren't supposed to care about worldly things like outward adornment, but somehow Jonathon always managed to look perfect no matter the circumstance.

"If I'm interrupting something—"

"No. No, not at all. I'm supposed to meet Lizzie for pie and coffee this afternoon, but I still have a little time."

"I wanted to see how you're doing after yesterday's scare."

"Much better, thank you. After what happened to Avery, I feel very fortunate." I sighed. "And a little guilty."

Jonathon's eyebrows shot up. "Guilty? Why? You had nothing to do with Avery's death."

"I keep wondering if he was killed because I got away."

"Oh, Hope. You can't let thoughts like that into your head. They will only torture you."

"I-I know. It's just . . ."

He walked over to where I stood and took my hands in his. "You have the best heart of anyone I've ever known. What happened to Avery had nothing to do with you. It had to do with malicious men who are spurred on by hate." He turned my right hand over and stared at my open palm. My heart fluttered inside my chest like a frightened moth trying to escape a trap.

"Papa went over to Avery's house to talk to his daughter," I said, not knowing why I said it.

"I know." His blue eyes bored into mine. "I heard you're no longer engaged to Ebbie Miller."

My heart must have moved from my chest to my throat because I didn't seem capable of speech. I couldn't even swallow. All I could do was nod.

"You must know how I feel about you, Hope. I'm not very good at hiding it."

I shook my head and struggled to find my voice. "No . . . I mean, I have no idea—"

Before I could get another word out, he leaned over and kissed me. It was the first time I'd ever been kissed on the mouth by a man. Ebbie and Papa had kissed me on the forehead and on the cheek, but this felt totally different.

"I hope you're not offended," Jonathon said softly, just inches from my face, "but I'm in love with you. I have been for a long time. I've wanted to tell you how I felt, but I couldn't because you were engaged to Ebbie." He let go of my hands and turned away. "Maybe it's too soon after breaking your engagement to think about another man." He swung back toward me, his expression taut and serious. "But I couldn't take the chance of not speaking to you now. Before you become engaged again. Do you understand?"

I nodded dumbly. "Please . . . I need time to think."

"I understand." He cleared his throat and leaned against the side counter. "I'm getting some people together to see if there's something more we can do to keep our citizens out of harm's way. If you'd like to join us—"

"I know I told you I wanted to help," I said, interrupting him, "but are you sure other people will want me involved? I mean, because I'm a woman."

"Hope," he said sharply, a frown darkening his handsome features, "you're one of the smartest people in this town. Why wouldn't we need you? You're just as talented and gifted as any man in Kingdom. Besides, there are already three other women who have asked to be at our first meeting."

His words gave me an odd sense of strength. Father had never tried to make me feel inferior as a woman, but he strongly believed women were the weaker sex and needed to be treated as such. However, it seemed to me that protecting Kingdom was the job of all our residents.

"When are you meeting?"

"Around three o'clock. At Noah's."

"Papa is with Noah," I said slowly. "If he'll be back for the meeting, Papa will be with him. I can't—"

"It's all right, Hope," he said with a smile. "I don't want to cause trouble with your father. I know he doesn't like me."

"He doesn't dislike you, Jonathon. He dislikes some of your beliefs. He's very old-fashioned when it comes to our Mennonite traditions."

Jonathon was silent for a moment. Then he gazed into my eyes. "And you? What do you believe, Hope?"

His question flustered me. What *did* I believe? I shook my head. "I wish I could tell you, but I can't. I don't condone violence, yet I also believe we should take care of the people we love. It's confusing. Ebbie says . . ."

I caught myself before I went any further, but it wasn't soon enough. Jonathon scowled at the mention of Ebbie's name.

"Ebenezer Miller thinks we should lie down and let our enemies slaughter us with smiles on our faces," he said in a subdued voice. "He believes there is some kind of honor in giving our lives for an ideal that has been passed down through our traditions. But traditions can be wrong."

I thought over his words. "Ebbie says we should pray for our enemies and let God defend us."

"Then why did God tell the children of Israel to fight and kill their enemies? Does that make any sense?"

I sighed. "Ebbie says Christ brought a different covenant.

That we no longer are under a covenant of judgment, but instead we're under a covenant of grace. And that means we must extend grace toward those who would try to hurt us. Just like Jesus."

Jonathon grunted. "Ebbie says. Ebbie says. You've been brainwashed by Ebbie Miller."

"No I haven't." My denial came out with more force than I'd meant to use, but his statement angered me. "I have my own mind, thank you. It just isn't as made up as yours."

He reached over and put his hands on my shoulders. "I'm sorry, Hope. You're right. It isn't easy for me either. I want to please God and handle this the way He wants me to, but I can't believe He intends for us to do nothing while we watch our brothers and sisters being murdered." He shook his head. "Seeing you in danger made me absolutely certain of my convictions. Maybe Ebbie could have watched you die, but I couldn't." He leaned down and kissed me again. This time his lips lingered a little longer.

Hearing the front door open, I quickly twisted away from him. Was Papa back already? Sophie stood in the doorway, a look on her face I couldn't interpret.

"Here you are," she said, looking at Jonathon. "Is the meeting still scheduled for three?"

Jonathon frowned at her. "Yes. I told you that a little while ago, Sophie. Don't you remember?"

She shrugged and stared at me the way a bird might look at a bug right before it becomes lunch. "I forgot. How long you gonna hang around here?"

"Actually, I do need to get going. I want to invite Aaron to our discussion." He smiled at me. "I hope to see you at three, Hope, but if you don't come, it's okay. I'll understand."

As he headed toward the door, Sophie shot me one last dirty look before she flounced out after him. It was obvious she had feelings for Jonathon. Feelings he didn't return. She was such a lost soul. Unrequited love certainly wasn't going to help her self-confidence. When I had a chance, I'd talk to Jonathon. He probably had no idea she cared for him. As irritating as she could be, I didn't want to see her hurt.

After checking the clock, I realized I was running late. Lizzie was probably wondering where I was. I hurried to the back room, cleaned up a bit, and then headed for the restaurant. I'd planned to leave Beau in the shop, but he got up and followed me out the door. Even though Lizzie had said Beau was always welcome in the restaurant, I was happy to find the dining room almost empty. I didn't want his presence to bother any of Lizzie's customers. Tonight was her busiest night. Most folks were waiting to come for the Friday night dinner specials, so finding only a couple of diners wasn't really a surprise. Lizzie was pouring iced tea for Harold Eberly when I entered. She motioned for me to take a seat at a table in the corner. I'd only been sitting a few minutes when she brought over a coffeepot and two plates with Dutch apple pie and ice cream.

I glanced at the clock on the wall. A little after two thirty. Jonathon's meeting would start in about thirty minutes. There was no way I could go. I couldn't lie to Papa. Even though he'd grudgingly agreed that I should have the right to make some choices of my own, his reaction to finding me with Jonathon and those who seemingly opposed our nonviolent beliefs would push him too far.

"Are you going to talk to me or stare into space?"

Lizzie's words made me jump. "I-I'm sorry. I was thinking about something else." I pointed at Beau, who had curled up next to my feet. "I can take him back to the shop if you'd like."

She grinned. "I told your father Beau could come in here anytime, and I meant it. We'll just make him our mascot." She leaned down to scratch Beau behind the ears and was rewarded with a big sloppy smile from the contented dog.

"Thanks, Lizzie. I'll stop worrying about it." I jammed my fork into the warm pie, vanilla ice cream dripping down the sides. Then I stuck it into my mouth. "Mmm. This is so good. You've outdone yourself this time."

"I added caramel and pecans to it," she said quietly. "Cora's recipe was great, but I wanted to add my own touch. Don't tell anyone, Hope. I don't want folks to think I'm saying I'm a better cook than Cora."

She actually was better than Cora, but I understood her loyalty to the woman who had given her a home in Kingdom. "Well, it's incredible." I sighed. "If you keep cooking this way, I'll end up as big as a barn."

She laughed. "I don't think there's any danger of that."

I nodded but didn't say anything.

"Is something wrong, Hope?" she asked. "You seem preoccupied."

"Ebbie and I are no longer engaged."

"I heard about the breakup. Word spreads through town pretty quick. Ebbie's parents are rather distressed."

"Oh, I'm sorry. I like them."

"Well, they're not upset with you. Ebbie took full responsibility for the whole thing."

"He did?" I wasn't surprised. He'd said he planned to take the blame. He could have easily held me at fault. Told everyone I cared for someone else. But he didn't. It was just like him.

Lizzie reached over and put her hand on mine. "Hope, you're my very best friend. Anything you tell me will stay between us. You know that, right?"

Abram and Miriam Zook got up from their table and, after laying some money down, smiled at us and left. The only other person in the room was Lutz Zimmerman, one of our church elders. He was on the other side of the room, seemingly engrossed in whatever he was reading, so I felt safe enough to talk openly. I quickly told Lizzie everything: Why Ebbie broke our engagement and what had happened between Jonathon and me before I arrived at the restaurant. By the time I finished, Lizzie's eyes were round saucers of surprise.

"Oh, Hope. Does your father know you care for Jonathon?"

I shook my head. "He's not certain, but he suspects it." I told her about Papa's contrition after our argument in the restaurant. "He apologized and told me he realized I was old enough to make my own decisions."

Lizzie looked confused. "You do realize that Samuel was right about Jonathon's feelings for you?"

"Well, yes. But he believed that before Jonathon said anything."

She looked at me strangely. "Oh, Hope. That doesn't make any difference."

I couldn't help grinning. "No, it doesn't. I guess I just don't want Papa to be right."

"But he was."

"I know."

Lizzie laughed.

"I'm so glad I have you to talk to, Lizzie. I feel better already."

"Look, Hope, I don't want to tell you what you should do, but—"

At that moment, the front door swung open and Jonathon walked in. He said hello to Lutz and then headed toward our table. I felt my face flush.

"Uh-oh. Is that your famous Dutch apple pie, Lizzie?" he asked with a smile.

"Yes, it is. Is that your subtle hint that you'd like a piece, Jonathon?"

He gave her an innocent look. "Now, where did you get that idea? You're way too suspicious."

She chuckled. "I'll get you some. How about a cup of coffee to go with it?"

"That would be wonderful." He lowered his voice. "Is Noah already upstairs?"

She shook her head. "He took Samuel over to Avery's house, but he said he'd be back in time for the meeting. You've got just enough time for pie and coffee before he gets here."

"Wonderful." He looked at me. "Do you mind if I sit with you? I don't want to interrupt your visit."

Lizzie stood up. "Nonsense. We were about done anyway. Have a seat."

She winked at me before she took off toward the kitchen. I felt my cheeks grow hotter. As Jonathon pulled out his chair, he noticed Beau. He reached down to pet him. "How's this guy doing?"

"Pretty good. He stays close to me though."

Jonathon frowned. "Was he in the shop earlier? I didn't see him."

I nodded. "He was lying down on his blanket behind the counter."

"I remember how he used to greet everyone when he came to town with Avery. That tail of his wagged so fast you could barely see it."

"He might not act like himself for a while. He's been through a lot." My voice caught. Thinking about Beau reminded me of Avery.

Jonathon must have felt the same way, because he didn't say anything for a moment. Then he cleared his throat before looking at me. "So are you coming to the meeting?"

I started to answer him, but at that very moment, Ebbie walked in the door. I suddenly felt incredibly guilty. Why did he have to pick this moment to come here? I reminded myself that we weren't engaged anymore and forced myself to meet his gaze.

His eyes went back and forth between me and Jonathon. "I-I'm looking for Noah. Is he here?"

I shook my head. "He took my father over to Avery's house to see Berlene. They should be back any minute. You can wait with us if you'd like."

Ebbie looked like he'd rather do anything than sit down at our table. His eyes darted around the room until he spotted Lutz. He appeared to be considering Lutz as an alternative, but the elderly man got up and headed out the door, grunting a quick greeting to the three of us as he passed by. Ebbie wasn't left with any choice. He sat down on the other side of our table, as far away from Jonathon and me as he could get.

At that moment, Lizzie came out of the kitchen with Jonathon's pie. "Ebbie!" she said warmly. "How nice to see you. I've got a piece of Dutch apple pie hot from the oven with your name on it."

"Um, no. But thank you, Lizzie. I'm waiting for Noah."

The sound of an engine coming up the road outside drew Lizzie's attention. She put Jonathon's pie down on the table in front of him and hurried to the front door. First she shot me a quick look of concern, suspecting how ill at ease I was.

"It's Noah," she called out.

As she waited by the door, the three of us sat in an uncomfortable silence. Papa was going to walk in and see me sitting with Jonathon and Ebbie. What would he think? Even more important, what would he say? I decided to leave.

"I . . . I'd better get back to the store," I said. "Excuse me."

Ebbie and Jonathon just stared at me without responding.

"Oh, Hope. You don't have to go yet," Lizzie said, looking my way. "You haven't even finished your pie."

For the life of me, I couldn't think of a response. Finally Noah came in the door. He kissed Lizzie and then noticed me standing near Ebbie and Jonathon. His eyebrows shot up. "Well, hello," he said, looking a little confused.

"Noah," I said, frowning, "where's Papa?"

"He decided to stay a little longer. Herman will drive him back to town when they're through visiting."

I was surprised, to say the least. "What are they talking about?"

Noah shook his head. "If you don't mind, I think I'll let your father explain that to you. I don't think it's my place."

I found the situation bewildering. What in the world would Papa, Herman, and Berlene have to discuss that would take so long?

Ebbie stood up. "I'd like a word with you, Noah. If you don't mind."

"If it's a continuation of what we talked about at the elders' meeting, there really isn't anything more for me to say."

The door opened and Sophie slinked in. Her eyes darted to Noah and then to Jonathon.

"Go on upstairs, Sophie," Noah said. "We'll be up in a minute."

Noah, Charity, and Lizzie lived upstairs in the small apartment where Lizzie stayed when she first came to Kingdom. It was a tight fit, but until their house was ready, it was the best place for them. Lizzie was grateful to have an option that kept them so close to the restaurant.

Ebbie glanced over at me before addressing Noah. I could see the conflict in his face. "I just wanted to encourage you not to go outside of what was decided in our meeting, Brother Noah. I'm concerned this could end badly. I know you're trying to protect our town, but isn't that God's job? Isn't He our protector?" He shook his head. "Please reconsider."

Lizzie walked to the door and turned the Open sign to Closed. I stood there like a trapped rat. My first instinct was to flee, but I honestly wanted to attend the meeting. Maybe it was mostly curiosity, but I felt the need to look at the argument from both sides. I'd already listened to Papa's opinion.

"Look, Ebbie," Noah said patiently, "as I explained at the

elders' meeting, I simply want to make sure we're exploring all our options. I still believe in peaceful resistance. We're not advocating guns or violence. We're simply trying to find a way to keep our citizens safe. There's nothing wrong with resisting our enemies in nonviolent ways. That's the kind of solution we're trying to find."

Jonathon stood to his feet, his face set and angry. "If either one of you had been on the road with me, watching Hope nearly run down, you wouldn't be so quick to rule out weapons." He focused on Ebbie. "You cared enough about Hope to want to marry her, yet you would have stood by and watched her die for some misguided religious belief? That's not love. That's exalting your principles over her life." He swung his gaze to back Noah. "You congratulated me for protecting her, but didn't I use my truck as a weapon? I threatened the man on the road with bodily harm, didn't I? What's the difference between that and showing these animals we're armed? It doesn't mean we'll actually shoot anyone. It's just a warning. Like my truck."

I watched Noah, wondering what his response would be. Frankly, I thought Jonathon had made a pretty good point.

"I understand what you're saying," Noah said slowly, "but I'm not prepared to shoot another human being. I just won't do it."

"You hit a man over the head with a chair when Lizzie's life was in danger," I said softly. "What's the difference between using a chair or a gun? Aren't they both weapons when used to hurt someone?"

"Hope's right," Jonathon said, jumping on my comment. "Are you sorry you hit that man?"

Noah was silent for a moment, staring down at the floor. Finally he lifted his head. "No. No, I'm not sorry."

"So answer Hope's question. What's the difference?" Jonathon repeated.

"I reacted in a situation that suddenly presented itself," Noah said harshly. "I didn't plan to go out and hurt anyone." He pointed his finger at Jonathon. "But you're preparing to confront other human beings, and you're planning to use violent means if you decide it's necessary."

Ebbie slowly rose to his feet. "I hear both of you justifying yourselves." He shook his head. "I understand why you reacted the way you did, Noah, trying to save the life of the woman you love. In your situation, I can't say I would have behaved differently. But that doesn't make it right. God created a world of peace. Maybe men brought unrighteousness and violence into that world, but God's original intent has never changed. Jesus was threatened, but he didn't defend Himself. He freely gave His life."

"Wait a minute," Jonathon interjected. "Christ's mission was to lay down His life for our sins. It wasn't Hope's mission to die on the road to Kingdom. And it wasn't Lizzie's mission to die at the hands of a man who wanted to steal her child. You're twisting the Scriptures to fit your purposes. Your argument doesn't hold up."

"What about being persecuted for righteousness' sake?" Ebbie asked. "Turning the other cheek? Not resisting your enemies? Do you just ignore these Scriptures?"

"No. I practice them, Ebbie," he answered, his words clipped and carefully measured, "but not at the expense of someone I love. If you fault me for that, then I'll accept it."

When Jonathon used the word *love* in reference to me, Ebbie flinched as if he'd been struck. I saw the hurt in his face, and I felt awful.

"Ebbie, why don't you come upstairs and talk with us?" Noah said. It was obvious to me that he was trying to calm rising tempers. "We need to hear what you have to say."

Ebbie shook his head. "No. I believe you've already made up your minds, and I don't want any part of it."

"But I haven't, Ebbie," I said softly. "And I would truly like to hear your opinion. What you've said makes sense to me."

His eyes searched mine, and for a moment I think he considered it.

"No," he said finally. "I don't think we have anything more to say to each other."

His words stung more than I thought they could, and I was unable to stop the tears that filled my eyes. Ebbie turned away from us and walked toward the front door. Just as he reached for the handle, the door swung open. Roger Carson, a young man I'd gone to school with many years ago, walked in. His wife, Mary, who'd been raised in Kingdom, followed him. She'd left town when she was eighteen and married Roger not long after that. Although Mary was raised as a Mennonite, she and Roger now attended a nondenominational church in Washington, where they lived. I'd run into Mary a few times during my trips to the fabric store and was happy to see her. Ebbie didn't say anything to either one of them. He just pushed the front door open and left. I stared out the window as he unhitched Micah and rode out of town. As I watched him drive away, an odd sadness washed through me.

Roger and Mary greeted everyone and followed Noah upstairs. Lizzie and Sophie headed up as well.

"What do you want to do, Hope?" Jonathon asked.

I stared at him for a few moments, my brain racing. "Let's go," I said, still unsure about my decision.

With that, we climbed the stairs, Beau trotting along behind us.

CHAPTER /7

I loved Lizzie and Noah's apartment. Homey, warm, and charming. The four rooms had been turned into two bedrooms, a living room, and a spare room with an extra bed, dresser, and desk. Lizzie liked to work on her accounts in the fourth room, keeping her papers and receipts in a small wooden filing cabinet. When she and Charity first moved here, Cora used the room for storage, but after Lizzie and Noah married, he set up shelves and storage space in the basement, freeing up additional space for the three of them. Even though Lizzie was excited about the new house, I knew she would miss this place. I wondered if the lovely rooms would sit empty or if someone else would move in.

We congregated in the living room. Noah grabbed a couple of chairs from other rooms so everyone would have a place to sit. Once we were settled, Roger began the meeting.

"We've gathered as much information as we could," he said, pulling a small notebook out of his pocket. "You've got to understand that the sheriff isn't what you'd call . . . helpful.

He's keeping a lot of information to himself. Besides, he has a really bad attitude about Christians."

"We've certainly seen that," Noah said. "What's his problem?"

Roger shook his head. "About ten years ago, he and his wife attended a small church in Washington. His wife worked as the church secretary. One day she took off with the pastor, who left his wife and children behind too. That explains why Sheriff Ford seems so bitter toward people of faith."

"That's awful," Noah said. "How can people call themselves Christians and make such selfish decisions? The havoc wreaked in the lives of their families can take years to repair."

"Well, it certainly sowed some bad seed in Sheriff Ford's life. You remember his son, Tom?"

I nodded. How could I forget? I tried to keep his leering grin out of my mind.

"Well, he was really hurt when his mother left. Tom used to be a nice kid, but he's changed. Now the sheriff has to deal with him too. Frankly, I feel sorry for the guy."

"I feel bad for him too," Jonathon said, "but he still has the responsibility to do his job. If he can't, he should step down."

Roger shrugged. "I agree with you there, but I wouldn't count him out. He may not like us, but I think he'll do what he can to find out who caused Avery's death."

While I searched my heart for some compassion for Tom, which was more difficult than it should have been, I couldn't help but notice Lizzie staring at Roger with suspicion. Although I was two years older than Lizzie, we were both terrorized by Roger when we were in grade school together in Washington. Children from Kingdom were treated like oddities by the regular kids. Roger had been one of our worst tormentors, and for some reason, Lizzie had been at the top of his list. In the past couple of months, tensions had eased some. Noah and Roger had become friends, and Roger had offered his heartfelt apologies to Lizzie for being such an "ignorant jerk." She forgave him, but I knew she still didn't completely trust him.

"Why are you helping us?" Lizzie asked suddenly. "You don't live here." She turned her attention to Mary. "And you moved away years ago. This isn't your fight."

Mary smiled at Lizzie. "First of all, just because I moved away doesn't mean I don't care about the people in Kingdom."

"I appreciate that," Lizzie said, "but your presence here still surprises me."

Mary frowned at her. "My parents live here, Lizzie. I'm trying hard to repair the misunderstanding between us. Things are actually going very well. I guess I feel if I can do something to help this town, people here may forgive my selfish actions."

Lizzie's expression softened. "Leaving wasn't selfish, Mary. I left for a while too. At the time I felt I had no choice."

Mary nodded. "I felt the same way. But ignoring my parents for years when I lived only a few miles away was wrong. They were good to me, and they deserved better."

"Your father was very strict. I remember when he pulled you out of school for eating lunch at a sandwich shop in Washington."

She smiled. "What you don't know is that he didn't take me out because I went to the deli. He took me out because I was extremely rebellious at home, and he was worried about me."

Lizzie stared at her for a moment without saying anything.

"All these years I had it wrong." She shook her head. "Not the first time, and I guess it won't be the last."

Mary laughed. "So am I allowed to stay?"

Lizzie waved her hand. "Please ignore me. I'm obviously an idiot."

"You're not an idiot. And thanks." She cleared her throat and the smile left her face. "Roger and I actually visited with several people who'd been harassed by these men." She tossed her head, her long hair flipping across her shoulder. She was no longer the shy, backward little girl with dull eyes and lifeless hair.

"So what did you find out?" Noah asked.

Roger spoke up. "Believe it or not, we think they're young guys. Late teens, early twenties. No one we talked to got a good look at them, but everyone's description was pretty much the same. Oh, and a couple of people mentioned a red truck. No license plate or anything. I wish we'd gotten that."

"Hard to worry about a license plate number when you're fighting for your life," Jonathon said with disgust.

"You've got that right," Roger said. He frowned at Jonathon. "Didn't you say you had another man who might be able to help us?"

"Yes, Aaron Metcalf. He offered to assist in any way he could, but right now he's so busy with the store I don't think we can count on him."

Roger shrugged. "I think keeping this town safe is a little more important than worrying about a business."

"It's not like that at all," Lizzie said sharply. "A lot of people are counting on Aaron, and he's got agreements set up with different distributors that can't be changed."

Roger noticed her tone and backed off. "Okay. I understand."

I held my hand up. "Could I ask a question?"

Mary smiled at me. "You don't have to raise your hand, Hope. This isn't Mrs. Gaskin's class."

Her mention of a particular teacher at Washington Elementary made me laugh. I put my hand down. "Does the sheriff have this same information?"

Roger nodded. "He should. We didn't have any trouble finding people who wanted to talk to us."

"Then I'm confused. If he's looking for the people behind these attacks, why are you doing the same thing?"

"I know it might seem redundant, but we don't trust him enough to leave the entire investigation in his hands. We want to make sure he doesn't miss something important."

Mary smiled and patted his leg. "Roger has always wanted to be a policeman. This gives him the chance to try out his investigative skills."

Roger colored with embarrassment, but he didn't disagree with his wife.

"Sheriff Ford threatened us when he came here after Avery was killed," Jonathon said. "He told us that if we made a big deal out of it, the media would be all over our town and that would open us up for more trouble than we had now."

"That's ridiculous," Mary said loudly. "That man really makes me mad. How in the world did he ever get elected in the first place?"

"Well, we sure didn't vote for him," Noah said with a deadpan expression.

Everyone burst out laughing, aware that the Kingdom community shunned involvement with the government or politics.

"Okay, you got me," Mary said, grinning, "but seriously, what can we do? How do we catch these guys, and how do we protect Kingdom?"

No one said anything for a moment. Finally Noah spoke up. "First of all, let me make one thing clear. I won't carry a gun or any other kind of weapon. I don't mind patrolling our borders . . . or doing anything else that might help, but my views are much closer to Ebbie's. I may have cracked a chair over a guy's head once who was trying to hurt Lizzie, but that's as violent as I'm ever going to get." He cleared his throat. "I hope." He gazed around the room. "So what are we signing on for here? I don't think you want me driving around with a chair in my truck just in case I happen upon one of these men."

Roger chuckled. "No. I think you can leave the chairs in the restaurant. Look, I've never been Mennonite, and Mary may be a fallen Mennonite"—he grinned at his wife—"but we're not into violence either."

Listening to Roger helped me to realize that Ebbie was wrong. No one here was promoting aggression. They were just trying to find a way to help our people in the most peaceful way possible.

I noticed that Sophie was scowling at Roger. No one appeared to be paying any attention to her. When she wasn't glaring at the rest of us, she was looking at Jonathon as if she were a dog and he a piece of meat. He didn't seem to notice.

"So all we're going to do is patrol?" Jonathon asked. "What happens if we see someone we don't know? How are we going to stop these troublemakers from coming into town?"

Noah stared at him blankly.

After clearing his throat, Roger spoke up. "Look, I understand how you all feel about this nonresistance thing—"

"It's not really nonresistance," Noah said. "We just don't believe in resisting evil with violence."

"The Bible says we're supposed to resist the *devil*, and he's evil," Sophie spat out. "So how are we gonna do that? Maybe Lizzie could make him a pie. That oughta do it." She shot daggers at Noah, anger distorting her features. "Do you have one single idea about how we can stand up to these people?"

"That Scripture you referenced also says we should submit ourselves to God first," Noah said gently. "Which is what we're trying to do." He shook his head. "And you're right. Our resistance should be against the devil. Not human beings."

Sophie snorted. "What in the world does that mean? You sound like my father. Saying things that don't make sense just so you can control everyone."

Noah frowned at her. "I'm simply saying we need to figure out how to protect ourselves in a way that won't betray our faith."

"Ebbie says we should just pray and let God protect us." The words popped out of my mouth before I could stop them. Everyone's eyes turned to me.

"I know," Jonathon said, "and I'm trying to respect him for his faith, but God uses people, Hope. And again, we're not advocating violence. We're just trying to find a way to . . . I don't know . . . a way to keep these people away from Kingdom. If we can do that, we'll be fulfilling the intent of Christ's teaching without giving them free rein over us."

"Look," Roger said, "I'm going to suggest something I'm pretty sure you're not going to like."

Noah nodded toward him. "Go ahead."

"Everyone here has a gun, right?"

"Well, rifles for hunting," Noah said.

"What if we set up different times to patrol the road into Kingdom, and we carry our hunting rifles? We're not going to use them, but no one needs to know that."

"Yeah, but everyone knows Mennonites aren't going to shoot anyone," Lizzie said. "How would that help?"

"Most people don't have a clue what Mennonites believe," Mary said. "Since leaving Kingdom, I've found that our . . . I mean, *your* community is a mystery to other folks. They think all you do is drive around in buggies, wear weird clothes, and shun electricity. To be honest, what the church believes isn't that interesting to them."

"So you're suggesting that we look like we're willing to shoot intruders even though we're not?" Noah shook his head. "I don't know. . . ."

I started to raise my hand again but stopped myself at the last second. "Isn't that dishonest?"

Lizzie nodded. "That's exactly what I was thinking. Besides, if they weren't planning to shoot us in the first place, waving a rifle at them could start something we don't want."

Jonathon stood to his feet. "I understand what you're saying, but these guys are playing for keeps." He directed his attention toward Noah. "If that had been Lizzie in that buggy—"

"I know. I know," Noah said harshly. "But this is different. This isn't a spur of the moment reaction. It's a prearranged strategy that could lead to someone getting hurt. Or worse."

"What if you carried a rifle that isn't loaded?" Roger asked. "Would that make you feel better?"

"That might do it," Jonathan agreed. "We wouldn't be in a position to really shoot anyone, but they wouldn't know that."

"We're splitting spiritual hairs here," Noah said. He looked back and forth between Lizzie and Jonathon. Finally he held his hands up in a gesture of surrender. "I'm an elder in the church. I appreciate what you're saying and how you feel, but I just can't do that. Carrying a rifle as a weapon, whether it's loaded or not, feels wrong to me. I'll do anything else I can to help, but I won't do that. You'll have to patrol without me."

Roger got up from his seat and walked over to where Noah sat on the couch. He put his hand on Noah's shoulder. "I respect that, Noah, and I think you're doing the right thing. Can I ask you to keep our plans to yourself though? I'm afraid if word gets out, it might make our efforts more difficult."

Noah chuckled. "You've never lived in Kingdom, Roger. You can ask Mary about it, but secrets are hard to keep here. I won't tell anyone, but I wouldn't be surprised if the whole town knows about it before long."

Roger patted Noah's shoulder once more, walked over to the window, and looked down on the street below. "All we can do is hope people understand."

"I believe they will," Jonathon said. "A lot of changes have already come to Kingdom. People are open to new ideas and have more freedom to make decisions on their own."

"No one is forced to do anything they don't want to," Noah said quietly. Even though his tone was light, he was obviously rebuking Jonathon. "The tenets of our faith are in place to protect us. To help us. Not to control us."

"You've got to admit it hasn't always been that way," Lizzie said. "I remember what it was like when my father was an elder."

"I do too," Mary said. "It's one of the reasons I left."

"I understand," Noah said, frowning, "but as you said, Jonathon, we're undergoing transformation. I guess I'm just trying to say that not everything we believe needs to change. Nonviolence is our way of following the teachings of Christ."

"But not everyone follows Jesus, Noah," Jonathon said. Noah started to say something else, but Jonathon held his hand up. "Look, we could go around and around about this, but what good would it do? We'll take unloaded rifles with us. There's no way we can hurt anyone with an empty weapon. Everyone here is trying to follow their faith the best they can. In my opinion, this is the perfect solution."

Silence followed his statement. Noah shrugged but didn't say anything. Jonathon and Roger got up and went downstairs to set up a schedule for patrols. Sophie and Mary followed behind them. Noah, Lizzie, and I were left upstairs staring at one another.

"I don't know how to feel about this," I told them. "Jonathon may have saved my life. If he hadn't come along when he did, I might not be here right now."

Noah took a deep breath and let it out slowly. "That's why I'm not trying to stop them. I don't have all the answers. I know what I believe, but when it came down to it, I used violence to stop the man who was trying to hurt Lizzie and Charity." Lizzie got up and came over to the couch, plopping down next to him and grabbing his hand. He kissed her fingers. "And if I had to do it again, I would." He shook his head. "You'll have to find your own way here, Hope. But

I can't carry a rifle, even if it's unloaded. Maybe if I wasn't an elder in the church, I could find a way to justify it. But for now I'll have to stand with the other elders and with our pastor. And I know they wouldn't approve of this plan."

I stood up. "Thank you both for being so candid—and for trying to do what's right. I've always believed in peace, but when I close my eyes at night I can still see that red truck coming toward me. I also think about Avery. I know that revenge belongs to God, but I must also be honest and tell you that there is anger in my heart against the person who killed him. I can't stand by and let another one of our friends die because I did nothing." I could feel tears on my cheeks. The emotion that had been building inside me since Avery's death seemed to be coming out on its own. Lizzie got up and came over to me, putting her arms around me. She held me while I sobbed.

"It's all right," she said softly, patting me on the back. "Everything will be okay."

I cried for a while, but when I was finally ready to stop, I looked up to see Noah standing next to us.

"I'm sorry, Hope," he said. "I should have realized how hard this was on you. Would you like to stay awhile and discuss how you're feeling?"

I shook my head and wiped my face. "Thank you, Noah. Maybe later. Papa should be home soon, and I don't want him to know I've been talking to anyone about these plans to protect Kingdom. He wouldn't be pleased."

"I'm sure he wouldn't," Noah said, frowning. "But I don't like the idea of hiding something from him."

"I have no plans to share my concerns with *my* father,"

123

Lizzie said. "He may have softened some in the past several months, but he still has very strong opinions. I'm certainly not opening that can of worms."

"Well, maybe it's wise to keep our conversation to ourselves for now," Noah said, "but I've found that almost every time I have to be secretive about something, it turns out to be a mistake."

"Not this time," Lizzie insisted, her dark eyes fastened on her husband. "We can't let another person die. And anyone in this town who doesn't agree is just . . . wrong."

Noah put his arms around his wife and held her. "I understand how you feel, Lizzie. I really do." He let her go and smiled. "I think Charity will be home soon. Don't you need to get tonight's specials started?"

"Oh my goodness," she said, her eyes wide. "It's Friday. I've been so distracted by everything, I almost forgot."

"Can I help you, Lizzie?"

"Thanks, Hope, but I think everything is under control. Callie's been such a wonderful assistant. With school almost out, soon she'll also be able to help with the cooking. I can hardly wait."

"And I'm sure you'll be happy to have more time with Charity," I said.

"Yes . . . well, I guess so."

Noah shook his head. "Charity's been . . . I don't know . . . going through something. We can't quite figure out what's wrong. She won't talk to us."

"I've noticed it too," I said. "I keep hoping she'll open up to me."

Lizzie smiled. "She loves you so much, Hope. You remind

me of Ruth Fisher. She was my confidante when I was a little girl."

I laughed. "Well, I love Ruth, but I must admit that I hope I don't look like her." Ruth was well into her eighties.

"Well, you *have* been looking a little tired lately," she said, grinning.

"Okay, that's it for me," Noah said. "You two are getting into a dangerous area that no man can tread safely through."

We both giggled.

"I've got to run to Washington for a few more supplies," Noah said to Lizzie. "I won't be gone long."

An idea suddenly popped into my head. "Noah, could I possibly go with you? I accidentally left something at the fabric shop in Washington, and I'd really like to get it."

Noah and Lizzie exchanged a quick look.

"If it's any trouble . . ."

"I'm happy to take you," Noah said slowly, "but you know that under normal circumstances men and women who aren't married are discouraged from being alone together."

Lizzie snorted. "Another silly rule. You and Hope are like brother and sister." She smiled at her husband. "I give you permission to take Hope with you. Does that help?"

"I guess it's okay," he said. "What about your father, Hope?"

I laughed. "Don't worry about him. Papa loves you like a son. Let's throw caution to the wind and not worry about the rules this once. Okay?"

"Maybe you can keep your head down as you leave town," Lizzie said. "No one will know you're in the truck."

"If Hope comes with me, we won't hide," Noah said sharply.

Lizzie nodded at him. "You're right. Sorry."

I looked over at the clock on a nearby table. "We should be back in plenty of time for dinner, and Lizzie can tell Papa where I am if he comes back before we return."

"Are you ready to go now?" Noah asked.

"I certainly am." I was excited about getting the fabric so I could finish Noah and Lizzie's quilt. I dismissed any concerns about what other people would think. Frankly, I was a little tired of worrying about the opinions of others. Trying to live up to everyone else's standards was tiring, to say the least.

"You two get going and be careful," Lizzie said. "I've got to get to the kitchen right this minute or I'll have some very unhappy customers tonight." She kissed Noah on the cheek. "I'll see you both when you get back." She took my hand in hers. "Why don't you and Samuel come to dinner tonight? My treat."

I shook my head. "Papa said he won't take any more free meals from you. He says if you don't quit giving away free food, you'll go broke."

She laughed. "Your father shouldn't look a gift horse in the mouth. It might bite him."

"He worries about you, Lizzie. You're like his other daughter."

"I know that, and I love him to pieces for it. But try to get him to come. Friday nights are fun around here."

I had to chuckle at her comment. Most families spent the weekends at home, so Friday was the last chance for them to eat out and visit with their neighbors. It was so nice to see a business that was once frowned upon turn out to be such a blessing. Even Pastor Mendenhall and his wife liked to come on Friday nights.

"I'll do my best." I squeezed her hand. "Maybe I'll see you later."

Noah and I started for the stairs, but before I could get to the door, Lizzie grabbed my arm. "I'm so grateful to God that you're okay," she said, her breath catching. "I love you, Hope. Promise me you'll stay safe. I couldn't bear it if anything happened to you."

"I love you too, my friend, but you know we're not supposed to make promises."

"I know. Just tell me you'll be careful."

"I'll be careful. Feel better?"

"A little."

I gave her a quick hug before Noah and I headed down the stairs. When we reached the dining room I found Jonathon, Roger, Mary, and Sophie hunched over a table, talking. Noah told me he needed to make a quick run to the bathroom before we left, so I started toward the front door. Before I could get there, Jonathon jumped up and intercepted me.

"I'd really like a few minutes with you, Hope," he said softly. "We need to talk."

"I think we do too, but I've got an important errand to run right now. Papa and I are going over to Avery's in the morning for the viewing. Then Papa will bring me back to town. He and some of the other men are going to Noah and Lizzie's house tomorrow after lunch to work, so I'll be alone. Why don't you come by in the afternoon?"

"Okay. I'll see you then."

I could tell by the look on his face that he wanted to kiss me again, but I knew he would never do that in front of anyone else. I said good-bye and hurried out the door. I waited only a couple of minutes before Noah came out, and we got into his truck. When we reached the main road that led to town, I could see Noah and Lizzie's house. The old Strauss home was only about a quarter of a mile from the intersection of the main road and the road to Kingdom. Even though I came this way once a month, I hadn't really looked closely at it for quite some time. It was really coming along.

"The house looks pretty good," I said to Noah. "How much longer until you can move in?"

He shrugged. "I'm not sure. We're making progress, but it's a lot of work. Of course, I've got plenty of help. You know how people are in Kingdom. Someone's always stopping by with lumber or paint. Or just wanting to donate their time."

"You know, your house is actually out on the main road. Do you worry about your safety?"

"Not really. I'm hardly ever there alone. Sometimes when we work late, we'll all just bed down on the floor and spend the night. We're about as safe as anyone can be right now, I guess. My understanding is that actual church buildings are more at risk than regular houses."

"I hope you're right. It wouldn't be hard for anyone to recognize you're Mennonite by the way you're dressed."

Noah snorted. "Please don't suggest we remove our hats. After your father's rebuke, I may nail mine permanently onto my head."

I laughed. "You really took his comments to heart, didn't you?"

He nodded, his smile gone. "I respect Samuel immensely, Hope. He stands by his beliefs without wavering."

"We all waver sometimes, Noah," I said softly. "None of us is perfect."

He was silent until we reached the main road and turned toward town. Then he said, "Are you wavering, Hope?"

I sighed. "I have to admit that I'm dealing with some confusion. It's like there are two voices in my head. One is fully committed to our doctrine of nonviolence under any circumstance. Another asks me what I would do if someone I loved was in trouble. What would I do to protect them?"

"Would you disobey God?"

I turned to stare at him. "Why would God want us to be defenseless? Like lambs led to the slaughter?"

He glanced over at me, his forehead creased in a deep frown. "I don't think He does. I believe our protection comes from our faith in His promises. Do you know Isaiah 54:17?"

"Papa quotes it often. 'No weapon that is formed against thee shall prosper; and every tongue that shall rise against thee in judgment thou shalt condemn. This is the heritage of the servants of the Lord, and their righteousness is of me, saith the Lord.'"

"That's right. But do you believe it?"

"I believe every word of God. My faith in His promises will never waver."

Noah chuckled. "I didn't ask you about *every* word of God. I asked you about that Scripture. Although God was talking to the children of Israel, He showed His heart toward His people. And we're His people."

I didn't say anything, but I felt conviction in my heart. My thoughts went back to what Papa had said about Ebbie. He believed we should spend our time in prayer, believing that God was our best defense.

"What I'm trying to say, Hope, is that as Mennonites, perhaps we should lay down the swords of men and pick up the sword of the Spirit."

I nodded slowly. "I understand, Noah. But if someone stood in front of you, holding a gun and threatening to kill you, would you be able to confront him with Scripture instead of a weapon?"

He grunted. "Yes, that's exactly what I'm telling you. Now, whether or not I would remember that when a gun was actually pointed at me . . . Well, that's a whole different story."

I grinned at him. "Let's pray you never have to find out."

"That's a prayer I can definitely agree with."

He was silent for a moment. "Can I ask you something, Hope?"

"Anything."

"You know I lived outside Kingdom for a while."

"Yes. You went to school out in the world for a couple of years."

"That's right. And Lizzie lived in Kansas City for five years."

I frowned at him. "I don't understand. What is it you want to know?"

He paused for a moment as if trying to gather his thoughts. "As I listened to everyone this afternoon I realized that the only people in the room who hadn't been away from Kingdom at one time or another were you, Sophie, and Roger. Of course, Roger never lived here, and Sophie is only seventeen. As an elder, I hear people talk about leaving for a variety of reasons. And some of them do." He turned his head to look at me. "But not you. Not once. Why?"

I looked at him in surprise. "It never occurred to me, I guess. Kingdom is my home and the only place I want to be."

"Even though bad things have happened to us?"

"Nothing will ever break my commitment to Kingdom. And it isn't because I'm afraid of the world. I'm not." I sighed. "I can't really explain it, but I know I'm where I'm supposed to be. I don't have any desire to live anywhere else, because my heart is in Kingdom—and it always will be."

"I feel the same way, and so does Lizzie. Kingdom is a very special place. I really do want to protect it."

"I know that. It's hard to know what to do, but in the end, we must trust God and make sure we are true to our hearts."

He smiled at me. "Exactly. And thanks for understanding why I couldn't get involved in Jonathon and Roger's plan."

We left our discussion about faith and moved on to more mundane topics. Noah explained the work that was going on in the house and what it would look like when completed. We also talked about the expansion of the electric company to Kingdom. Many of our citizens were availing themselves of the new opportunity. Each request for electricity had to pass through the elders first for approval, but most requests were being granted, especially for the farmers who lived outside of town. Two residents who had dairies were given permission as well. If the recent transformation hadn't happened in our church, I was certain no one would be the recipient of this once-shunned prospect. I wondered if Papa would ever agree to sign up for it. Our quilt shop got so cold in the winter, even with the potbellied stove we used to provide warmth. And in the heat of summer, it could be stifling.

When we finally arrived in Washington, Noah dropped me

off at Flo's while he went to the building supply store to pick up his order. Flo had my fabric under the counter, waiting for my return. We visited while I waited for Noah. Most of our conversation centered on Avery's death.

"When I heard that someone in a buggy had been killed," Flo said, "my heart almost stopped in my chest. I was so afraid it was you."

I reassured her that I wouldn't be out on the road by myself again until the men behind the attacks were caught. By the time Noah came back to pick me up, she had calmed down considerably.

We started back to Kingdom a little later than we'd planned because Noah's order wasn't quite ready at the supply store. I hoped Papa wasn't worried. Although I'd purposely tried to not think about the wisdom of going to Washington with Noah, on the way home I began to worry about the consequences. The idea that anyone would be concerned about our being alone in Noah's truck seemed ludicrous, but I had no desire to cause trouble for Noah. Had I pushed to get my way without thinking it out first? Though Lizzie, Noah, and I had no problem with our decision, that didn't mean everyone else would feel the same way. Would the move toward grace in our church cover us, or would we be chastised for breaking the rules? I really had no way of knowing, but a tickle of fear began to wriggle its way around inside me. I'd just decided to discuss the situation with Noah when I heard the sound of another vehicle coming up behind us. I checked the side mirror, and a feeling of horror made my current concerns seem unimportant. Behind us, and drawing closer, was a large red truck.

CHAPTER 8

"Noah, I think that's the truck that tried to run me off the road." I fought to keep my voice even, but it shook, betraying my fear.

"Hold on, Hope," Noah said loudly, trying to be heard above the red truck's loud engine. "I'm going to try to outrun him."

I grabbed the handle over the passenger door and braced myself with the other hand on the dashboard. Noah pushed on the accelerator and we sped up, our tires spinning on the gravel beneath us. I kept my eyes peeled on the mirror outside my window. The red truck caught up to us quickly. We were still several miles from the turnoff to Kingdom, but even if we could make it there, would we be able to take the road home? Wouldn't we lead the man behind us right to our town? I glanced over at Noah, wondering if I should say something, but the look on his face choked back my words. His attention was fully focused on getting us out of harm's way, and I knew I needed to be quiet and let him concentrate.

As we sped down the road, I began to pray softly for God's

protection. The words from Isaiah came back to me. "'No weapon that is formed against thee shall prosper; and every tongue that shall rise against thee in judgment thou shalt condemn. This is the heritage of the servants of the Lord, and their righteousness is of me, saith the Lord.'" I began to speak the verse over and over in a low voice. After a couple of times, Noah began to say it with me, although I could barely hear him over the roar of two engines racing down the road, both of us going faster than we should.

Before we could put enough distance between us and the red truck, another truck sped past us. Although I didn't know a lot about trucks and automobiles, I could read a speedometer. I looked at ours. Noah was going almost seventy miles an hour. The new truck, older and black, had to be going at least eighty. I tried to see inside the cab as it went by, but just like the red truck, the windows were heavily tinted. All I could see was the shadow of a man at the wheel. I couldn't make out his features.

He drove ahead of us and then suddenly slowed down, whipped his truck around, and blocked the road. Noah slammed on his brakes, but the gravel beneath our wheels caused us to skid and we spun around, finally coming to a stop a few feet from the black truck. Noah and I watched our mirrors as the red truck slowly approached us from behind, effectively blocking us in.

"I should have pulled out into the field," Noah said in a low voice.

"We could have gotten stuck in the ditch." I reached out and put my hand on his arm. "You did everything you could. This isn't your fault."

Noah pushed a button and locked our doors.

The red and black trucks sat with engines idling. No one got out.

I stared at Noah. "What can we do?"

He didn't answer me, but I saw that his eyes were glued on the rearview mirror. A quick look told me he wasn't staring at the truck parked behind us. He was focusing on his hunting rifle in the rack behind the back seat. I wanted to tell him to forget about his gun. That grabbing it was wrong. But I couldn't force the words out. If the men in the truck came after us, what would happen? What would they do? Would they beat us? Kill us? Was I in danger of an even worse outcome? The fear inside me rose like a growing flame, threatening to overshadow everything else. Even my faith. I began to whisper, "'No weapon that is formed against thee shall prosper. No weapon that is formed against thee shall prosper'" over and over.

"Get down, Hope," Noah growled. "And stay down." He'd just turned to reach for the rifle when a high-pitched sound split the air. We both froze. A siren. The drivers of the trucks obviously heard it too. The truck in front of us backed up, turned around, and took off, and the red truck raced its engine. It was an angry sound, making it clear its owner was frustrated that his plans had been interrupted. But like the black truck, he backed up and then sped around us, following his friend the other way.

The dust they left behind shielded them from our sight. I tried desperately to get a glimpse of their license plates, but not only did the dust hide them, the red truck's plate was smeared with mud in what I perceived was a deliberate attempt to conceal the numbers. Even still, as they roared away, a feeling of relief washed over me, combining with the fear that still held me in its grasp. I began to shake uncontrollably.

"We're all right, Noah," I said, blinking back tears. "We're all right."

He didn't respond, just sat there staring into the rearview mirror. A few seconds later, a patrol car pulled up behind us. I turned around to see Sheriff Ford climb out. He strolled over to our truck but had to knock on Noah's window twice before he rolled it down. Noah's face was ashen, and I wondered if he was in shock.

"You two okay?" Ford said. "Truck broke down?"

Noah shook his head. "We didn't break down. Two trucks forced us to a stop. Probably the same people who killed Avery."

Ford frowned and stared at me. "You both look fine to me. If someone was out to get you, why ain't you both a little worse for wear?"

"Are you serious?" I said, emotion making my voice higher than normal. "Do you think we're making this up? We were threatened, Sheriff. If it hadn't been for you, we might be dead."

He shook his head, his basset-hound jowls jiggling. "Didn't see nobody botherin' you, girlie. You sure 'bout this?"

I'd had enough with the sheriff, and my patience was about as thin as it could get. "If you didn't see the men who stopped us," I snapped, "why in the world were you speeding down the road with your siren on?" I tried to control the anger in my voice, but it seemed to take over. At least I'd stopped shaking. I lost the battle to control my tears, but they weren't tears of fear. They were tears of rage.

"You need to settle down, little lady," the sheriff growled. "I got a call that someone was broke down on the road. That's why I came out to check. Since I can hear your engine, I think you need to move on. Go back to that little town of yours and stay there. It ain't a good idea for any of you Mennies to be out here."

"Why would you say that, Sheriff?" Noah said, seeming to finally find his voice. "I mean, if there's nothing to worry about, why should we stay in town?"

"I didn't say there wasn't nothin' to worry about, young man. I just said I didn't see anyone out here botherin' you right now. Don't mean there won't be in the future."

I glared at him. "May I ask you one question, Sheriff? Who called to report we were stranded? The only people we've seen out here are the men who chased us. Not one other car passed us. Not one."

He scowled at me. "Are you calling me a liar?"

Rage boiled up inside me. "Yes, sir. I'm calling you a liar."

The sheriff's eyes widened and he walked away from Noah's window, came around the front of the truck, and knocked on my window. For a brief second I considered leaving the window up, but I rolled it down.

"You listen to me, you little troublemaker. Did it occur to you that there are farms out here?" He pointed to a farmhouse set back from the road, not far from where we were. "I never said the call came from a vehicle, did I?"

I didn't like being confronted by the rude sheriff, but I had no answer for him. He was right. There were actually two houses nearby. Someone from either one of them could have called. Something else suddenly occurred to me. I swallowed hard, trying to find the courage to push the sheriff's buttons just a little more. "Maybe . . . maybe you could talk to whoever called. I mean, they might have seen the trucks. Might help you to believe our story. Maybe they'll even recognize the vehicles."

His eyes narrowed and a vein in his temple began to throb. For some reason, I couldn't take my eyes off that vein.

"You take the cake, young lady. What's your name?"

"H-Hope."

"Well, Hope, I intend to do just that. Why don't you two get goin' and let me do my job." He stuck his finger in my face. "And I don't wanna see either one of you for a while. You understand me?"

I wanted to argue, but I felt like a wrung-out dishrag. Frankly, the only thing on my mind was getting back to Kingdom. Noah and I nodded simultaneously, and I was reminded of the funny little bobblehead dog Flo kept on the counter in her shop. She liked to flick its head because it always made me laugh. But today I didn't feel like laughing.

Sheriff Ford shot us both one more threatening look and walked back to his patrol car. He got in, started his engine, and then sat there, just like the man in the red truck had.

"I think he's waiting for us to go," I said to Noah.

He put his truck in gear and started slowly down the road. I glanced back at Sheriff Ford's car, but he didn't move.

"If you're wondering if he's really going to talk to anyone about what happened, I wouldn't get your hopes up," Noah said.

His expression concerned me, and I studied his face carefully. "Are you all right?" I asked finally. "I know that was frightening, but shouldn't you be relieved we're okay? God protected us, Noah. We're safe." I noticed that his knuckles were white as he grasped the steering wheel.

He was silent for several seconds. When he finally began to speak, it was almost as if each word caused him pain. "When it mattered, Hope, when I had the choice to choose God or to choose my gun, I almost chose my gun. How am I going to be able to live with that?" He shook his head. "I may have to step down as an elder. I'm not worthy of the position."

My mouth dropped open in shock. "That's ridiculous, Noah. You're a wonderful elder. Our lives were in danger. And besides, you *didn't* pick up your rifle. Even though you thought about it, you didn't. Please don't make a rash decision based on what *might* have happened. Our church needs you." I reached over and touched his arm. "I need you, Noah. Anytime I have a question or a problem, I know you'll lead me in the right direction."

He shook off my hand. "I didn't lead you in the right direction today, did I? I should never have taken you with me. It was wrong, and I knew it. My rebellious nature almost cost you your life."

Tears stung my eyes. "But that wasn't your fault. I talked you into—"

"That's enough," he snapped. "I don't want to talk about this right now."

I wiped my face with my apron. "Please, Noah. Please pray about this before you do anything."

He turned toward me, and his expression softened. "Don't cry. I'm sorry. I'll pray about it, I promise. Let's not discuss it now. Please. I need to think."

I didn't respond, just nodded. We drove back to Kingdom in silence. I dreaded telling Papa what had happened. I almost asked Noah if we could keep it to ourselves, but I knew he would never agree. It was important for everyone to know that traveling the road outside of Kingdom truly wasn't safe. Even in cars and trucks.

When we got back, Noah pulled up in front of the restaurant. I could see an old green truck parked in front of the quilt shop. I wondered if it belonged to Herman Hightower, Berlene's husband. Sure enough, the front door of the shop swung open, and Papa and Herman emerged. Papa kept his eyes on me even though he spoke to Herman for a while before he climbed into his truck and drove away.

Noah got out, came around, and opened my door without a word. He headed toward the restaurant while I waited for Papa to reach me. He didn't look happy.

"Where have you been, Hope?" he asked immediately.

"Noah took me to Washington, Papa." I held out the sack of fabric I'd picked up from Flo. "I forgot this the other day. It's for the quilt I'm making for Lizzie and—"

Papa held up his hand, and I stopped talking. This wasn't going to be easy.

"I know we talked about you making your own decisions, but this was not a good one. I know nothing inappropriate happened between you and Noah. Nor would it. But you must remember that Noah is an elder. He must keep a spotless reputation. You should have waited to go to Washington. Your lack of patience may have caused Noah a great deal of harm."

I wanted to defend myself, but I couldn't. I hung my head.

"You're right. And that isn't the worst part, Papa. Something happened out on the road."

Papa's already disturbed expression darkened as I told him about the trucks that had confronted us and what Noah had said about leaving his position with the church. When I finished, he shook his head.

"I am grateful to God that you are safe." He pointed his finger at me, exactly the way Sheriff Ford had done. I was beginning to get tired of fingers in my face. "This is the second time your life has been in danger, and I will not allow it anymore."

"I have no intention of leaving town again," I said. "You don't need to worry about me. I'm perfectly happy being home, where it's safe."

The creases in Papa's face relaxed, and he reached over to gently pat my face. "I am happy to hear that. Just make sure you follow through." He stared over at the entrance to the restaurant. "I am concerned about Noah. To think that he would walk away from his eldership troubles me greatly."

"He respects you so much, Papa. Maybe you could talk to him?"

He nodded. "Yes, I will do that."

"Please, Papa. And before he has a chance to do something he'll regret."

"I will speak to him tonight." He studied me. "Are you hungry?"

Although I hadn't been thinking about food, I realized I was ravenous. "Very hungry."

"Then let us have supper at the restaurant. It will give me a chance to speak to Noah."

I nodded. "You haven't said anything about your visit with Berlene and Herman. Is everything all right?"

"I would not say everything is all right, Daughter. My visit with Herman and Berlene was . . . interesting though. We have a lot to talk about. Herman and Berlene have no desire to leave their lives in Summerfield, so they will not be able to run Avery's store." He shook his head and stared down at the ground. I didn't say anything, just waited for him to finish as I wondered what that could possibly have to do with us. "They want to sell the store to me, Hope. But that would mean we would have to close the quilt shop."

My mind was reeling from Papa's news when the front door of the restaurant burst open and Lizzie ran down the steps toward us, her eyes wide and wild.

"Hope, Samuel. You've got to help us. Charity is missing!"

CHAPTER 9

I grabbed Lizzie by the shoulders and tried to get her to calm down. "What do you mean she's missing? Wasn't she at school?"

She nodded, huge tears running down her cheeks. "She's supposed to come home right after school on Fridays. I thought she was upstairs. About an hour ago, I went to check on her, but when she wasn't there, I assumed she'd gone with Noah." She took a deep, shuddering breath.

"But when Noah came into the restaurant, you found out he didn't have Charity."

She nodded again and sniffed.

"Look, we'll find her, Lizzie. I promise."

At that moment, Noah came running down the stairs, headed for his truck. "Her schoolbag's not upstairs. She never came home." His eyes were wide with alarm. After what we'd just been through, I felt sure he was worried that something awful had happened to Charity.

"Noah," Papa said sharply, "calm down. Charity is around here somewhere. She would never leave town. You and I need to start looking for her." He scanned the small group of people who had begun to assemble. Some of them had been in the restaurant and overhead Lizzie and Noah's frightening discovery. "The rest of you, if you want to help, ask around. See if anyone has seen her."

Leah Burkholder, who had come over to see what was going on, stepped up next to Lizzie. "She left class at the usual time. I can't imagine where she could be." Her face was pinched with worry.

"What about the other children?" I asked Leah. "Could any of them have seen her out on the street? Noticed where she went?"

"I-I don't know," Leah said. "But it's certainly possible."

"Leah, will you stay here with Lizzie?" I said. "Harold Eberly's daughter, Mercy, goes to the hardware store every day after school. She may have seen something. I'll be right back."

As I ran down the street toward Eberly's Hardware, I could hear Papa giving instructions to those who had volunteered to help. Although I had to agree with him that Charity would never leave town on her own, I knew from firsthand experience that evil lurked right outside the safety of Kingdom. Could it have made its way inside? Was Charity in danger? I prayed as I hurried to the hardware store. When I got there, I pushed the door in and found Harold at the cash register and Mercy sitting on a stool beside him, obviously doing her homework.

"Gracious, Hope," Harold said. "You look upset."

"Charity Engel is missing. I need to ask Mercy if she saw her after school today."

Harold turned to his daughter, "Mercy, do you remember seeing Charity?"

The girl stared at her father with wide eyes, obviously frightened by our intensity. Mercy, almost sixteen years old, was a quiet girl who kept to herself and wasn't usually the center of attention. "I don't know. I can't remember."

I took a deep breath, trying to appear calm so she would relax. "Mercy, I didn't mean to scare you. I'm sure Charity is fine. We just need to know where she is."

She studied me for a moment, her sky-blue eyes fastened on mine. I could tell she was trying to recall what had happened after school. Suddenly, revelation flashed across her features.

"Now that I think about it, I did notice her," she said slowly. "Usually she goes straight to the restaurant or to your shop after school. But today she walked the other way. Toward the edge of town."

I tried to keep the panic off my face. Why would Charity walk *away* from Kingdom? It was the worst thing she could possibly do.

Harold frowned at his daughter. "Didn't you try to stop her, Mercy? Ask her where she was going?"

Mercy looked puzzled. "I figured she was going to the Strauss house. Don't her parents own it?"

"Yes, they do," I said. "But right now, it's best if no one goes near the main road alone."

Mercy looked over at her father with a curious expression. Harold nodded at her. "We'll talk more about it after Hope leaves." He swung his gaze to me. "I should have addressed this before now. It's just hard to explain this kind of thing to your child."

I didn't say anything more. It was painfully obvious why Mercy should be warned not to go near the main road. In the light of Charity's disappearance, nothing I could say would make it any clearer. "Thank you," I said to Mercy. "You've helped a great deal." I smiled at her. "I've got to get back and let Charity's parents know what you saw."

"We'll pray that she is found right away and that God will keep her safe," she said.

"Thank you. I appreciate that and so will her folks." I nodded at Harold and left the store, more worried than I'd been before I arrived. Lizzie and Noah were waiting on the steps of the restaurant when I returned. Papa wasn't anywhere to be seen. I assumed he was aiding in the search for her.

"Does Mercy know where she is?" Lizzie asked as soon as I reached them.

"Mercy saw her walking west down Main Street," I said gently.

"Out of town?" Lizzie said, her voice breaking. "Oh no. But why? Why would she do that?"

"Mercy assumed she was going to your house. Has she ever done that before?"

Lizzie shook her head. "She knows better than that. Especially in the light of what's been happening. We talked about staying close to home."

I found it ironic that Noah and Lizzie had explained the dangerous climate outside of Kingdom, yet Charity was missing. Harold hadn't taken the trouble to give Mercy the same instructions, yet she was safe at home.

"You both stay here," Noah said. "I'm going to the house to see if she's there."

"You are not going alone." Papa had come up behind us. "After what happened to you and Hope today, no one should go near the edge of town unaccompanied. I will go with you."

Noah didn't bother to argue. He jumped in his truck and waited for Papa to climb in the other side. Papa barely got the door closed before they took off down the street. Several horses tied to hitching posts reacted with alarm. Lizzie and I joined several other residents in calming them. When we finished, I followed her into the restaurant, where she collapsed into a chair.

"I can't believe I didn't know she wasn't here," Lizzie said, shaking her head.

I grabbed her hand. "Oh, Lizzie, you're a wonderful mother. Charity almost always goes straight upstairs after school. Anyone would have assumed the same thing. Don't blame yourself for something that isn't your fault."

Before she had a chance to answer me, Callie came up to the table. People were beginning to file in for dinner.

"What do you want to do?" Callie asked softly. "Should we tell everyone to go home?"

"I don't know," Lizzie said. "Maybe I should get back to the kitchen."

"No," I said firmly. "Either close the doors or let Callie and me handle everything."

Lizzie shook her head. "You can't do it alone."

I squeezed her hand. "Nonsense. Is everything already cooked?"

She nodded slowly. "I've started all the specials. The chicken needs to be fried, though, as well as the chicken-fried steak. The spaghetti's already done, and so is the beef stew."

"Come back to the kitchen and supervise us," I said. Frankly,

I thought it would be more appropriate to close the restaurant, but I knew Lizzie would just sit and worry. At least this way she'd have something else to think about.

Although she protested some, she followed us into the back room. Callie and I worked hard at obeying her instructions, but I couldn't get my mind off of Charity. Would the men who confronted us on the road today kidnap a child? They'd already proven they would kill for their twisted hatred. I loved Charity. Thinking of her in the hands of those awful men was almost more than I could bear.

We'd been working for nearly an hour when the door to the kitchen swung open. Callie had a huge smile on her face as she held it ajar. Noah walked in with a very embarrassed-looking Charity by his side. Papa stood behind her with Beau next to him.

"Charity Lynn!" Lizzie cried. "Where in the world have you been? You had me scared out of my mind." She ran over and put her arms around her daughter. The seven-year-old girl didn't say anything, but as she hugged Lizzie she began to cry softly.

"She was at the house," Noah said. "Waiting for me."

Lizzie let go of Charity and straightened up. She stared at Noah, confusion on her face. "I don't understand." She gazed solemnly at her daughter. "Why didn't you let me know you wanted to go to the house? I had no idea where you were."

Charity kept her eyes focused on the floor, tears streaming down her face.

Noah cleared his throat. "Seems we have some talking to do. Someone told her that Clay Troyer is her father. And that he's in prison."

Lizzie seemed to wither right in front of my eyes. This was something she hadn't wanted to explain until Charity was much older. Lizzie had gotten pregnant after Clay took advantage of her. Then he'd tried to take Charity from her after attempting to kill Lizzie first. Not only was she worried about what Charity would think of her mother becoming pregnant out of wedlock, she was also concerned how she'd take the news that her father wasn't someone to be proud of.

"Why didn't you tell me about Clay Troyer, Mama?" Charity asked in a quiet voice. Even though she was seven, she still had some problems with pronouncing the letter *r*. It made her sound like such a little girl that my heart ached even more for her.

"I planned to tell you, Cherry Bear," Lizzie said, "but I wanted to wait a while. Maybe I was wrong, but I thought you should be old enough to understand." She frowned. "Honey, if you wanted to know about Clay, why didn't you just ask me? I thought we could talk about anything."

"She was afraid to upset you," Noah said. "She figured I'd tell her the truth."

Papa, who looked uncomfortable with the scene unfolding in front of us, suddenly spoke up. "Maybe the three of you should be alone to talk this out. Hope and I do not want to intrude on your personal business."

"I'm sorry. You're right," Noah said. "We shouldn't air our problems in front of you."

"No, my friend," Papa said with a small smile. "We are more than willing to share your burden, but I do not want you to feel we are encroaching on something that should remain private."

"You're family," Lizzie said. "We have no need to keep secrets from you, but you're right. We should talk this out."

"Lizzie, why don't you all go upstairs? Callie and I have everything under control here. We can finish out the evening without you."

She stared at me, biting her lip and slowly shaking her head. "I can't ask you to do that."

"There are people driving in from their farms," Noah said, "and we have no way to let them know we won't be open. I would hate to let them down."

"What can I do?" Lizzie said, unable to keep the emotion out of her voice. "I really need to be with Charity tonight."

"You go on," I insisted. "We're fine. Really."

Lizzie started to protest, but I held my hand up. "I won't hear another word about it. If we need help, we can always come upstairs and get you. Okay?"

"And I'll help too," Noah said. "You and Charity need some time alone. I've worked in the kitchen before. The three of us can do this without any problem. You two get upstairs. I mean it."

Lizzie looked at each of us. "All right. I appreciate it. And like Hope said, if you need me, I'll just be upstairs."

"You and Charity take all the time you want," I said, trying to look more confident than I actually felt. I went over to Lizzie's daughter and took her hand. The look in her eyes made me want to cry. "Charity, I want to tell you something. I remember when you were born. Your mama was so happy. There isn't a mother alive who loves her child more than your mother loves you. She has loved you all your life. Every single second. She would do anything for you. I had a good mother too, but she died a long time ago, and I would give anything to have her back." I let go of Charity's hand and smiled at her. "Being loved is the most important thing in this world. More important than anything else. Do you understand?"

"Yes," she said in a small voice. "I understand."

Beau left Papa, walked up to Charity, and leaned against her legs. She looked down at him and then slumped to the floor, wrapping her arms around his furry body. The little dog seemed to understand and didn't flinch a bit.

Lizzie shook her head as she watched a dog that had been through so much reach out to a little girl who needed comfort. I heard Papa sniff and caught him wiping his eyes with his sleeve.

Charity finally let go of Beau and gazed up at me. As I looked into her dark eyes, I couldn't help but be amazed at the difference I could see in her over the past few months. When she'd come to Kingdom, she's been such a child. Now there was a maturity in her face and manner that was beyond her years. Maybe it was a blessing. Perhaps she would be able to understand that her mother wasn't perfect. That none of us are.

"Thank you," Lizzie said, hugging me. "Let's go, Charity."

We watched them leave and then swung into action. Even Papa pitched in. Seeing him deliver plates, pour coffee, and clean up tables made me giggle. Somehow, we made it through the evening and closed the doors around nine thirty, pretty late for a town that usually clears the streets by eight o'clock.

Not long after the last customer left, Callie took off. She'd done almost all of the dishes, wiped down the tables, and swept the dining room. There was very little for Noah, Papa, and me to do. When everything was finally put away, Papa ordered us into the dining room.

"I need to talk to both of you," he said sternly, using a tone he reserved for serious conversations.

I glanced over at Noah. He didn't look happy. "It's pretty late, Papa," I said, "and I'm sure Noah wants to get upstairs to Lizzie and Charity."

"This will not take long. I believe there are some things we must discuss."

Noah and I sat down next to him. I had a pretty good idea what he was going to say. I turned out to be correct.

Papa frowned at Noah. "You were wrong to take Hope with you to Washington today. Even though your intentions were honorable, it was not wise to put yourself in a situation that looked questionable."

I started to say something in Noah's defense, but Papa held his hand up, signaling me to be quiet.

"Please be still, Hope," he said. "No one knows better than I that you and Noah are friends and there is no reason to be concerned about something untoward happening between you. But you must realize that there are others in town who do not know you as well as I do."

"I get a little tired of living my life based on the judgmental attitudes of narrow-minded people," Noah said. "As we loosen some of the religious viewpoints that have bound us for many years, we must also begin to extend grace and trust toward our brothers and sisters. Why must we always believe the worst?"

Although I'd been directed to stay silent, I nodded in agreement with Noah.

Papa sighed deeply. "Please understand that I agree with what you say in theory. But here is the problem. There are those whose motives are not as pure as yours. Opening a door like this could have serious consequences for people whose faith is not strong. I am reminded of Sheriff Ford and his wife. Perhaps if their church had followed stricter guidelines, their terrible betrayal would not have happened. Also, please remember that God's Word warns us to abstain from all appearance of evil. For you, Noah, this is even more important. You are an elder in our church."

Noah nodded. "I know you're right, Samuel. Even though I get tired of trying to live up to others expectations, I realize it was careless of me to take Hope to Washington. I should have carefully considered the things you've just pointed out. At the time, it seemed so harmless. So innocent."

Papa reached over and patted Noah's shoulder. "I know that, Son. There is no doubt of it in my mind. However, I do believe you should discuss this situation with our pastor and the board of elders. I am confident they will find it unnecessary for any further rebuke. But if anyone should bring up the matter or try to claim false charges against you or Hope, you can refer them to our church leaders. Bringing this into the light will quench any further fiery darts the enemy may send your way."

"Right after this happened I thought very seriously about removing myself from the eldership," Noah said.

I started to protest, but Noah shook his head at me. "It was something said out of emotion, Hope. I've reconsidered and no longer feel the need to take such a drastic step. But I will certainly take your suggestion, Samuel. Thank you."

I stayed quiet, relieved that Noah was no longer thinking about leaving his position. Although I completely understood Papa's advice, I was still a little upset. It was irksome, always being watched and judged. There were days when I wished I could just do whatever I wanted to do without fear of breaking some rule of the church.

"Now I want to talk about what happened to you on the road," Papa said. "We have asked our people to keep their buggies in town, but now, it seems that even riding in motor vehicles may put us at risk."

Noah shrugged. "I don't know what to do, Samuel. We have to be able to travel. Unfortunately, Kingdom doesn't have everything we need."

I cleared my throat. "Jonathon and a few others intend to keep an eye on the main road, but obviously they can only do so much."

Papa's eyebrows shot up. "I suppose it is a good idea to post watchers at the crossroads. As long as all they plan to do is watch."

Noah and I gave each other a quick look. Papa saw it.

"Do they plan to carry weapons, Noah?" he asked, frowning.

"I don't know for certain, Samuel, but it's a possibility. They mentioned taking their hunting rifles but not loading them."

Papa's expression turned dark. "We cannot allow this. Surely you will have nothing to do with their plan."

"I told them I couldn't participate if they carried guns. Unloaded or not."

"Good." Papa stared down at the table for a moment. Then

he took a deep breath and let it out. "I certainly understand their passion. My beloved daughter has been attacked twice now, but I still cannot agree to using aggressive means to defend ourselves." He fastened his gaze on Noah. "Have you talked to the other elders about this plan?"

"No, but I will. I have no choice." He stared at me for several seconds, and I knew he was thinking about the moment he started to grab his own rifle out on the road. I had no intention of mentioning it to anyone. Noah would have to sort out his own feelings. I was too busy trying to figure out my own.

"We must go," Papa said suddenly. "I am tired, and I am sure Hope is as well. You must spend time with your wife and daughter, Brother."

"Thank you, Samuel," Noah said, standing to his feet, "for your advice and for your help tonight. I'm grateful."

Papa nodded. "Good night, my friend. If we can do anything else to help you, please let us know. You and your family are very special to the both of us."

"We feel the same." He and Papa shook hands. Then Noah walked over and held the front door open. After Papa and I stepped outside onto the sidewalk, we heard Noah lock the door behind us.

"I hope they'll be okay," I said. "Charity looked so confused."

"I am sure of it," Papa said. "They love each other very much, and Charity knows that."

I nodded, the look in Charity's eyes still burning in my mind. "Papa," I said, "if you will allow me to change the subject, we need to talk about your meeting with Berlene.

155

You can't really want to close our quilt shop. You know that Mama taught me to make quilts. I've always felt like a part of her is still with me—inside our store."

He sighed. "It is very late, Daughter. I would rather talk about this tomorrow."

"Please, Papa. It's on my heart, and if we don't discuss it now, I don't know if I'll be able to sleep tonight."

He shook his head. "I know you are unhappy with my decision, Hope. But Avery's business produces much more income than the quilt store ever will. You know money does not mean much to me, but someday when I am gone, I want to know that you will be taken care of. I will be able to put aside some of the profits from the saddle and tack store for your future."

I looked sideways at him. "In case I never marry, Papa? Is that what you're concerned about?"

"I am not saying that, but your mother and I married when she was seventeen and I was nineteen. You are twenty-six, and you just canceled an engagement that would have been perfect for you."

I raised my eyebrows in surprise. "Must I remind you again that Ebbie canceled our engagement?"

"You gave him reason to do so, Hope."

I didn't respond since the truth of what he said was obvious.

"Regardless, I must consider the possibility that you will not marry. If this is the case, I do not want you to be destitute."

"We're not destitute, Papa. We get by just fine with what we make through the quilt shop."

He shook his head. "Unfortunately, that is not the case.

Most of our food comes from our garden, as well as the eggs and milk from our chickens and cows. Without me, I am not sure you would be able to keep up with all our resources."

I had to admit that milking cows and raising chickens weren't my favorite things to do. I wasn't very good at it. Papa also traded milk and eggs with a couple of other families for meat, fruit, and other staples. If he wasn't around, I probably wouldn't be able to stay on top of everything.

"Wait a minute," I said, making a face. "Why are we talking as if you're not here? You're a young man, Papa. You're not old enough to worry about dying."

His face hardened. "I do not see any reason to continue this discussion, Daughter. There is simply no way for us to oversee both stores effectively. I have no choice but to sell the quilt shop and buy the saddle and tack store."

"Surely I have a say in this. The store belongs to me as much as it does to you. I love it, and I have no desire to sell it."

"I wish it could be different, Hope, but my mind is made up. Berlene and I have already agreed to the terms of sale. We will begin taking over her father's store by the end of the month."

He turned and walked toward the hitching post, where Daisy stood waiting to carry us home. I followed him to the buggy, but I couldn't take my eyes off the front of our quilt shop. How could this be happening? I would have to grieve the demise of my engagement and my precious shop within a few days of each other. I climbed up into the carriage and Beau jumped into my lap. The four of us began the journey home, my heart heavy with sorrow for what I'd lost.

CHAPTER 10

I'd planned to open the shop as usual the next morning, but I was still so exhausted that Papa took one look at me and ordered me to stay home. I'd told Jonathon I would be there, but I was too tired to worry about missing him.

Papa had planned to take me to view Avery's body. In Kingdom, visitations were held in the home a day or two before the funeral. Although I wanted to show my respect to the family, I was secretly happy to miss the viewing. There were so many emotions raging inside me that the thought of having to look at Avery made me feel as if I'd break apart.

I was still worried about Jonathon and the rest of the group that was out watching the entrance into Kingdom. Were they in danger? Jonathon's willingness to go against the church because of his concern for all of us touched me deeply. But as my feelings for him grew, my concern for his safety increased too.

I was also uneasy about Noah. Would he be disciplined by our church for taking me out of town without supervision? Would he be removed as an elder after he'd decided to stay?

As I sat at home, Beau at my feet, turning these things over in my mind, I found myself working on my wedding quilt. I dreaded finishing it without any names in the final square, but there was nothing to be done about it. The quilt needed to be completed. It would still be a blessing during the long, cold winter months.

Sunday after church, Jonathon found me. Papa was busy helping with Avery's funeral arrangements and had asked Noah and Levi's mother and stepfather, Dottie and Marvin Hostettler, to take me home. They lived close to us and had readily agreed. But after Jonathon insisted on talking to me, I told them I didn't need a ride after all. I felt guilty about it but had no intention of telling Papa I'd changed his plans.

Jonathon had left his truck at home, choosing instead to bring one of his family's buggies. "On a beautiful day like today," he explained, "I love riding in an open carriage so I can enjoy the smell of the spring air and feel the sun on my face."

I understood his sentiments and found his enjoyment of our old-fashioned mode of transportation rather endearing. As he helped me into his carriage, Ebbie rode past us with his parents. Although he didn't acknowledge our presence, I could tell by the stoic look on his face that he'd seen us.

Once we turned down the road toward our house, I felt a little more relaxed. "Were you out on the road last night?" I asked him.

He nodded. "Sophie and I took the evening shift, and Roger and Mary relieved us around two in the morning."

It dawned on me that spending time in the dark with Sophie, a girl who was obviously smitten with him, was even worse than my ride into town with Noah. However, I decided to keep my thoughts to myself for now. It was such a nice day, and finally I felt some peace inside. There would be plenty of time for talking to Jonathon about Sophie.

"So you're watching the road into town only at night?" I asked.

"We can't watch it twenty-four hours a day," he said with a sigh. "Most of the attacks against churches have occurred after dark. I assume it's because the people behind these acts of violence don't want to be seen."

"They're cowards," I said. "But they've come after me twice now, and both times it happened during the day."

Jonathon frowned. "Twice? I thought it was just that once."

As I shared with him what had happened on Friday, he grew pensive. "I wish someone would have told me about that. Obviously none of our people are safe on the road whether they're in a buggy or in a car. Any man wearing a hat like ours or a woman with a prayer covering is in danger. These men are becoming bolder."

"Now that you know about the second confrontation, will you still patrol only at night?"

He shook his head. "I don't know. Without additional help, I doubt we can do much more than we're doing now. Besides, these men didn't set out to hurt you, Hope. They accidentally stumbled upon you when you were alone in your buggy and then again when they ran into you and Noah in his truck. They were presented an opportunity to cause more destruction, and they took it."

I was silent while I mulled that over. For some reason, the idea of trying to kill another human being because of an unplanned twist of fate seemed even more sinister than something prearranged. I shivered, though it wasn't the least bit chilly.

"I didn't mean to upset you," he said. "I'm sorry."

"Oh no. You're just being honest."

He cleared his throat. "Speaking of honesty, I think we need to finish the conversation we started the other day."

I looked down at my hands, feeling embarrassed. "What conversation is that?"

"Don't be coy, Hope. It doesn't suit you."

I looked over at him in surprise. "I wasn't trying to be coy."

"Yes you were. You know exactly what conversation I'm referring to."

"I may know what you're talking about, but that doesn't mean I was trying to be coy." Jonathon's attitude irritated me.

"Okay. Forgive me. One of the things I appreciate about you is your candor, and I don't like being manipulated."

"Well, that's good, because I wasn't manipulating you. It's just that I'm not used to talking about my feelings with a . . . man."

He laughed lightly. "You and Ebbie didn't talk about your feelings?"

I thought about his question before answering. "We shared many things, but we hardly ever talked about our feelings for each other. Not until—"

"The engagement was broken?"

I nodded. "Doesn't make much sense, does it?"

"No. No, it doesn't."

He was silent for a while, and it gave me time to think about Ebbie. When we'd both realized our friendship had turned into something deeper, we'd just accepted it. There wasn't really a reason to talk about it. We both knew we would be together. Would it have made a difference if we'd been more open with each other? I had no idea, but it didn't matter anymore. Ebbie's face floated into my mind. I remembered seeing love for me reflected in his deep brown eyes.

"Look, Hope," Jonathon said finally, "if you and Ebbie were meant to be together, you wouldn't have let him go so easily."

"I guess so."

We were coming to a fork in the road. One way led to our house and the other led to a nearby creek. Jonathon urged his horse toward the creek.

"You're going the wrong way," I said.

"No I'm not. You and I are going to talk this out. I can't go another day without finding out if we have a future together. It's all I think about."

I felt my face flush, and it had nothing to do with the warmth of the spring day.

Jonathon drove the carriage across a small bridge until we reached the other side of the creek. Then he got out and tied his horse to a nearby tree. Without saying a word, he held his hand out and helped me down. We walked to a place near the water, and Jonathon sat down on a large tree stump. He patted a spot next to him, and I sat beside him.

The sound of water bubbling over the rocks and birds singing in the background made me feel more tranquil than I had since Thursday afternoon. I lifted my face toward the sun and let the gentle breeze wash across my face. For some reason, I reached up and took off my prayer covering. I felt the need to feel the sun on my head. We sat there for several minutes, both of us enjoying God's creation in silence.

"I love to come here," Jonathon said softly. "It's so peaceful."

"It's wonderful. Just what I needed."

I had my eyes closed, but I felt it when he leaned toward me. His lips were soft and gentle on mine. When he moved away, I opened my eyes and looked at him.

"I love you, Hope. I want to officially court you. It won't be easy. Your father will probably oppose us. You'd have to care about me enough to stand against his displeasure and the negative opinions of others in Kingdom."

Jonathon was right. My engagement to Ebbie had been announced in church, as was our custom. Everyone would soon know that the wedding had been called off. How could I begin a relationship with Jonathon so soon after my breakup with Ebbie? Jonathon waited for a response, and I was desperately trying to come up with one. What could I say? I felt drawn to him, but fear gripped my heart. I finally said the only thing I could.

"Will you give me some time, Jonathon? Being seen together so soon after Ebbie seems . . . wrong. I don't want to embarrass him. And I know my father won't give his approval right now. We need to wait. Maybe he will change his mind. For now, we must keep our feelings for each other secret."

He sighed. "You're right." He gazed into my eyes and put his hand under my chin. "I want to be with you so badly, I just didn't think. It will be incredibly hard for me to wait. Even a day spent away from you is painful."

I was so swept away by the moment I could barely breathe. "I want to be with you too, Jonathon. But we must do things the right way. If we don't, I'm afraid we'll regret it."

He kissed me once more, and I laid my head against his chest. It was a perfect moment except for an ant that scurried across my skirt. All of a sudden, I heard Ebbie's voice in my head. *"They're the most incredible creatures, Hope. Every time I watch them, I'm reminded that with God nothing is impossible. If they can lift fifty times their body weight, what can we do through God who strengthens us? I believe ants are a message sent from God to encourage us."*

As Jonathon and I sat there together, a tear rolled down my cheek and landed right in the spot where the ant had been only moments before.

CHAPTER 11

Monday morning Papa and I rose even earlier than usual. I put together a nice big salad for the meal after Avery's funeral, and we rode to the edge of town. Avery's body was being brought to the church in a horse-drawn hearse. A couple of men from our church had driven the hearse to Washington to pick Avery up at the funeral home. Noah and Herman followed them in Noah's truck, watching for danger. Some of our farm families who lived off the main road joined behind the hearse as it made its way back to Kingdom. No one really expected problems, since troubling a long line of buggies was a lot more intimidating than confronting a single woman or an elderly man traveling alone. More eyes, more chances of getting caught.

Normally, Papa and I would have driven to Avery's and joined the procession, but under the circumstances, Pastor Mendenhall asked those who lived in town to wait at the crossroad and join the other buggies there. A little while after we arrived, the hearse turned off the main road and headed for town. We waited until the other carriages passed by us and then pulled Daisy to the end of the procession. One by one, others followed us.

After we got to the church, several men carried Avery's plain wooden coffin into the large meeting room. Mennonite funerals were simple occasions. There were no flowers, although some may be placed on the grave after the burial service. And there were no elaborate speeches about the deceased. Pastor Mendenhall preached for quite a while, urging forgiveness be extended toward whoever had killed Avery.

"When Christ was born, the angels announced that peace had come to Earth," he said. "Our Lord continued this message throughout His time in this world, imploring us to love our enemies, and to do good to those who persecute us. Our church has been given an opportunity to put His teachings into practice in a way we never have before. Can we walk the path of Christ and forgive? Can we refuse to seek revenge for our dear brother and leave judgment in the mighty hands of God? We have professed our willingness to walk the path of peace in this church for many years. Now it's time to see if we truly believe what we say."

He shook his head and stared down at the simple wood podium he stood behind. "As a people, we have been viewed by many in the world as weak, but I tell you from my heart that walking the path of peace takes more strength than striking back when a wrong is done to us." He looked up, tears in his eyes. "Many of us feel anger toward those who believed our brother's life was so inconsequential. It is not wrong to feel anger, but it is wrong to act on it. It is not wrong to resist evil, but it is wrong to return evil for evil. How strong are we? Are we strong enough to pray for the men who perpetrated this heinous act? Are we strong enough to stand unbroken in the love of Christ?"

As Pastor Mendenhall led us in prayer for the men who killed Avery, I couldn't help but think about his words. Resisting evil wasn't wrong, but resisting it with violence was. So what did that leave us? What was our part and what was God's part? Should we just pray and stand up to evil with faith as our only weapon? Are we strong enough to stand resolute, protected only by the love of Christ? I looked across the aisle and saw Jonathon staring at me. Was he also stirred by the pastor's words? Realizing I was looking around when I was supposed to be praying made me feel uneasy, so I turned my head and closed my eyes until Pastor Mendenhall finished his prayer.

After that, folks were allowed to offer words of respect for the deceased, but any praise for Avery wasn't flowery or effusive. Humility was prized by our members. We preferred that any praise received at our "home going" come from God alone. Only He knew our hearts and could judge us rightly.

When the service concluded, we all rode to the cemetery at the other end of town and laid Avery to rest. Then we proceeded back to the church to share a meal together. Big tables were set up outside the building. Lizzie brought large pans of fried chicken, mashed potatoes and gravy, roast beef, and green beans. Others in the community filled the tables with other dishes. Many were German recipes passed down through generations. Jaeger schnitzel, sauerbraten, fat sausages with sauerkraut, steaming red cabbage, and German potatoes sat among wonderful desserts like cinnamon swirl kuchen, and sugar zwieback. And, of course, there were all kinds of strudels. Ruth Fisher always brought an incredible walnut and raisin strudel to our gatherings. Just thinking about it made my mouth water.

Before everyone descended on the food, I searched for Ruth's strudel, finally finding it among all the desserts. I quickly grabbed a slice before it was gone. I should have felt ashamed of my selfishness, but when it came to Ruth's strudel, I found it easy to lean fully on the forgiveness of God.

We all ate, visited, and offered our condolences to Berlene and Herman. I helped Lizzie serve the food she'd brought. Jonathon came through the line twice. It was obvious he wanted me to slip away for a while, but I couldn't leave Lizzie without assistance. Ebbie brought his plate up once, and I put a serving of roast beef on it. He mumbled his thanks, but he didn't look at me.

After everyone appeared to have eaten their fill, including Herman, who filled his plate four times, I excused myself and found Berlene. She was sitting next to Herman at a table under a large oak tree.

"I'm so sorry for your loss," I said. "Avery was such a good friend to all of us."

"I appreciate that, Hope," she said, a smile on her large round face. "My father loved this town."

I nodded and started to walk away, but Berlene called me back. "You know we've been talking to your father about taking over the saddle and tack store?"

"Yes. Papa told me about it."

"And how do you feel about that?" she asked, frowning.

I stared at her, not sure what to say at first. "I'm grateful for the opportunity," I said slowly, "but the quilt shop—"

"The quilt shop means a lot to you, doesn't it, Hope?"

I nodded, horrified to feel tears fill my eyes. Berlene had just lost her father, and here I was, concerned about a business. Shame made me feel even worse.

She got up from the table and came over to me. "Hope," she said quietly, "how old are you?"

Her question took me by surprise, and I faltered. "I-I'm twenty-six."

She grabbed my hand. "Why can't you run the quilt shop and let your father take care of Dad's store? I don't see why you both can't do what you really want." She smiled at me. "This solution seems so obvious to me and Herman, but you've never even considered it, have you?"

"No, but to be honest, there hasn't been much time to think. With your father's death, and everything else going on recently, my head has been full of so many different thoughts."

"Well, now that your head has this idea in it, why don't you talk to your father about it? Herman and I will do whatever we can to make it easier for you to run both businesses. If you need anything or can think of something we can do to help you, please let us know. Okay? We're staying around for a while. We need to clean out Dad's house and sell it, along with his land. Then we'll deal with his store. You have some time to figure out how to keep your quilt shop open." She squeezed my hand. "I remember your mama, you know. I still have a quilt she helped me to sew when I was a young girl. She was a special lady, and I think she'd want you to keep the shop open. Don't you?"

I could only nod. The lump in my throat made it difficult to speak. Berlene, who wasn't known for her sociable attitude,

171

suddenly hugged me. "You look so much like Hedda. She was one of the most beautiful women in Kingdom."

I hugged her back and managed to whisper thank you before hurrying away. My intention had been to console her. Instead, she had given me hope.

I was trying to find Papa when someone called my name. Belle Martin waved me over to a table where she was sitting alone. Most people had finished eating and were busy visiting. I slid onto the bench next to her.

"It's so sad, isn't it?" she said. "Avery was such a nice man. He was always coming by the house to see if he could help us. He took care of so many tasks that would have been difficult for Mama and me."

I nodded. "Yes, it's very sad. I'll miss him." I gazed around at the large crowd filling the church grounds. "We're not the only ones who feel that way."

She smiled, but I could see sadness in her green eyes. "He touched the lives of many, many people. I guess that's the legacy of his life. I only hope I can impact those I love in such a positive way."

"You already bless us, Belle. You're always so encouraging. Just being around you makes me feel uplifted. I know life hasn't always been easy for you."

"No, it hasn't, but God is good. I know He has a wonderful plan for Mama and me."

Belle wasn't born in Kingdom. She and her mother had fled her abusive father when Belle was just five years old. For the first couple of years after they moved here, she and her mother, Priscilla, lived in fear that he would find them. They rarely ventured out of the house. But over the years, the fear had vanished. Now Pricilla and Belle were happy, friendly people who loved to help the community.

I noticed that Belle seemed rather distracted, looking past me. I followed her gaze and discovered that she was watching Aaron Metcalf, who was talking to Clara Barlow. It was obvious that Clara wasn't happy. I wondered what they were talking about.

"Aaron's a nice man, isn't he?" I said.

Belle colored and turned her attention back to me. "Aaron? I guess so. I don't really know him very well."

I grinned at her, and although she tried to keep a straight face, she lost the battle and giggled, putting her hands over her face. When she took them down, she was so red that for a second I was worried about her. But then I remembered how easily she blushed. Maybe it had to do with her light coloring. It was always easy to know when Belle was embarrassed.

"I really like him, Hope, but he doesn't even know I exist. Clara follows him around like a calf at a new gate."

"You're not seeing what I see."

She wrinkled her forehead and looked confused. "What should I be seeing?"

"Aaron keeps looking away from her. He's not really paying attention. If he really liked her, he'd be hanging on her every word. I think that's probably why she looks so upset. She knows he's not interested in her."

"You don't think he likes her?" Belle's tone was so hopeful it made me smile.

"No. He's just being polite. You watch. He'll try to get away from her as soon as he can." Sure enough, Noah walked past them, and Aaron said something to Clara. Then he caught up to Noah and quickly began a conversation.

Belle broke out into a wide smile. "Oh, thank you, Hope. I feel so much better."

"You might want to talk to him sometime, you know. Let him know you like him."

She shook her head vigorously. "Oh, I couldn't be that bold. What if he acted the same way toward me as he did with Clara? I would feel so foolish."

I laughed. "But if you don't speak to him, how will you know?"

She nodded. "I know you're right, but it scares me. Not knowing whether or not he likes me seems better than finding out he doesn't." Belle was quiet for a moment, and her expression grew solemn. "Hope, I heard you and Ebbie aren't engaged anymore. It's not any of my business, but—"

"It's okay, Belle. We just decided that getting married right now wasn't a good idea."

She looked at me and wrinkled her nose. "I must confess that I overheard something very different, but I probably shouldn't repeat it."

I frowned at her. "If it's about Ebbie and me, I think I have the right to know. Please tell me, Belle. It will stay between us. We're friends."

She bit her lip and stared down at the ground. I could tell she was mentally wrestling with my request. "Well . . ." She raised her head and looked around quickly, as if checking to see if anyone else was near enough to overhear us.

My curiosity was certainly aroused. Had Ebbie said something bad about me?

After more hesitation, finally she said, "Ebbie was called before the elders and Pastor Mendenhall to explain the reason he wasn't keeping his commitment to marry you. He told them the broken engagement was his fault—that he just wasn't ready for marriage. He confessed his fault and was forgiven, but he has been asked to step down from his position."

"What?" I could barely believe what I was hearing. "But . . . but . . ."

"Oh, Hope," Belle said, her eyes wide with distress. "I shouldn't have said anything."

"Who told you this?" I asked, trying to remain calm.

"Aggie, Elder Scherer's daughter. She said her father told her. Maybe she wasn't telling the truth."

I shook my head and wiped away the tears that spilled down my cheeks. I was surprised to find myself crying. "Excuse me, Belle," I said, getting to my feet. "I-I have to talk to Ebbie right away."

I heard Belle calling my name, but it was as if she were a long way off. I started searching the crowd and finally found Ebbie talking to Pastor Mendenhall under a tree in back of the church. I called out Ebbie's name, and both men turned to stare at me as I marched toward them.

"Ebbie Miller, I need to talk to you," I said loudly, my voice breaking.

Pastor Mendenhall looked at me with concern. "Perhaps I should leave."

"No. Please stay, Pastor."

I glared at Ebbie. "I hear you told the other elders that you broke our engagement."

He looked alarmed. "I did. I'm the one who—"

"That's not completely true, and you know it." I turned

175

my attention to Pastor Mendenhall, who was looking at me as though I'd lost my mind. "Pastor, Ebbie ended our relationship because he knew I had feelings for someone else. He did it because he wanted my happiness more than he cared about what people would think. He was concerned about my reputation. That's why he didn't tell you the whole story. And now, you've . . . you've taken his eldership away from him. It's not fair, Pastor. It's just not fair."

Pastor Mendenhall looked at Ebbie, whose face had gone white. "Is this true, Ebbie? You called off the wedding because you found out Hope cared for another man?"

"Tell him the truth, Ebbie," I said. "I will not let you lose your position because of me. If you won't tell him, I'll spread the truth all over town until everyone knows. If you are really concerned about my reputation, you won't let that happen."

Ebbie's eyes fastened on mine. "Why are you doing this? There's no reason to—"

"Yes there is," I said, my voice quivering. "You're a virtuous man. Probably the best man I've ever known, and I won't allow you to ruin your life for me."

Pastor Mendenhall cleared his throat. "Well, he is hardly ruining his life, Hope. Ebbie was asked to step down for only a month, so he could give himself to prayer and repentance. He has not lost his position in the church."

At that moment, I wished the ground would open up and swallow me. "Oh. Well . . . well, he shouldn't have to step down for even a month." I drew myself up as straight as I could. "That's all I have to say. Thank you for your time." I turned and walked away as quickly as I could without running. Belle called out to me as I hurried past her. I loved her to pieces, but if I stopped, I might be tempted to thrash her. And *that* was definitely not in line with our Mennonite tradition. Not knowing what to do or where to go, I decided to walk to the quilt shop. I found Papa and told him I was leaving. He was busy talking to Herman and Berlene and just nodded absentmindedly at me.

When I got to the shop, I opened the door and was greeted by Beau, who'd been locked in while we were gone. I sank down to the floor and wrapped my arms around him. He leaned into me and allowed a silly Mennonite girl to bawl her eyes out after embarrassing herself beyond measure. After a few minutes I heard the door open behind me. Papa! If he found me weeping, he'd want to know why. I could only hope he would think I was crying about Avery, but when I turned I found Ebbie standing there.

"You didn't need to do that, you know," he said gently.

"I couldn't let you take the blame for something that was my fault. It wasn't right."

"I appreciate it, Hope, I really do, but I wish you'd just let me handle it." He knelt down and held out his hand. After a moment I took it, and he pulled me to my feet. We stood there, close to each other, and for some reason I couldn't let go of his hand.

"I'm so sorry, Ebbie," I said, tears falling down my cheeks. "I've caused you so much hurt, and I never meant it. Can you ever forgive me?"

He brought his other hand up to my cheek and stroked it softly. "Forgive you? I already have." He shook his head slowly. "I was so sure . . . so certain we were meant to be together. I never would have agreed to the engagement unless

I had believed God told me . . ." He dropped his hand and stared into my eyes. "I have to apologize to you too, Hope. Somehow I missed God's leading. I guess my love for you made it hard to hear His voice."

It was easy to see that no matter what Ebbie said, he still loved me. I could see it in his eyes. He'd always worn his feelings on his sleeve. In that moment I wanted to turn back time. To go back to the way things had been before Jonathon. Before I could say anything, Ebbie dropped my hand and backed away from me. The pain on his face made my chest hurt.

He took a step toward the door, but before he could leave, Beau trotted over to him and leaned against his legs, effectively blocking his path. Ebbie was obviously glad to see his little canine friend and knelt down next to the dog. After scratching him behind the ears, Beau promptly dropped to the floor and rolled over on his back. Ebbie laughed and began rubbing the dog's stomach. Beau's tongue lolled out the side of his mouth, making him look comical. In spite of my distress with the situation, I had to giggle. I leaned down and stroked Beau's stomach too. My hand accidentally touched Ebbie's, and he pulled it away as if I'd just burned him.

"Ebbie," I said, "when you broke up with me, you said you would always be my friend. But I don't feel like we're friends at all. You won't speak to me, and whenever I see you, you ignore me."

He took off his hat and ran his hand through his hair. "I meant it when I said it, Hope. But it's much harder than I thought it would be." He frowned at me. "I'm sorry. I'll try harder. That is, if you're still interested in being my friend."

I nodded. "I'd really like that."

"All right. And thanks, Hope, for charging in to save me even though I didn't really need you to."

I sighed. "Pastor Mendenhall must think I'm insane."

He chuckled. "Actually, he thought it was pretty brave. He thinks very highly of you. You have nothing to worry about."

"Thank you for saying that."

"You're welcome." Ebbie put his hat back on. "I'd better go. My parents will be wondering where I am."

"I understand."

He leaned down, petted Beau once more, and then left. I walked over to the window and watched him walk away. Beau came up and sat down next to me, and I looked down at him. "Well, at least I've still got you, Beau. Maybe you and I should just stick together. You're easier to understand."

I stood by the window until I couldn't see Ebbie anymore. A feeling of sadness washed over me as I thought about him. He'd always been there for me. Always stood by me, no matter what. Maybe he didn't make my heart race the way it did around Jonathon, but no one had ever understood me the way Ebbie had. Would it ever be the same? Could we really be friends? I wasn't so sure.

Beau licked my hand as if to comfort me. I reached down and stroked his head. After a while, I went back to my wedding quilt and was still working when Papa came by to pick us up and take us home. We were just climbing into our buggy when we saw an old truck barreling down the street. It stopped next to us, dust from the dirt road swirling up in the air. Papa jumped down and grabbed Daisy's halter. The door to the truck flung open, and Levi, Noah's brother, jumped out.

"We need help," he yelled. "Noah and Lizzie's house is on fire!"

CHAPTER 12

After telling me to stay in town, Papa climbed into Levi's truck and they took off. I stood in the street, trying to calm Daisy. Beau, who obviously sensed something was wrong, stood next to me and whined. I told him to get into the buggy, and we rode to the church. A big crowd was gathered there, mostly made up of women and children. I tied Daisy to a nearby hitching post and ran toward the assembled group. The food was still on the tables, but Lizzie was nowhere to be seen. I saw Belle talking to Callie and hurried toward them, Beau right on my heels.

"What's going on?" I asked when I got there. I grabbed Belle's arm. "Levi said Lizzie and Noah's house is on fire."

Callie nodded, her expression grim. "Someone set it on fire while we were all here for the funeral. After the service, Noah wanted to get Ebbie's advice about some of the work being done on the house, so they decided to run over there. Noah said they saw the smoke from the road even before they could see the house."

"How bad is it?" I asked, afraid that Lizzie's dream house was gone.

"We don't know," Belle said. "They just rode back here and asked for help. Aaron called the fire department from his store. All the men left to see if they could put out the fire."

As soon as the words left her mouth, we could hear sirens in the distance.

"How does Noah know the fire wasn't caused by some kind of accident?" I asked. "Not every fire is arson."

"I . . . I don't know," she said slowly. "But there's no electricity there. Nothing he thinks that could have ignited flames without help."

"Oh, Hope, after what's happened, it was only a matter of time," Belle said, shaking her head. "It would be obvious to anyone that our people were working on that house—just by the way we dress. They'd know the house belonged to Mennonites."

Belle's reasoning seemed sound, but I just couldn't jump to that conclusion yet. Knowing that Lizzie and Noah's house was out on the main road, I'd wondered how safe it would be. But all the other buildings that had burned were churches. Not private homes. It seemed these men hated everything and everyone who had a relationship with God.

Lizzie had obviously gone to the house with Noah. I asked about Charity. Callie told me Leah had taken her and some of the other children over to the school for a while.

No one seemed to have any idea what the damage was. I thought about taking Daisy down the road so I could see what was going on, but Bethany Mendenhall, the pastor's wife, circulated through the crowd, telling us that Noah had asked everyone to stay off the road and away from the house. There was nothing for the rest of us to do but to clean up from the dinner and wait. As I worked I prayed silently that the men fighting the fire would be safe and that Lizzie's house would be spared from too much damage.

We'd been waiting almost an hour when Harold Eberly's truck came down the road. When it finally reached the church, several of us ran over to see what we could find out. Harold parked and got out. I was frightened by his demeanor.

"Harold, what's happening?" I asked.

He shook his head. "The fire's out, and the damage isn't as bad as it could have been. With a little work, Noah can get it fixed. The house is still structurally sound."

"That's good news," Callie said with a smile.

"Where is everyone?" Belle asked. "Are they on their way back?"

He nodded. "Soon."

Harold didn't look relieved by the news he'd brought us. "Harold, is everyone all right?" I asked. "Was anyone hurt?"

He paused for a moment and then took a deep breath. "Someone got hurt real bad. Burned. Ambulance took him to the hospital. We're all prayin' he's gonna make it."

Papa was there, as were Noah, Jonathon, and Ebbie. My voice shook with fear as I asked, "Who was it, Harold?"

"Didn't see him myself," he said, "but I heard someone say it was Ebbie. Ebbie Miller."

I felt as if all the blood drained from my body. All I could do was stare at Harold. Callie took my arm.

"I'm sure he'll be fine, Hope. God will take care of him. We'll pray—"

I wrenched my arm away from her and ran to my buggy. My fingers shook as I untied Daisy. I quickly climbed inside, and Beau jumped in next to me.

"Get down, Beau," I said firmly. "You stay here."

Usually a very obedient dog, he stayed put and refused to look at me. I told him once again to get out, but he continued to ignore me.

"Fine. Have it your way."

I urged Daisy forward, snapping the reins to let her know I wanted her to run, not something we did very often. I could hear the cries of people behind me, calling out to me not to go. I turned a deaf ear to their pleas.

As we raced down the road, all I could think about was how much I cared for Ebbie. I couldn't lose him. Not now. Not after I'd caused him so much pain. I knew tears were running down my cheeks, but I didn't care. Let everyone see how important he was to me. It just didn't matter anymore. I was halfway to Noah's when a truck passed me. I heard someone call my name, but I kept going. The truck turned around and began to follow me. Someone was yelling at me to stop, but I couldn't. I had to find out if Ebbie was all right. Finally the truck pulled past me and stopped in front of the buggy. Aaron Metcalf got out. I pulled back on Daisy's reins because I had no other choice.

"Hope, where are you going?" he asked, frowning. "The fire's out. Everyone's headed back to town."

I tried to speak but could only sob. He came up next to the buggy. "Goodness gracious, Hope, what's wrong?"

At first I couldn't get any words out. I took a deep breath and tried to calm myself. "Eb-Ebbie," I finally choked out. "I-I heard he was hurt. How bad is it?"

Aaron's mouth dropped open. "Ebbie? Ebbie Miller?"

"Harold said he was badly burned. That he'd been taken to the hospital."

I felt someone touch my shoulder and swung around. Ebbie stood there, looking at me. I cried out and flung my arms around him. "You're . . . you're okay. I . . . I thought you were dying."

"Hope, it was Eddie," Aaron said gently. "Eddie Stutzman. And he's okay. Just slightly burned. He was taken to the hospital in Washington, but the last we heard, he's already on his way home."

I heard Aaron's words, but for some reason I couldn't let go of Ebbie. Somehow he seemed to understand and continued to hold me.

"Hope, I'm fine," he whispered into my ear. "Really. Everything's okay."

I finally let him go. When I looked around, I realized that Aaron had gone back to his truck. I could see some buggies and other vehicles coming back from the house. Aaron moved his truck to the side of the road, and Ebbie and I moved out of the way. I wasn't sure who was driving past us. It could have been Papa or Jonathon, but I didn't care. I took Ebbie's hand.

"If anything had happened to you . . ." I choked up before I could get my words out.

Ebbie smiled. "Seems like I remember a scene very similar to this when I thought you'd been hurt."

I'd forgotten all about Ebbie's reaction when he'd thought I'd been killed out on the road. I shook my head. "How odd. We were both so upset, yet we're both fine."

He cocked his head to the side and stared at me strangely. "It is odd, isn't it? Almost seems like a coincidence. Of course, I don't believe in coincidences."

I sighed and tried to calm my trembling body. The fear that

had grasped me so tightly was draining away, and I felt like a squeezed-out dishrag. "So you think this means something?" I looked into his face. "And what would that be?"

He smiled. "I think that's a question you'll have to ask yourself, Hope."

He gently withdrew his hand from mine and went back to the truck. Aaron pulled around me and drove back toward town. I got into my buggy and turned Daisy around, Ebbie's words echoing in my mind.

I found Papa waiting for me when I returned. He got into the buggy and we headed home. He told me that they'd found a homemade bomb outside of Lizzie's house. Thankfully, whoever threw it hadn't aimed very well. One side of the structure was scorched, but it was fixable. Eddie had tried to snuff out a section of the fire with a blanket, but it caught fire and burned his arms. Not too bad. Leave it to Harold to embellish the story.

"I shouldn't have believed him," I said to Papa as the buggy bounced along the dirt road to our house. "Why does he always make things bigger than they are?"

Papa smiled. "Harold has a good heart, he just gets overly excited. Obviously, he misheard and thought someone said Ebbie instead of Eddie."

I sighed. "And then I took off with it."

He nodded slowly. "Yes, Daughter, I would say you did."

Papa informed me after we got home that he and Herman planned to spend all day Tuesday working on the transfer of Avery's business. Avery got some of his inventory through the mail, but the rest had to be purchased in Junction City. That meant Papa would have to find a way to go to Junction City every couple of months. That wasn't going to be possible in a buggy. Not only was it too far, but there was no way our buggy could carry all the things Papa would need to pick up.

"So what does that mean?" I asked him.

Papa hemmed and hawed for a while, finally telling me that Herman planned to give him Avery's truck as part of the deal. I found it funny that Papa would have to learn to drive, but he assured me rather huffily that he knew how to drive before he came to Kingdom and it couldn't have changed all that much.

As we sat at our kitchen table finishing supper, Papa made a surprising announcement. "Herman is taking me to Junction City to meet Avery's suppliers. We will be gone for two days."

I couldn't remember the last time Papa had left Kingdom for more than an afternoon. "When do you leave?" I asked.

He finished off his roll before answering. "Tomorrow. I do not want you out here alone, Hope. I asked Lizzie if you could stay with her. She has happily agreed. She will be by herself as well, since Noah and some of the other men plan to stay out at the house. Noah does not want there to be another fire. Until these men are caught, he plans to remain there."

"What about you and Herman, Papa?" I said. "Will you be safe on the road?"

Papa smiled. "Herman was asked this question by his wife. His answer was that no one in their right mind would take on someone his size. I guess I am to be the beneficiary of his large frame."

I laughed. Papa seemed to be in a good mood about his upcoming trip and hadn't said anything directly about seeing me out on the road with my arms around Ebbie. I was relieved. He would have asked me to explain my reaction. Yes, Ebbie was a dear friend, but the overpowering fear I'd felt when I thought he was injured seemed like something else. Felt like something else. I couldn't understand it, and I couldn't define it.

The next morning we rode into town and met Herman in front of the quilt shop. Papa kissed me on the forehead before he got into Herman's truck.

"You will be safe, Hope. I thank God every day that His angels have charge over you." He held my face in his hands and looked deeply into my eyes. "Remember that God offers us blessing and protection, but we must receive it by faith. By trusting Him. God does not force blessings on us, Hope. Especially blessings of the heart."

I nodded, but to be honest I wasn't sure what he meant. As the truck rumbled out of town, his words came back to me, and I wondered what "blessings of the heart" I was missing. A small voice whispered the answer, but I pushed it away.

CHAPTER 13

Tuesday morning went by slowly with only two ladies stopping by for supplies. Around three o'clock, the front door opened and Charity walked in.

"Hi, Hope," she said, shyly. "Is it okay if I'm here?"

"I was hoping you'd come by," I said with a smile. "How about a glass of lemonade?"

She nodded. "It was hot in school today. Lemonade sounds really good."

I got the other stool out of the corner and moved it to the front of the counter. Charity promptly climbed up on it, plopping her schoolbag down.

I went to the back and got the lemonade. Then I put some sugar cookies I'd made over the weekend on a plate and carried them out too. Charity's face lit up when she saw the cookies. Lizzie tried to limit Charity's intake of sweets, but I felt she needed a treat today. And to be honest, I did too.

"Did you hear about the bad men that burned our house?" she asked as I put the plate on the counter.

"Yes, I did. I'm so glad it's okay."

189

"Me too. Mama says God kept it safe, just like He keeps us safe."

I smiled. "That's right."

Charity picked up her glass and took a big drink. It seemed we were done talking about the fire. I was surprised but relieved to find her so calm.

"You're almost finished with school, aren't you?" I asked. "How's it going?"

"Well, I think I'm doing okay in English, but not so good in math." She frowned at me. "I don't see why I have to learn all that stuff. No one ever asks me to add or subtract anything. I don't think it's very important."

I laughed. "I use math every day, Charity."

She wrinkled her little nose. "How?" The skepticism in her voice was clear.

I stood up. "Okay, let's say you want to buy this package of needles for sixty-five cents, and all you have is a dollar. So, you give me the dollar; how much change would I owe you?"

Charity shook her head. "I don't know. That's your job, not mine."

I grinned at her. "Okay, let's turn this around. You told me once that you love the quilt shop and you want to work here with me when you're old enough. Do you still feel that way?"

"Yes. So you mean I might have to give someone change?"

"Of course. It's part of working in a store."

"And that's math?"

"Yes, that's math. And what about measuring things? How many inches are in a foot? If someone wants three-fourths of a yard of fabric, how will you handle that if you don't know your math?"

Charity rolled her eyes and sighed deeply. "Okay, okay. I guess I do need math. But it isn't very easy."

I handed her another cookie. "Do you have a math worksheet you need to do tonight?"

She nodded her head. "Uh-huh."

"Is it in your bag?"

She said yes, although it sounded more like "yeth" due to a mouthful of cookie crumbs.

"You finish your snack, and we'll work on it together, okay?"

She smiled, a look of relief on her face. I was thankful we were only working on second-grade math. I'd had a tougher time with some of my more advanced math classes in school and wasn't sure I'd be much help with those kinds of problems.

"Hope, can I ask you a question?" Charity had a very serious expression, and I assumed she was either going to ask about her father or say something else about the fire.

"Of course you can. What do you want to ask me?"

"Are you gonna marry Jonathon Wiese?"

I was so surprised that for several seconds I couldn't think of anything to say. "Charity Lynn Engel, where in the world did you get that idea?"

She shrugged. "I overheard Sophie Wittenbauer tell Miss Leah that Jonathon said you were going to marry him."

I had no idea how to respond. Why would Jonathon say something like that to Sophie? We weren't even officially dating yet. And of all the people to tell, Sophie was the last person in town who needed this information. First chance I got, Jonathon and I would have a serious conversation. With

Sophie running at the mouth, it wouldn't be long before the story reached Papa. I suddenly realized that Charity was waiting for an answer to her question.

"No, honey. We're not planning to get married. Sophie was wrong. Who else heard her say this?"

Her forehead wrinkled in thought. "Well, like I said, she told Miss Leah."

"And what did Miss Leah say?"

Charity grinned. "She told Sophie she shouldn't be going around spouting off about stuff she doesn't know nothing about."

I was fairly sure Leah had used better grammar, but I was gratified to know she'd corrected Sophie for gossiping.

"And I think Ebbie Miller knows."

My heart skipped a beat. "And why do you think that?"

"'Cause he was there. He came to fix a couple of our desks."

"Are you sure he heard Sophie?"

"Well, she talks really loud."

I'll bet she purposely raised her voice so she could be certain he heard her. "Thanks for telling me, Charity. Gossiping about other people's private business is wrong. You know that, right?"

She nodded, but then she frowned. "I know it's wrong, but it sure is interesting. That makes it harder, doesn't it?"

As upset as I was, I couldn't suppress a smile. "Yes, it makes it very hard sometimes."

She took a big gulp of her lemonade and put the glass down. "Some people have been gossiping about me," she said, looking down at the floor.

"What are they gossiping about?"

Silence.

"You don't have to tell me, Charity. It's your business."

"My daddy is in jail. Millie Sims heard her mama talking about it, and she told me." Charity's head hung down, her dark hair hiding her features.

My heart skipped a beat. "Does that bother you?"

Charity sighed. "It did at first, but then Mama and I talked about it."

"And what did your mama say?"

She raised her head and her eyes met mine. "She said we should pray for him. That he needs Jesus. But then she made me remember that God sent me another daddy to take his place. A good daddy." She smiled sweetly. "God must love me very much, I think."

I returned her smiled. "Yes, I believe He does. Very, very much."

"So now I don't worry about it. But I told Millie Sims that she shouldn't spread stories."

"And what did she say?"

Her smile widened. "She said she was sorry, and that she thought I knew. I forgave her and now we're best friends. I think everything turned out pretty good."

I chuckled. "I think it turned out great. Now let's get to your homework, okay?"

"Okay."

As we worked through Charity's math problems, I felt a lot of joy seeing how her situation had resolved itself, but I was worried about Ebbie. He had broken off our engagement, and then a few days later he heard that I was engaged to Jonathon. My mind spun with bewilderment. Was I really going to marry Jonathon someday? Whenever I was around him I felt flushed, and my heart beat faster. Didn't that mean that I loved him? He was a good man who loved God. His kindness and his concern for me touched me deeply. So why in the world was I worried about what Ebbie thought?

While Charity worked on an addition problem, I prayed silently. *God, I'm so confused. My feelings say one thing, and my mind says another. I can't separate them from each other. Please show me what to do. I have such deep feelings for Jonathon, but I can't stop thinking about Ebbie. Please, please give me wisdom.*

We worked for more than a half hour, and although we got through it, I could see that Charity's weakness for math had nothing to do with Leah's teaching skills. Numbers just weren't the girl's forte. Yet I'd read some of her stories and had seen many of her drawings. She was bright, artistic, and expressive. God had given her many gifts, but a good grasp of mathematics wasn't among them.

She left around four thirty, excited to find out I was spending the night with them and happy Beau was coming with me. I missed Papa, but the idea of having an entire night with Lizzie and Charity had me almost walking on air. I could hardly wait to lock up the shop and go to the restaurant. I'd packed a small valise with my nightgown and fresh clothes for tomorrow. At five o'clock I quickly grabbed it, called to Beau, and we both took off for the restaurant. When we arrived, the dining room was only about half full. Callie saw me and waved me over.

"Lizzie's in the kitchen. She said you could take your things upstairs and then come into the kitchen with her and Charity."

"Thanks, Callie."

I worked my way through the dining room, Beau's nails clicking on the floor behind me. We had to stop several times so people could greet him. He turned out to be much more popular than I was. Beau dutifully stopped to visit every person. It was obvious he enjoyed the attention, but his tail continued to hang limp. I'd even gone so far as to check it out after the accident, making sure it hadn't been injured in some way, but it was perfectly sound. The problem wasn't physical. It was inside him. Even though he seemed happy most of the time, I could see something in his eyes. A shadow of pain. I could only pray that someday it would disappear completely. Until then, all I could do was love him and make sure he knew he was safe.

After making the rounds, we headed upstairs. I put my bag in the spare room and started toward the stairs, calling Beau to follow me. Instead of obeying, he turned around several times and lay down on the rug in the middle of the floor. I walked over and scratched him behind the ears.

"I don't blame you, boy. It's much quieter up here, isn't it?"

I left him where he was and headed downstairs and into the kitchen. Lizzie was standing over the fryer, pulling chicken out and putting it into a large metal pan.

"Hope," she cried when I came in, "you're here!" She put a large piece of chicken in the pan and came over to hug me. She smelled of sweat and chicken, and I loved it. And her.

"What can I do to help?"

"Nothing," she said, smiling. "It's not very busy tonight.

Everyone got to visit at the church supper yesterday, so most of them are staying home. I plan to close early so we'll have lots of time to visit." She pointed at the small table she kept in the kitchen for Charity, who was eating her supper. "Have a seat. What are you hungry for?"

"I'm having chicken," Charity said. "It's my favorite."

"Well, your fried chicken looks and smells wonderful, but I think I'm in the mood for meatloaf tonight." Lizzie's meatloaf was an often-picked choice from the menu. It was by far the best meatloaf I'd ever tasted, and with a side of her pan-fried potatoes, there just wasn't a better meal to be found anywhere. Of course, with Lizzie's food, it was hard to find a favorite dish. Everything she made was delicious.

She slid a pan of meatloaf out of the oven and sliced off a large piece, much too big for me, but when I protested, she just laughed. "Can't have you telling folks I don't feed you enough."

While Charity and I ate supper, Callie and Lizzie filled the last orders. A little before seven, Lizzie closed the restaurant, and by seven thirty, all her customers were gone. We cleaned up quickly, and then the three of us went upstairs.

Charity squealed when she saw Beau and petted him with exuberance. Then Lizzie sent her downstairs to take a shower, reminding her exactly how to turn on the water so she wouldn't scald herself. Once Charity was gone, Beau got up and came over to where I sat. He plopped down on the floor next to me, his head resting on my foot.

"I can't believe how that dog has taken to you," Lizzie said. "He was so close to Avery, I was afraid he wouldn't adjust to anyone else."

I reached down and ran my hand over Beau's head. "It's funny, but he acts like he's lived with us his whole life."

Suddenly, an odd squealing sound filled the room. Lizzie shook her head. "It's the pipes that run from the shower in the basement. I have no idea why they make that sound. The water seems to run just fine, but every time we turn on the shower, it makes that noise. I love this place, but I can hardly wait to have a shower that isn't two floors down and doesn't scream like someone is being murdered."

"And you have to use the bathroom in the restaurant," I said. "I'm sure you'd rather have your own."

She nodded. "Living in the new house will be wonderful. I'm so thankful it was spared." She sighed. "It's hard to understand how people who don't know us would try to destroy our home."

"I know. I'm just grateful you weren't home when it happened."

Lizzie snorted. "I think they knew we were gone. These men are cowards. Going after women and old men on the road. People who won't fight back."

"Maybe their cowardice will work for our good," I said.

Lizzie raised an eyebrow. "What do you mean?"

"Perhaps it will keep them from coming into town. Too many people to face."

Lizzie sighed. "I wish I could believe that, Hope. But if they are convinced we won't fight back, what will stop them?"

It was a good question, and one I couldn't answer. "I'm so confused by the different opinions I'm hearing. Ebbie believes one way, and Jonathon believes another. Papa stands by our teaching of nonviolence, but the idea that he wouldn't try to protect me if I was threatened makes me feel—"

"Unloved?" Lizzie said with a smile.

I shook my head with vigor. "No. I know my father loves me. It's just . . ." I sighed and put my hands up. "I don't know. To be honest, I don't know what I believe anymore. I wish I was more like you. You seem to know exactly what you believe. No doubts at all."

Lizzie laughed and tossed her head back. "Oh, Hope. I have doubts, but I know I'm accepted by my heavenly Father. If I'm wrong about something, and it's important, He'll let me know."

I turned her words over in my head. My love for God was unshakable. But was my faith that He would lead me in the right direction as strong? Did I trust Him to show me the way?

"Hope, can I ask you something?"

"Of course. Anything."

"What's going on with you and Jonathon? I heard from my daughter that there may be an engagement soon." She frowned. "I was surprised because you hadn't said anything."

"She overheard Sophie Wittenbauer telling Leah that we're engaged. It's not true."

"And where did she get that idea?"

"I have no idea. If it was Jonathon, I'm surprised. We certainly haven't talked about marriage. We're not even courting yet."

Lizzie was quiet. Too quiet.

"What's wrong, Lizzie?"

She shook her head slowly. "I hope you'll be careful, Hope. Don't move too soon. I don't want you to make a mistake."

I held up my hand. "Trust me. I have no intention of moving forward with anything right now. I'm still trying to recover from my broken engagement with Ebbie. Besides, I wouldn't do anything to embarrass him. Seeing anyone else right now wouldn't be appropriate."

Lizzie picked up one of the pillows on the couch, punching it lightly. "I have a hard time believing that Jonathon would share personal information with someone like Sophie. I know he's uncomfortable with the way she acts around him."

"I think he likes it." I knew I sounded snippy, but being the center of gossip unnerved me. Let alone the knowledge that this rumor could reach Papa.

Lizzie snorted. "Wow, your nose is really out of joint. You must have some unresolved issues about Jonathon."

"Well, I guess I do." I stood up, walked over to the window, and looked out at the empty streets. After the restaurant closed, downtown Kingdom became a ghost town. "I don't know, Lizzie. I think I love Jonathon. He has so many good qualities, but for some reason I keep comparing him to Ebbie. It's stupid, I know. To be honest, when I was engaged to Ebbie, I constantly measured him against Jonathon, and he came in a distant second." I turned around to look at my friend, who was staring at me with sympathy. "What in the world is wrong with me?"

"My dear, dear friend. There is nothing *wrong* with you. You're just torn between two men. It happens. The important thing is that you wait until you're absolutely certain you know your heart and you've heard from God. Don't do anything until that happens. Okay?"

I smiled at her. "Thanks. Sometimes I feel that life is passing me by and I have to decide everything quickly. Twenty-six is old for a woman to still be single."

Lizzie pointed her finger at me. "You should get married when you're ready, Hope, not because it's expected of you. What if you move too fast and miss the husband God has for you? I had the choice to marry someone besides Noah. If I'd done what looked right, I could have ended up in misery, or even dead." She frowned at me. "You're not on earth to do the will of your earthly father or anyone else. You're here to find that special path God has for you. Don't sell out."

"I wish I could find that path," I said quietly. "Jonathon seems to be everything I've been looking for. He's good and kind. And he loves God." I sighed. "Whatever I do, I won't hurt Ebbie anymore. I just can't. You should have seen the look on his face when he heard Papa accuse me of being in love with Jonathon. I'll never forget it."

"Yes you will, honey. Someday when you're married to whoever is meant for you, and Ebbie is married to the woman meant for him, you'll realize that things turned out exactly the way they were supposed to."

"I hope so. Papa says that God may have a plan for all of us, but we can choose to follow it or not to follow it. The trick is to make God's will more important to us than our own. Sometimes I'm not sure I'm doing that. My emotions seem to pull me one way and then another until I don't know what I want."

Lizzie grinned. "Well, Jonathon isn't going to lose interest. That boy's got it bad. I see it every time he looks at you. Just relax and take your time. You wait until you're sure what God's will is for you."

A loud knocking sound came from downstairs, startling me. Before Lizzie had a chance to respond, a voice called out, "Lizzie? Where are you?"

"That's Jonathon," I said, following her downstairs, Beau on my heels.

When we got to the bottom of the stairs, Jonathon was standing in the middle of the dining room. It was obvious he was upset.

"What's going on?" Lizzie asked. "Is something wrong?"

"Yes, something's wrong," he said tersely. "Is Noah here?"

"No, he's at the house," she said. "Why?"

Jonathon took off his hat and ran his hand through his hair. "Have you seen Sophie?"

"No," Lizzie said, "but she hardly ever comes here."

I stepped around Lizzie. "What's wrong, Jonathon?"

He sank down into a nearby chair. "She's made several comments about wanting to carry a loaded rifle when we're out on the road. Roger and I both told her no. We don't allow her to touch our guns, loaded or not. I finally told her I wouldn't let her come with us anymore if she didn't stop arguing about it."

"Are you and Roger still carrying unloaded rifles?" Lizzie asked.

Jonathon shook his head. "I don't. When it came right down to it, I just couldn't do it. It didn't feel right."

"What about Roger?" she asked.

He shrugged. "I told him how I felt, but he has to make his own decision about that. I have no idea if his rifle is loaded."

"Has something happened with Sophie?" I asked.

"I keep a rifle in my truck just like a lot of us do. It's always there in a rack behind the back seat."

Lizzie started to say something, but he held his hand up. "It's for hunting, Lizzie. That's all."

I felt the blood drain from my face. "Where's your rifle now, Jonathon?"

"I don't know. That's the problem. Sophie was hanging around earlier today while I was helping Noah out at the house. I left there around six to go home for dinner. On the way, I noticed my rifle was gone. I think she's got it, and it's loaded." He stood up. "I've got to find her before she does something stupid."

"You mean stupider?" Lizzie said sarcastically.

He nodded. "Yes, stupider." He sighed deeply. "I don't know what to do with Sophie. She follows me around like a little puppy dog. I've spoken to her about it, tried not to hurt her feelings, but it's like she doesn't hear me."

"Maybe you're not trying hard enough," Lizzie said.

He shrugged. "What can I do? Tell her she's never allowed to talk to me again? That seems cruel."

"Right. And look what being kind has gotten you." Lizzie was clearly exasperated, but I could see Jonathon's point. Hurting Sophie, a girl so obviously in need of some attention, would be very difficult.

"I've got to go. I'm afraid she's gone out to the road with my gun." He put his hat back on his head and turned toward the door.

"Wait a minute. I'm going with you," I said.

He swung around, his hand on the doorknob. "No you're not. It could be dangerous."

"Don't be silly. You're just trying to locate Sophie. She's not going to shoot us. Besides, I need to talk to you, and this would be a perfect opportunity. Papa's with Herman in Junction City." I looked over at Lizzie. "I won't be gone long. Do you mind?"

"Not at all. This will give me time to get Charity to bed so we'll have lots of gab time when you get back." She grinned lopsidedly. "Besides, I have a feeling we'll end up with a lot more to talk about if you go with Jonathon." She looked down at Beau sitting next to me. "Beau can stay here with us. Charity will never speak to me again if you take him with you."

"Thanks, Lizzie. I appreciate it." I leaned down and patted Beau's head. "You stay here, boy. I'll be back soon."

He licked my hand as if to show me he understood.

Jonathon raised his eyebrows at Lizzie's comment about having more to talk about when I returned, but at least he didn't argue anymore. Instead, he held the door open. After saying good-bye to Lizzie, I scooted past him and hurried to his truck. He opened the passenger side door so I could get in, and then ran around to the driver's side. When we got to the edge of town, I turned toward him.

"About Sophie . . ."

"Hey, I get it, okay? I didn't handle this well."

"That's not what I'm talking about."

He looked at me with a confused expression. "Okay, what *are* you talking about?"

"Seems that Sophie was overheard telling Leah Burkholder that we're engaged."

He stepped on the brakes, slowing the truck down and

forcing me to brace myself by putting both hands on the dashboard. "She said what?"

"You heard me." I shook my head. "All the kids in Leah's classroom overheard her. It won't take long before it gets back to Papa."

He put his arm across the back of the seat. His long hair fell over one eye, and he brushed it aside with his other hand. "I never said anything like that to Sophie. Why would I? That would be crazy."

"Maybe you thought it would get her to leave you alone?" I asked it as a question, but I was aware that it sounded more like an accusation.

He shook his head. "No. In fact, except for seeing her at Noah and Lizzie's for the meeting, I haven't spoken to her. She was at the funeral supper, but I was too busy to pay any attention to her."

I sank back against the seat. "Then where did she get that? How could she know about us?"

"I have no idea, but I can guarantee you it wasn't from me."

I stared out the windshield, dirty from the dusty roads in Kingdom. "Sophie's smarter than you think she is. She may think that starting a rumor around town about our impending marriage will actually split us up. It's not a secret that Papa doesn't like you."

"I know he disagrees with my views," Jonathon said, hurt in his voice. "But I'd hoped he didn't actually dislike me."

I reached over and touched his shoulder. "I'm sorry, Jonathon. I shouldn't have said that. Papa knows we need to walk in love with each other."

He raised one eyebrow. "So he has to 'walk in love' with

me on purpose? Great. I knew asking him if I could court you would be difficult, but now I'm really worried about his reaction."

"Look, let's not talk about this now. I think finding Sophie is our first priority. Especially if she's out near the main road. After what happened at Noah's house, it's obvious she's not safe there."

He put the truck into gear and started down the road again. "I have a few questions for that girl when I find her. I'm trying to consider her feelings, but she's beginning to make me mad." He glanced over at me. "And I won't have her causing problems between us."

I couldn't help but smile. "Just a thought, but you might want to get your rifle back before you chastise her."

He blanched. "Yeah. Hadn't thought of that."

Within a few minutes we reached the edge of town, but I didn't see Sophie anywhere. "Where could she be?"

"You know something funny?" he said as he pulled his vehicle over to the side of the road. "She's been disappearing a lot lately. And when I ask her where she's been, she won't tell me." He sighed. "Her parents don't keep an eye on her, so I try to. I could swear she's up to something, but I have no idea what it is."

Believing Sophie was "up to something" wasn't the least bit difficult for me. Every time I was around her, I felt distinctly uncomfortable. I didn't trust her as far as I could throw her.

Across from us was a long fence put up a couple of months ago by several of the men in Kingdom. On the other side was a deep ravine. There had been several accidents when automobiles or horses accidentally veered off the narrow road and tumbled over the side. The new fence helped provide a measure of safety for our buggies, although the wooden posts wouldn't offer much protection for a heavy car or truck. Jonathon pointed toward a tree several yards from the ravine, where a large horse stood.

"That's Sophie's horse. She's here all right. When we watch the intersection, we usually stand over there. That tree keeps us hidden, but we can clearly see the road."

I scanned the area. "She shouldn't be out here alone, Jonathan. What if those men spotted her from the main road? She could be in serious danger."

"I'm aware of that. She's been told not to come here by herself, but she does it anyway. You may have noticed that Sophie doesn't take advice well."

"Yes, I've noticed." I looked around the area carefully. "I don't see her anywhere. Are you scheduled to watch the road tonight?"

He shook his head. "Roger's on this evening. Mary has the flu, so he'll be alone."

"Even so, Sophie had to know that it wouldn't take you long to find out your rifle was missing."

"I have no idea what she's thinking. Figuring Sophie out is beyond my abilities." He put his hand on the door handle. "I'm going to look for her. That ravine worries me." He got out and trotted across the street. I watched as he leaned over the fence and then walked around to where the structure started. After looking down into the ravine, he suddenly disappeared.

I waited for several minutes, but when he didn't reappear,

I jumped out of the truck and ran toward the last spot I'd seen him. Had he fallen? Was he all right? As I neared the fence, I heard a loud popping sound and felt a sharp pain in my chest. It was only as I collapsed to the ground that I realized I'd been shot.

CHAPTER /14

"Hope? Hope, can you hear me?"

I could hear Jonathon's voice, but I couldn't figure out where I was. Then suddenly I remembered the sound of the gunshot. I opened my eyes and looked up to see Jonathon's worried expression.

"I think I've been shot," I whispered. "Am I going to die?"

He shook his head. "No, you're all right. I'm so sorry—"

"But my chest hurts."

"You weren't shot, although it's a miracle you weren't. The bullet struck the tree, and a piece of bark smacked your torso. I'm sure it hurts, but you're going to be fine."

I sat up, more humiliated than sore. "I could have been killed. Was that your rifle?"

He took my hands and helped me up. "Yes. I found Sophie hiding from me. When I tried to take the rifle from her, she grabbed it, and it hit the ground. It went off." His taut expression revealed his anger. "It was a stupid thing to do. She could have killed you. Or at the very least seriously injured you."

It was at that moment I saw Sophie standing a few feet away, her usual sullen expression planted firmly in place.

Something rose up inside me, and I stomped over to her. "You could have really hurt someone," I yelled. "Me or Jonathon. What in the world is wrong with you?"

"It was a mistake. Get over it."

In my whole life I'd never seen anyone look at me with such contempt, but that's what I saw in her face. It made me take a step back.

"Don't talk to her like that, Sophie," Jonathon snapped. "You took my rifle without permission, and then you came out here after I told you not to. You not only put yourself in danger, you could have cost someone their life. I've had it with you."

Jonathon's rebuke caused her face to crumple. Tears fell down her cheeks. "I-I'm sorry, Jonathon. I just wanted to help. Like you and Roger."

"Roger and I are men," he said crossly, "and we're used to guns. You're not."

"Mary patrols with Roger, and she's not a man."

The indignation in Sophie's voice seemed to upset Jonathon even more. "They're a team, Sophie, and Mary doesn't do dumb stuff like this."

It was clear that Jonathon was getting weary of the young girl's protestations. I didn't want to feel sorry for her, but I knew what it was like to be on the outside of life, feeling as if you don't quite belong. Ever since Mama died, I'd felt different from most of my friends who had both parents. As if they belonged to a club I couldn't join.

"Look, Sophie," I said, trying to sound a little gentler,

"maybe we can work together to help Jonathon and Roger. Something that won't be so dangerous." I looked over at Jonathon. "Is that possible?"

"I'm not going to talk about that right now. I need to get you both back to town. It's almost dark, and it's not safe out here."

I pointed toward the northwest. "Noah said he and the men staying with him will help keep an eye on the road. Surely that will help."

"If they were actually watching out for strangers, that might be a great idea, but they're so busy working, someone could easily slip past them."

I frowned at the bitter tone in his voice. "You're angry with them?"

He stared past me, his mouth tight. "I'm trying hard not to be, but I guess I resent their attitudes a bit. They could come out here with us. We're trying to guard *their* town. *Their* families. *Their* homes. Instead, they treat us like we're up to no good. Maybe if Noah had decided to join us, his house wouldn't have been targeted. I only hope these men don't feel emboldened to do more to us since they got away so easily with setting Noah and Lizzie's house on fire."

I frowned at him. "What do you mean?"

"Did Noah call the sheriff about the fire?"

I shook my head. "No, because the sheriff would just tell him there was no way to know how the fire started or who started it."

Jonathon snorted. "My point is that whoever caused that fire got away with it. Noah did nothing to protect himself or to try to bring the perpetrators to justice. He could actually be putting the rest of us in more danger. And he's still not out here trying to help us." His frustration had made his voice grow louder.

"Maybe if you and Roger weren't carrying guns, he and a few men might be willing to join you. They're good men, Jonathon. You know that."

"I'm not carrying a gun."

"But Roger is."

He shrugged. "I guess so."

"Why don't you ask him to put his rifle away? Then approach Noah and the others."

"I don't know. Maybe." He let go of a frustrated sigh. "Roger wants to be in law enforcement someday. He loves patrolling. At first I thought he was committed because of Mary and her folks. Now I'm not so sure that's his main priority. I'm not certain I can talk him into putting his gun away, but I'll try. And I'll talk to Noah tomorrow." He shook his head. "Still seems like I shouldn't have to chase him down for help, but I'll do whatever it takes to keep Kingdom secure."

"A lot of good talkin' to him is gonna do," Sophie said sharply. "Noah cares more about what those church people think of him than he cares about keepin' the rest of us safe."

"That's not true, Sophie," I said, trying to control my irritation. "He cares very much, but he's trying to do what he thinks is right. I'm sure it's very difficult for him."

Sophie pushed her dark prayer covering back. Strands of greasy dishwater-blond hair fell out onto her face. "It's not the least bit difficult. If some creep tries to hurt someone I care about, I'm gonna put a hole through 'em." I noticed her quick glance at Jonathon but he hadn't seen it.

Jonathon sighed with exasperation. "We're not going to 'put a hole through' anyone, Sophie. Frankly, after this incident, I'm beginning to question this whole idea. Something really tragic could have happened here today." He pointed his finger at her. "No more. I don't want you touching another gun, and I don't want you out here again. Do you understand me?"

She didn't answer, just hung her head.

"I mean it, Sophie. I'm very close to disbanding this group. This doesn't seem to be working. Maybe we need another plan."

Her head snapped up at his comment, a look of fear on her face. "You wouldn't do that. We gotta protect Kingdom."

Jonathon slowly shook his head. "The attacks happened out on the main road. These guys have never tried to come into town. Maybe they don't know we're here."

"It would have been easy to follow one of our buggies, Jonathon," I said. "I don't think we should assume they don't know where Kingdom is. They obviously know where Noah and Lizzie live."

He shrugged. "Well, with only one road in, it would be difficult to get out without being seen. Why go to the trouble when it's easier to hit churches in Washington and other towns?"

"Why?" Sophie asked angrily. "Because they know there's a bunch of people here who won't protect themselves! I'm telling you, they're coming. You gotta believe me!"

I watched her grow increasingly upset. Sophie was lonely, looking for some place to belong. The idea that she might lose her "group" seemed to terrify her.

"I don't know," Jonathon said. "Maybe you two are right,

but I'm not going to talk about this right now. Let's get out of here." He glared at Sophie. "You ride your horse back to your house and stay there tonight. I'll drive Hope home." As he looked at me, his eyes widened, and he stared at my chest. I looked down to see a small red stain on my apron. I pulled it down and found a larger spot on my dress that was slowing growing. As I stared at it, I felt a little nauseated.

"You need to tend to that right away," Jonathon said. "It should be cleaned and bandaged."

I guess I swayed a bit because he hurried over and grabbed me. "Sorry . . . sorry," I mumbled. "After being thrown from my buggy, you'd think I'd be getting used to seeing my own blood."

He chuckled. "I'm not so sure anyone should get used to something like that." He pointed at Sophie. "Get going, Sophie. Now."

I got a quick look at her face before she whirled around and headed toward her horse. I was glad she no longer had a gun in her hands. This time, shooting me might not be an accident.

"Just lean on me," Jonathon said. "I'll help you to the truck."

"Thank you. I'm sorry to be such a baby."

He laughed. "I still remember putting up a fence and slicing my finger open on a nail. Blood spurted out all over the place, and I fainted dead away. Fortunately I fell over on a soft mound of dirt." He shook his head. "It's a normal reaction, Hope. Nothing to feel embarrassed about."

I laid my head against his chest and felt safe with his arms around me. He smelled of sweat and soap. It was almost intoxicating.

"It's getting dark," he said after we were both in the truck, "and I'm not comfortable letting Sophie ride all the way home alone. I think we should follow her."

A full moon would have provided enough light for Sophie to safely find her way, but I had to agree that the small sliver in the sky didn't provide very much illumination.

"You've spent a lot of time following women around in your truck, haven't you?" I said with a smile.

He chuckled. "Well, that sounds wrong. Maybe you shouldn't repeat that to anyone else."

I laughed. "You're right. I won't. Especially to Papa."

Jonathon turned the truck around and drove slowly toward Sophie's horse. When he reached her, he had me roll my window all the way down. He leaned across the seat so Sophie could hear him. "I'm going to drive behind you, Sophie. I don't want you riding home in the dark by yourself. My headlights should help you see the road."

She shrugged her shoulders, not even looking our way.

Jonathon shook his head and pulled around behind her, leaving several yards between us.

I glanced sideways at him. "You know she has feelings for you, don't you?"

He looked at me with surprise. "She's like my sister, Hope. I feel sorry for her. Her parents don't pay any attention to her, and she doesn't have any friends."

"She doesn't have friends because she's pushed everyone away who's tried to reach out to her. I've tried to befriend her, Lizzie's tried, Leah . . . lots of us have offered our friendship only to be rebuffed."

"When's the last time one of you really put out any effort?"

I couldn't stop my mouth from dropping open. "Are you blaming us for her bad attitude?"

"No, not really. But I've got eyes. When she's in town, no one talks to her. Same thing at church."

"That's not fair, Jonathon. We've all tried. Many times. She doesn't want anyone in her life. She's made that very clear. Except for you, of course."

He shrugged. "It's not my job to tell you what to do, but I think you're wrong. I think she wants friends very badly. She's just afraid you'll reject her like her parents have. There are some people you have to keep working on, Hope, and she's one of them."

I was quiet as I thought about what he'd said. Maybe he was right. After being rejected more than once, I'd basically given up on Sophie. Had I quit too soon?"

"All right. I'll make you a deal," I said. "You give Noah another chance, and I'll give Sophie another chance."

"Well, okay, but like I said, I'm not upset with Noah. I'm beginning to think that he was right all along."

"So you're really thinking about breaking up your little group?"

"My *little* group? You make it sound like we're a bunch of children playing a game."

"I know you're very serious, and I appreciate everything you're doing to help us."

"You think I'm wrong to consider it?"

I sighed. "I can't answer that question, Jonathon. I'm just as confused as everyone else."

"I know what you mean. I believed we were doing the right thing until tonight. You could have been really hurt, Hope.

If anything bad had happened, I would have blamed myself the rest of my life."

"But I'm fine," I said. "Besides, Sophie is responsible. Not you."

"I understand what you're saying, but I'm the one who started this whole mess. In the end, the responsibility lies with me."

I honestly didn't know what to tell him. Until recently, I'd been proud of the stance Mennonites took against violence, but when actually faced with its consequences, my faith had been sorely tested.

We slowly followed Sophie. A gentle breeze blew through the truck, and the scent of wild honeysuckle mixed with moisture drifted through the air. I was certain that before the night was over, we'd have rain. We rode in silence for several minutes.

"What time is Roger supposed to patrol tonight?" I asked. "It's getting pretty dark."

He shrugged. "I'm surprised we didn't bump into him back there. He must be running a little late."

I nodded, not sure Jonathon could see me in the shadows.

"So you're mad because some people might think we're engaged?" Jonathon asked suddenly.

"I'm worried about Papa. If he hears it, he'll be angry. And hurt."

Jonathon sighed. "What if he doesn't want me in your life, Hope? Will you go against him? You're old enough to make your own choices, you know. How long will you let your father tell you what to do?"

"I don't know. He told me I could make my own decisions,

but I still want his blessing. Not because I'm afraid of him, but because I love him." I reached over and touched Jonathon's arm. "If God wants us to be together, He'll work it out. I just know it."

"But you want to be with me, right?"

I turned my head and smiled at him. "I think I need you. You seem to be saving me all the time. Without you, I'm not sure I'd make it."

He chuckled. "Speaking of your near-death experiences, how are you doing?" He pointed at my chest.

I gingerly pulled down my apron again. Thankfully, the stain hadn't gotten much bigger. "I'll live, but I sure am running through dresses. Glad I brought an extra one to Lizzie's."

He smiled. "You'd look beautiful no matter what you wore."

This was the second time he'd told me I was beautiful. I felt self-conscious and warm inside, all at the same time.

"Did I embarrass you?" he said softly.

"A little."

"I'm sorry, but you are beautiful, outside and inside."

I turned my head and smiled in the dark interior of the truck, not wanting him to know that his compliments pleased me.

We rode quietly until we reached Sophie's turnoff. Jonathon pulled past her and got out. Then he walked behind the truck to where Sophie sat on her horse waiting. He spoke to her briefly and then watched as she rode off. When he returned I asked him what he'd said to her.

"I told her that we both forgave her for making a mistake."

"Good. What did she say?"

He put the truck into gear and started back down the road. "Not much. Just begged me again not to abandon the patrols." He shook his head. "She's obviously more concerned about being a part of something than she is about the original reason we got together. I feel sorry for her, Hope, but I don't know what to do."

"You know, even if you decide to stop watching the road, that doesn't mean everyone will."

He looked over at me. "What are you talking about?"

"Well, Roger seems pretty intent on staying put."

He turned his head to the side. "You and Lizzie don't like Roger much, do you? Want to tell me why?"

I filled him in on our days back at school and the way Roger treated us.

"I had no idea. Noah introduced him to me, but he didn't give me much background."

"You can see why Lizzie isn't thrilled to have him around."

Jonathon was quiet for a minute. Then he said, "Why is it we're all worried about whether or not we have the right to defend ourselves, but we're not concerned about unforgiveness?"

I was surprised by his statement. "I didn't say she hadn't forgiven him. I just meant that she doesn't trust him completely."

"Aren't they the same things? Forgiveness and trust?"

"I . . . I don't think so." I frowned at him. "Are you trying to make a point? If so, I'm not sure I understand."

"I don't know," he said, drawing his words out slowly. "I guess I'm trying to say that it isn't always easy knowing what's right and wrong. For the most part, we're all trying to do our best. Roger too. And judging his actions now by something that happened when he was a child . . . Well, I'm not so sure how fair that is."

"You might be right. Maybe Lizzie and I need to work on our attitudes. I don't want to hold something against Roger that occurred so long ago."

"Sophie could use some forgiveness too. What she did was stupid and careless, but it would be nice if we both show her we've moved past it."

I nodded. "As long as she understands it can't happen again."

"I agree."

We drove into town and Jonathon pulled up to the restaurant. "You and Lizzie have a good evening. I'm going to drive back over to Noah's and help out for a while. Talk to him about the incident with Sophie. I also want to check with Roger."

I reached over and grabbed his arm. "Wait a minute. Are you sure you should say anything to Noah? I know he's your friend, but he's also an elder. If you tell him the truth, he may be forced to take some kind of action. What Sophie did could get her into a lot of trouble. I don't trust her father. I've suspected that he hits her."

"I hadn't considered that." He thought for a moment. "I guess I won't bring it up, but I don't like hiding things from Noah."

"It's up to you, Jonathon. Just be aware of the consequences."

"I don't want to make things any tougher for Sophie. She's been hurt so much, and I'm confident one of these days she'll turn around."

I smiled and squeezed his arm one more time before removing my hand. "I'm glad she has a friend like you."

He got out of the truck, came around, and opened the door for me. "Do you want me to go in with you? I don't want Lizzie to think I had anything to do with your . . . injury."

I laughed. "Don't worry about it. I'll make sure she knows it wasn't your fault."

"How are you going to explain what happened? If you mention Sophie, she might tell Noah."

"She won't," I said, cutting him off. "Lizzie and I share all kinds of things that we don't tell anyone else."

"But this is a little different, Hope. Do you really think she'll keep something like this from her husband?"

"I don't know," I said slowly. "But I can't lie to her."

"I wouldn't expect you to. You do whatever you need to do. Whatever happens, we'll deal with it." Jonathon bent down and kissed me on the forehead. "I'll talk to you soon." With that he got back into his truck and drove down the street toward the edge of town.

I stood there for a moment, trying to decide what to say to Lizzie. Finally I trudged up the steps and into the restaurant.

"I thought I heard Jonathon's truck," Lizzie said when I came in. She was sitting at a table with Charity, playing Candy Land, Charity's favorite game.

"Mama, Hope's hurt," Charity said, her eyes wide. Beau, who was lying under the table, got up and came over to me, whining softly.

Lizzie stared at me, seeing the bloodstain on my apron. She jumped to her feet. "Hope, are you all right?"

221

I smiled. "I'm fine. Just a stupid accident. If you two don't mind, I'm going upstairs so I can change my clothes."

Lizzie came over to me to get a closer look. She lifted my apron and inspected my dress. "This looks pretty bad. How did it happen?"

I gently pushed away from her. "I told you. It was an accident. You two go ahead and play. I'll be right back." I hurried away before she could ask anything else, but I could feel her eyes on me as I went up the stairs. She wouldn't let this go. I was certain of that.

When I got to the apartment, I went into the spare room, where my satchel sat on the bed. It only took me a few minutes to remove my stained clothes and put on a fresh dress. I inspected the wound. It was deeper than I thought it might be, and I knew I should clean it. I also needed to rinse out my bloody clothes with cold water so the blood wouldn't set. Since the only water was downstairs in the bathroom or the kitchen, I bundled them all up and hurried down to the dining room.

"I need to wash these out, Lizzie," I said. "Can I use the sink in the bathroom?"

She nodded but didn't say anything. I went into the bathroom and rinsed out my dress, apron, and bra. I also washed the cut on my chest with soap and water. It stung when the soap touched it. I'd just pulled up my clean bra when someone knocked on the door.

"Can I come in?" Lizzie asked.

I quickly yanked up the top of my fresh dress to cover myself. Then I turned around and opened the door. Lizzie stood there with a bottle and a box of bandages.

"I want to make sure your cut is clean. Soap and water isn't good enough. Do you want me to take care of it? If not, you need to do it yourself."

I shook my head. "I can do it. Thanks. I appreciate it."

She handed me a spray bottle of antiseptic cleaner and the box. Then she shot me a look that made it clear I was going to have to explain what had happened.

After I closed the door, I lowered my dress again and sprayed the liquid on my wound, having to bite my tongue to keep from crying out. Although it stung, I felt better knowing it wouldn't get infected. As I dried my skin and applied the bandage, I thought about what Jonathon had said. How could I not tell Lizzie about Sophie? I didn't want to get the girl in trouble, but was it right for me to ask her not to tell Noah? I'd been taught that the husband is the head of the house and asking a wife to keep secrets from her husband is wrong.

When I finally came out, Lizzie had hot chocolate and cookies ready for us. We played two games of Candy Land before Lizzie sent Charity upstairs to bed.

"But I don't want to go to bed," Charity whined. "Hope's here."

"You have school tomorrow," Lizzie said firmly. "This is the last week. We'll have Hope back after you're out for the summer, but tonight, you've got to get to bed. I already let you stay up later than normal."

Faced with her mother's irrefutable argument, Charity grudgingly accepted her fate. After good-night kisses for both of us and a trip to the bathroom, she headed up the stairs. Beau got up and followed after her. It was as if he knew Charity needed him more than I did right now.

"Call me when you're in bed, and I'll come up and pray with you," Lizzie called after her.

There was no response, and Lizzie grinned at me. "I can hardly wait until she's a teenager. Should be a barrel of laughs."

I wrinkled my forehead, and Lizzie shook her head. "A barrel of laughs means . . ." She frowned for a moment and then burst out laughing. "Oh my goodness. I have no idea where that phrase originated. It really doesn't make any sense at all."

We both giggled. I'd spent my school years in Washington, so although my speech wasn't as proper and old-fashioned as Papa's or most of the older residents of Kingdom, there were still phrases I didn't comprehend. Lizzie had spent five years living in the world, so every once in a while she said something I'd never heard before. Usually she could explain it to me. This was the first time she hadn't been able to.

"We may not be very modern in Kingdom," I said, still chuckling, "but at least we know what we're saying."

Lizzie nodded. "You've got me there." She took a sip of her cocoa, watching me over the rim of her cup. When she set it back down on the table, she cocked her head to the side and stared at me through narrowed eyes. "Okay, now give. What happened to you? How did you get hurt?"

Stalling for time, I bit into my cookie and chewed slowly. What should I do? I truly didn't want to cause trouble for Sophie. If she had a chance of turning her life around, it would take lots of compassion and understanding.

"Is it really so bad you can't tell me?" Lizzie asked, obviously not fooled by my hesitation. "You know I'll keep it to myself." She looked hurt, and it made me feel guilty.

"What if you can't tell Noah?" I asked softly. "I don't want to put you in an uncomfortable situation."

"Wow. I mean, I don't always tell Noah everything, but I'm not sure how I feel about purposely keeping secrets." She wrapped her hands around her cup. "You can trust him too, Hope. You know that, don't you?"

I shook my head. "I'm afraid he wouldn't be able to keep this to himself. It could put him in an awkward position. I'm trying to avoid that."

She didn't say anything for quite a while. I could hear the clock on the wall ticking. She'd just opened her mouth to respond when we heard Charity calling from upstairs.

"You wait here. I'll be right back. And I won't say a word to Noah if you don't want me to."

She dashed up the stairs as Charity continued to holler for her. I pushed my chair away from the table and walked over to the large window by the front door. The moisture I'd felt in the air earlier had been a precursor of rain, as I'd predicted. A light drizzle wet the streets and shimmered in the light. Besides the illumination from a small lamp near the entrance to the restaurant, there was now a new streetlight outside the general store. The streetlight marked the beginning of even more changes in Kingdom. Although I worried sometimes about losing some of the doctrines that set us apart from the world, I loved the soft light that now flooded the street. The streetlight had been added as a safety measure because in the winter the store would be open while it was still dark outside. I liked being able to see our town more clearly at night, and I knew Lizzie and Noah appreciated it too.

The only other person living downtown now was Leah,

who had a small apartment in the back of the school building. Although the elders had approved the use of electricity for the store, a few folks in Kingdom weren't quite as supportive. Elmer Wittenbauer, Sophie's father, had stated clearly that he would never set foot inside Metcalf's General Store. But I figured that would last only until he really needed something. Brother and Sister Wittenbauer's convictions were subject to change based on need.

As I waited, I wrestled with my decision to tell Lizzie about the incident with Sophie, but in the end, I felt the need to share it with her. All I could do was hope she would still be able to keep her word after I told her the truth.

Another thought was swirling around in my brain. Lizzie had cautioned me to not make any decision about Jonathon until I was sure I knew God's will. The more I thought about it, the more I realized she was right. "God," I prayed softly, "I want your will. I'm at a crossroads with no idea which way to go. If I'm ever to be married, I want the man you have for me. So until I'm sure, I'm not going to do anything. All I've done so far is made a mess of things, and I've hurt a good man." I turned my face upward. "I won't change my mind, and I won't break this covenant, Lord. No matter what. Your will, not mine." A feeling of peace washed through me for the first time in days.

By the time Lizzie returned, it was raining harder. Before she'd gone upstairs, she'd turned the lights down in the restaurant, saying it would be best for us to stay downstairs until Charity fell asleep. The low lights and the sound of the rain gave the room a cozy feeling that I loved.

Our house had a balcony on the second floor, but there

was no door to access it. On rainy nights, I liked to climb out my window and sit there. Our overhanging roof kept me dry unless the wind blew the wrong way. Tonight I had the same feeling of protection and peace I experienced when I sat out on my balcony. I knew it was because I'd finally released my future to God instead of trying to plan it myself. I was also feeling a sense of freedom not having Papa around. More like a grownup and less like a child.

"So where were we?" Lizzie asked as she came down the stairs.

I twirled around and smiled at her. "You were trying to wrestle information out of me."

She put her finger up in the air. "Oh yes. I believe you're right." She pointed at our table. "Spill it, girl."

We both sat down as the sound of the rain hitting the roof above us grew a little louder. "Okay, but what about Noah?"

She sighed. "I'll do my best, Hope. But if I feel it's important and he needs to know, I'll have to tell him. That's the best I can do. Of course if you've killed someone, all bets are off." She crossed her arms across her chest and scowled at me with a rather comical look on her face. "You haven't killed anyone, have you?"

"No. I don't think you need to worry about that."

"Well, if that's not it, you'd better tell me what's going on."

The peaceful atmosphere and the tranquility I felt inside helped me to finally get the words out. I told her about going after Sophie and how the rifle had gone off.

"Hope!" she exclaimed when I finished. "You could have been killed! How could Jonathon allow Sophie to get anywhere near that gun?"

"It's not like he told her to break into his truck and take his rifle. She did that on her own."

Lizzie bit her lip as she stared at me. I was already beginning to regret my decision to tell her what happened. I'd been worried about Sophie getting in trouble with the elders. For the first time, I realized that Jonathon could be implicated as well. Lizzie's first admonition hadn't been directed at Sophie. Her anger was toward him.

"Look, I know I told you I wouldn't say anything to Noah, but has it crossed your mind that Sophie might be dangerous?"

"Lizzie, she wasn't trying to shoot me. She dropped the rifle, and it went off accidentally. I think you're overreacting. She's not really a bad person. Her parents have a very negative influence on her."

"You're right about that," Lizzie admitted. "And now they're paying the price for their neglect. She won't pay any attention to anyone, and they don't seem to know how to control her. I think they've just given up."

"No wonder she's so angry." I picked up another cookie even though I didn't need it. Lizzie was such an incredible baker, and her oatmeal raisin cookies practically melted in my mouth.

"Leah told me that when Sophie was going to school, she'd come without a lunch almost every day. When Leah asked her about it, Sophie mumbled something about being allowed to eat only once a day because she was being punished."

"Well, she's getting food from somewhere. She doesn't look like she's missing any meals."

Lizzie cleared her throat. "I wonder where she'd find food in Kingdom."

My mouth dropped open. "Elizabeth Lynn Housler. You're feeding her?"

"Kind of."

"How in the world do you 'kind of' feed someone?"

She shrugged. "I *kind of* send food to the school every day at lunchtime. There are only twenty-one children attending right now, so it's not a lot. Besides, most of those children eat the lunches their parents send with them. This food is just something extra that the kids can have if they want it—or need it." She pointed her finger at me as I made a clucking sound with my tongue. "Would you rather I throw the food out? And just so you know, I send fruit, sandwiches, and—"

"Dessert?" I asked.

"Hmm. Maybe sometimes," she said innocently.

"But Sophie doesn't go to school anymore."

Lizzie grinned. "She might not officially be enrolled, but that doesn't mean she's not welcome to eat lunch with everyone else."

"Oh, Lizzie. You're just too much." I shook my head, unable to hide my amusement at her big heart. I was about to make a comment about what kind of food Sophie's parents were serving her at home, but before I could get the words out, I was interrupted by the sound of a vehicle outside.

"Maybe Noah changed his mind and decided to stay in town tonight," Lizzie said, jumping up and hurrying to the front of the restaurant. She suddenly stopped a couple of feet from the large picture window. Without any warning, she reached for the light switch, and the dining room became dark.

"Lizzie, what in the world—"

She shushed me. "Hope, didn't you say that the person who harassed you on the road drove a red truck?" Her voice shook as she spoke, causing a cold thread of fear to wrap itself around me.

I nodded in the dark, not realizing that she couldn't see me. "Yes. Red with a dent in the driver's side door."

Lizzie gasped and threw herself against the wall—away from the window. "Get down on the floor, Hope. Now! I think that same truck is sitting in the street, right outside our door."

CHAPTER 15

"What are we going to do?" I whispered loudly. "Did he see us? Is he coming inside?"

"I don't know. With our lights turned down so low, it's possible he didn't see us." She took a sharp intake of breath. "Oh!"

"What's wrong?"

"The door. I don't remember locking the door."

"Oh, Lizzie." I hated the way my voice sounded, squeaky with fear, but I couldn't help it. The terror I'd felt on the road back to Kingdom had just returned full force.

"Just stay where you are." I could barely see her as she lowered herself to the floor and crawled to the front door.

When I heard a click, I breathed a sigh of relief.

Slowly she scooted back to the wall that hid her from prying eyes outside. "Noah keeps telling me to lock that door. Why don't I listen?"

"Because you don't like being told what to do," I hissed.

"Are you really going to start a conversation like that now?" she replied with exasperation. "Can we save the criticism for a little later?"

"Sorry." I kept myself as close to the floor as possible, which might have been a good idea if Lizzie had taken the time to sweep up after closing the restaurant. I could smell something that reminded me of corned beef and cabbage, and when I moved my hand, I felt a small piece of food crunch under me. No telling what it was.

"What's he doing?" Lizzie murmured.

I raised my head a bit but couldn't see clearly, so I crawled a little to the left. Some new piece of dropped food crackled under my knee. "Couldn't you have swept the floor?" I griped.

She let out a deep sigh. "Well forgive me for not planning to be stalked by *your* crazed truck driver."

"He's hardly *my* crazed—"

"Hope, will you be quiet and tell me what you see?"

He was still there, his engine idling. Was he looking for someone? For me? I'd just started to tell Lizzie what the truck was doing when it began to move slowly. "He's leaving," I said softly, wondering why we were keeping our voices low. It wasn't as if the man in the red truck could hear through walls. I waited until he drove past the window, and then I picked myself up from the floor, dusted the food off my dress, and walked slowly over to where Lizzie stood, plastered to the wall.

"Where's he going?" she asked as I stood next to her.

"Down to the end of the street." I moved closer to the window, several feet from her, trying to watch the truck. His taillights disappeared from my sight. "I've got to step outside," I said. "I don't see him anymore."

Lizzie grabbed my arm. "Don't you dare! He'll spot you!"

"Nonsense. He's way down the road. We've got to know

if he heads out of town. Unless you plan to stay here hiding in the dark all night."

She loosened her grip on me. "You've got to be careful. If he turns around—"

"I'll get back inside before that happens."

"Okay."

She let me go, and I slowly crept toward the door, watching the windows for any sign the driver was returning. When I was certain it was safe, I unlocked the front door and gingerly stepped out onto the porch. I watched as the truck's taillights reached the edge of town. Then without warning, they disappeared.

Had he abruptly turned the corner? It wasn't until the last moment that I realized the awful truth. He'd switched off his lights and turned around, driving slowly back up the street. I heard him before I saw him coming toward us and jumped inside, slamming the door behind me. I quickly locked it before grabbing Lizzie and wrapping my arms around her. It was the only way we could both cower behind the wall between the door and the picture window without being seen.

"He's heading back," I said, my voice breaking. "And he turned off his headlights."

"We've got to get help, Hope," Lizzie said in a loud whisper.

"How? No one's close enough."

"I've got a phone."

"Who are you going to call?"

"I don't know. Several people in Kingdom have phones now."

"Anyone who could get over to the house and bring Noah

and the men back to town?" My voice shook so badly my words were hard to understand.

The drone of the truck motor grew louder. The driver would be in front of the restaurant within seconds.

"I-I don't know. What about Jonathon?"

"He lives too far out of town, and we need help now."

"Leah's got a car and she's only a couple of blocks away."

I sighed. "But she doesn't have a phone. Besides, I'm not going out into the street, and I wouldn't ask her to do it either. It's too dangerous."

Lizzie was quiet for a moment. "Hey, I know. What about Berlene? They've got a truck, and Avery's house isn't that far from the main road. Fairly close to our house. If she could get word to Noah—"

"Papa and Herman took Avery's truck to Junction City, and I don't think Herman's truck is running."

"Well, for goodness' sake, Hope, what are we supposed to do?"

The noise of the engine grew louder. It was just outside now. Lizzie and I held each other, both of us shaking. I began praying quietly.

"God, we need your protection. You said you would be our strong tower and our refuge in times of trouble. Help us, dear Lord. Please keep us safe."

As if the driver of the truck actually could hear us, he suddenly sped up and drove past the building. About a minute later, the sound of his engine faded away. Lizzie and I didn't move for several minutes. Then she said, "Should we check again?"

"Stay here. I'll look."

I prayed silently as I opened the front door and once again stepped outside. I looked down the street in the direction the truck had gone, as well as the other way. Downtown Kingdom wasn't large. It wouldn't take much time to circle around it and show up in front of the restaurant again. However, the street was completely silent. I waited for a while, hearing nothing but the rain. Finally I went back inside.

"I think he's gone," I said, locking the door behind me.

"But we have no idea if he's coming back," Lizzie said as we stood in the dark room. "I know you won't like this, but I'm going downstairs to get Noah's extra rifle."

"Lizzie, no!" I cried. "The last time I was near a gun, I got hurt. Please don't—"

"Listen, Hope," she said firmly, "I have a child upstairs, and I have no intention of trusting that flimsy door to protect her from some nut who wants to kill us."

"But we prayed, Lizzie. God will protect us. I know He will." I quoted the Scripture verse in Isaiah that Noah and I had prayed when we were penned in by the trucks on the road.

She was silent for a moment. "I believe that promise, Hope, and I do trust God to help us. Has it occurred to you that maybe He's telling me to get the rifle? I pray I won't have to use it, but I don't intend to leave us unprotected."

There it was again, the dichotomy of faith. Believe in God but have another plan in case He fails you. I didn't argue with Lizzie, because Charity was her child, not mine. Somehow it didn't feel right, but this wasn't the time to argue over our interpretation of Scripture.

Lizzie jogged to the kitchen and turned on the light before going to the basement. The glow from the kitchen brought some illumination into the dining room. I went back to the window, watching in case the truck returned. A couple of minutes later, Lizzie entered the room, rifle in hand. She leaned it up against the wall. After what had happened earlier in the day, just seeing it made me shiver.

"We've got to get a message to Noah," she said. "I'm going to call Berlene. Even if she doesn't have their truck, Avery's horse is there and she can ride it down to the Millers' house. They don't live far away. Ebbie can hitch up their buggy and drive to our house."

"But that will put him out on the main road," I said, my voice catching. "What if that man is out there? What if he sees Ebbie? He'll try to run him down the way he did Avery!"

Lizzie twirled around, and I could see the worry in her face. "Do you have a better idea, Hope? The only other people with phones are too far away or too elderly to help us. This is the only thing I can think of."

"I couldn't take it if Ebbie was injured," I said, tears filling my eyes. "If anything happens to him because of me—"

"But it's not just you, Hope," she said firmly. "It's all three of us. It's Charity too."

I nodded, not knowing what to say. Lizzie went to the kitchen to call Berlene while I sat down at a nearby table and stared at the shadow of Noah's gun in the corner. Somehow, looking at that rifle made the debate between Jonathon and Ebbie seem clearer than it had before. Both men wanted to protect the people they loved, and both men were torn between their faith and their fear. Was a gun a symbol of our human strength? Was it a substitute for our ultimate trust in God?

I didn't know the answer, but for the first time, I understood the question. Jonathon and Ebbie were good men. Both trying to find the right way. And sometimes the *right* thing was hard to see. I still wasn't sure what I believed, but I was able to quit judging either one of them. God knew their hearts and He loved them. No matter what.

A few minutes later, Lizzie came back into the dining room. "Have you seen him again?" she asked, walking toward me.

"No. It's quiet outside. I think he's gone."

She sat down next to me. "Listen, I'm sorry if I sounded harsh earlier. I didn't mean to. I'm just upset that we have to go through this. To think that some numbskulls think they have the right to terrorize innocent people makes me angry. Forgive me for taking it out on you."

"Of course I forgive you," I said. "You're my best friend."

She reached over and gave me a quick hug. "I love you, Hope. You know that, right?"

"Yes, I do. And I love you too."

"I don't doubt that at all. No matter how rotten I act, you never treat me any different. I've learned more about love from you than from anyone I've ever known." She chuckled. "Except Noah, of course." She grabbed my hand. "You've always been there for me. When I needed to get away from Kingdom, you were willing to put yourself on the line to help me."

Lizzie was referring to an incident that occurred when she was only eighteen years old. An unhappy teenager who felt ostracized by an unplanned pregnancy, she'd asked me to help get her and her baby away from Kingdom. On one of my trips to Flo's, I took her to Washington, where she got on a bus and traveled to Kansas City so she could start a new life.

"You know, the strangest thing about helping you leave was that no one could believe I had it in me." I shook my head. "I know people think I'm very mild mannered, what you'd call a wimp, but most of the time, I'm just content." I stared down at the floor. "I'm not like Jonathon. I don't have any causes. I only react when I have to. Unfortunately, I seem to be doing a lot of that lately."

"But, Hope, that's wisdom, isn't it? Picking the battles that are important? When it comes down to it, you're the strongest person I know. You won't compromise what you believe."

I smiled. "Maybe that's my problem now. I don't know exactly what I believe. Sometimes I wonder if I ever will. I can see everyone's point of view, and they all sound right. At least tonight I've decided not to worry about it anymore. God's the ultimate judge. Not me."

Lizzie nodded. "You'll find the truth, and when you do, no power on earth will be able to change your mind. Noah's a lot like that."

"I don't know if I ever told you this, but I'm so glad you and Noah found each other." Even as I said the words, I wondered if I would ever have the kind of relationship Lizzie and Noah had.

"Me too. And you'll find the same thing someday. I'm sure of it."

"I hope you're right. Were you able to reach Berlene?"

"Yes. She's going to drive her truck over to the Millers. It's having transmission problems, and she can't get it out of second gear. If it wasn't messed up, she'd drive all the way to our house and alert Noah herself. Hopefully she'll make it. She did say she'd call back and let us know what's going on. Oh, and Berlene gave me the number of the motel where your father's staying. She suggested you call him and tell him what's going on."

I shook my head. "If I do that, he'll rush home. Running Avery's store is important to him. I don't want him to cut his trip short."

"I think he would want to know that man was here in Kingdom, Hope, but it's your decision."

"I'll tell him when he gets back. Anyway, I don't think we're in any real danger now. If he planned to return, surely he would have done it by now. With God's help, Ebbie should reach Noah before long."

We sat in the dark for quite a while, waiting for word from Berlene. About thirty minutes later, the phone rang and Lizzie jumped up to answer it. I listened to the rain while I waited.

As I sat there, I began to wonder about the red truck. Maybe it wasn't the same one I'd seen on the road. Although the thought made me feel a little better, there was one big hitch with that theory. No one in Kingdom had a red truck. Almost all our vehicles were painted black or dark blue. Avery's dark green truck was about as daring as anyone ever got. Although I'd never said it out loud, down deep inside, I felt that if you had to paint your car black to keep your neighbors from being jealous of you, your neighbors had problems bigger than any amount of paint could ever fix.

The door to the kitchen swung open, and Lizzie came out. "Great news. Berlene got to Ebbie's house, and he's on his way to get Noah." She came over and sat down next to me. "Berlene said Ebbie was really upset, and after she told him about the red truck, he hitched Micah up and drove down the road like someone had set him on fire."

"Yes, he would," I said softly.

Lizzie made a grunting sound. "I hope you don't mind my saying this, but Ebbie doesn't act like someone who's moved on. I think he's still crazy about you."

"He's the one who broke the engagement."

"Because he believed you loved someone else."

I was silent for several seconds. "Jonathon is a wonderful man, you know. He already saved my life once. And the way he cared for me after Sophie's gun went off . . ."

Lizzie frowned at me. "Of course, if he hadn't started this whole vigilante thing, Sophie might not have had access to a gun, and you wouldn't have been put in danger in the first place."

"He's trying to keep us safe, Lizzie. I . . . Oh, never mind. I'm exhausted, and I don't want to talk about this right now. Besides, I put the situation in God's hands tonight. I don't intend to be with anyone until I know for certain he's the man God has picked especially for me."

Lizzie reached for my hand. "Oh, Hope. I'm so glad to hear that. I hope you'll stick to it."

I smiled and patted her hand with my other one. "This is one decision I won't change. I'm determined to wait on God."

"I can always count on you to do the right thing. You're so—" She suddenly stopped and sniffed at the air. "Do you smell something?"

I nodded. "Could you have left the stove on? It smells like something's burning."

"I was just in there. I think I would have noticed, but I'll look again." She jumped up and hurried into the kitchen while I waited. The strong aroma of smoke continued to get worse. A few seconds later, Lizzie came out of the kitchen, a puzzled look on her face. "The stove's turned off, and I checked everything else." Suddenly her eyes got wide. "Charity! I'll be right back." She rushed up the stairs. I got up and ran after her. When I reached the landing, the smell was stronger. Lizzie came into the living room from Charity's room. "Nothing's burning up here. What in the world . . . ?"

At that moment, I caught a glimpse of something out of the living room window that made my blood run cold. I rushed over to get a better look. Flames were coming from a building down the street. I turned to look at Lizzie with horror.

"It's the church! Oh, Lizzie! The church is on fire!"

CHAPTER 16

Lizzie and I ran down the stairs as fast as we could. For the first time I realized Beau hadn't followed me. The reason was obvious when we got to the dining room. He was sitting next to the front door, not fooled by the source of the smoke.

"I've got to call the fire department in Washington," Lizzie said as she raced toward the kitchen. I stood in the middle of the room, not knowing what to do. A minute or two later, she came out. "They're on their way. I just hope they get here in time." She went to the door and grabbed the knob, but I pushed her arm away.

"Wait a minute! What if the man in the truck started the fire as a way to get us to come out? We can't take the chance of walking right into a trap."

"Oh, Hope. Why would he go to all that trouble? He could break in here and shoot us if he wanted to. We can't just let the church burn down. Besides, what if someone's inside?"

Although I doubted seriously that anyone was there at this time of night, it was true that sometimes Pastor Mendenhall worked late in the church office.

"I don't know." I said. "What if . . ."

Lizzie whirled around and jogged across the room, leaving me standing there as Beau whined softly. She grabbed the rifle and stomped back to the door. "I'm going. You stay here and keep an eye on Charity. No sense in both of us being in danger."

I shook my head. "No way. If you go, I'm going too. Lock the door behind us. I'll come back after we find out what's going on to check on Charity. Besides, you told me she's a sound sleeper. She probably won't wake up."

Lizzie flung the door open. "Suit yourself, but stay behind me." She turned and looked at me intently, her expression resolute. "If that guy's out here, and if he tries anything, I will defend us, Hope. No question about it."

I didn't say anything, just nodded, but my mind was seized with trepidation. What were we getting ourselves into?

We both walked out onto the street and looked around. No red truck. After locking the door to the restaurant, Lizzie took off toward the church, and I followed her. Even though it was still raining, it didn't seem to have any effect on the fire. Flames licked the sky as if there were no moisture in the air at all. Lizzie held her rifle in front of her, keeping an eye on our surroundings. I was worried about the man in the red truck too, but I couldn't seem to tear my eyes away from our church burning down in front of our eyes.

"What can we do?" I yelled at Lizzie.

"I don't know. There's a water pump behind the building, but it wouldn't help. I'm still worried that someone might be in there."

"We can't go inside, Lizzie. It's too dangerous."

"Has anyone called the fire department?" Jonathon ran up next to us. I was surprised to see him in town.

"Yes, they're on their way," Lizzie said.

We turned as we heard hoofbeats behind us. A horse was galloping up the street, pulling a buggy behind it. The buggy rocked back and forth as the driver urged the horse on. When the buggy got closer, I could see it was Bethany Mendenhall, her expression one of sheer terror.

Jonathon grabbed the horse's bridle when the buggy reached us. "Where's Daniel?" he yelled.

"He's working late. He's in the church!" Bethany jumped out of the buggy and started to sprint toward the burning structure.

I ran after her, grabbed her around the waist, and held her tight. She began to fight me, and I wasn't sure how long I could hang on. "You can't go in there," I screamed. "It's too dangerous."

"He's not supposed to be here," Jonathon said. He looked at us wild-eyed. "Hold her!" He grabbed a blanket from inside the buggy and hurried around to the back of the church. It only took a minute for me to realize what he was planning. He put the blanket under the water pump and soaked it. Then he put it over his head and ran as fast as he could toward the building's front entrance.

Lizzie had come over to help me with Bethany, but the pastor's wife had gone limp and wasn't fighting anymore. "Don't let her go!" I instructed Lizzie. Calling Jonathon's name, I started to go after him, but something sent me stumbling to the ground. Beau stood in front of me, blocking my way. I was starting to get up to my feet when someone grabbed me from behind.

"What do you think you're doing?"

I looked up into Ebbie Miller's face, and my emotions overcame me. I broke out in tears. "Jonathon's in there," I sobbed. "He went after Pastor Mendenhall."

A voice shouted from behind us. "Pastor Mendenhall's inside?"

Holding on to Ebbie, I pulled myself up. Noah stood next to Ebbie while several other men came running across the church lawn.

"He . . . he said he was working late," Bethany cried. "Then I saw a strange glow in the sky, so I rode down here as fast as I could. I just knew something was wrong."

"All of you stay here," Noah ordered. He and Ebbie took off toward the church even though flames shot out of the windows around the huge double front doors.

"No!" I screamed. "Please don't go in there!"

Before Lizzie, Bethany, or I could say anything else, a figure exited the front doors, holding something in his arms. The edges of the blanket covering Jonathon were smoking. Ebbie pulled it off him, tossed it to the ground, and stomped on it to put it out. Jonathon lowered Pastor Mendenhall's limp body onto the grass.

Bethany shrieked and ran toward him. Ebbie and Noah dropped to their knees, checking to see if he was alive. Ebbie put his head on Daniel's chest for a moment. Then he started to compress the pastor's body. After several compressions, he placed his mouth over Daniel's and began breathing into him. Lizzie and I held hands and prayed while Bethany cried loudly, calling her husband's name.

From the street, trucks, cars, and buggies began to pull

in, people streaming toward the burning building. Then the sound of sirens broke through the hum of voices and the whinnying of horses. A large fire truck drove right onto the grassy area near the church. The firemen jumped out and started grabbing hoses. Since Kingdom had no hydrants, they'd brought a tanker truck that carried its own water. As the firemen began to pump water out and direct it toward the blazing structure, I realized it wouldn't be enough. Our church was lost. Suddenly, the light rain turned heavy, as if trying to aid in putting out the fire.

I hurried over toward the spot where Pastor Mendenhall still lay on the ground and was thrilled to see Ebbie helping him sit up. Jonathon stood a few feet away, coughing. I went over to check on him.

"Are you all right?" I couldn't tell if the moisture on my face came from my tears or from the rain, but I didn't care.

He nodded, still coughing, unable to speak.

"Stay here," I told him. "I'm going to get you some water." It seemed like a strange thing to say since we were being drenched with rain, but Jonathon needed a drink to calm his throat. I ran down the street as fast as I could until I reached the restaurant. When I unlocked the door, I found Charity standing in the dining room, her dark eyes wide with fear.

"I heard a loud noise," she said when I came in, "and Mama is gone."

I quickly explained that the church had caught fire, but the firemen were putting it out. She followed me as I went to the kitchen, searching for something to carry water in. Lizzie had a big stack of pitchers sitting next to the dishwasher. I grabbed one and filled it quickly from the sink.

"You stay here, Charity," I said. "Your mother is fine. I'll tell her to come back and check on you."

"I don't want to be here by myself. I want my mama."

I hesitated a moment, not sure what to do. "Okay," I said finally, "but you've got to stay right next to me. Will you do that?"

She nodded slowly, looking scared. I held the pitcher of water in one hand and took Charity's small hand in the other. "Everything will be okay," I said gently. "Your daddy's there too."

A look of relief crossed her face, and I smiled at her. Although she didn't actually smile, at least some of her fear seemed to dissolve.

I led her to the front door, put the water pitcher down, and opened the door, almost running smack into Lizzie.

"Charity!" she cried. "I was just coming to check on you."

"The sirens woke her up," I said, reaching down to pick up the pitcher. "I need to get this to Jonathon. Do you mind if I go?"

"Of course not. Thanks for taking care of her."

I nodded and flew out the door, down the steps, and headed toward the church, trying not to spill all the water before I got back to Jonathon. As I neared the church grounds, I saw someone standing behind a tree, watching the fire. For a brief moment, I thought it looked like Sophie, but as I got closer, whoever it was ran off. Strange, but I quickly forgot about it. I was focused on Jonathon. I found him sitting on the grass by the fire truck, an oxygen mask on his face. He pulled it off when he saw me.

"I . . . I . . ." Another bout of coughing hit him.

"Here, drink this," I said.

He laughed when he saw the large pitcher of water but reached for it and downed almost the entire amount in just a few seconds. "Thank you," he croaked. "I couldn't seem to catch my breath."

"He breathed in a lot of smoke," said a fireman who was standing nearby. "His voice will be raspy for a while, and he'll cough for the next few days." The man smiled at my worried expression. "He'll be okay, ma'am. I don't think there's any permanent damage." He looked down at Jonathon. "You're a real hero, you know. You saved that man's life." Another fireman called his name, and the man walked away.

"He's right," I said. "You *are* a hero."

Jonathon shook his head. "Anyone would have done the same thing. You know that."

"Doesn't matter," someone said from behind me, making me jump. "You did a brave thing." Ebbie stuck his hand out to Jonathon. "You're a decent man, Jonathon. I'm sorry we've been at odds."

Jonathon struggled to his feet and pulled Ebbie to him. "And I'm sorry if I did anything to hurt you. You're my brother, and I love you."

Ebbie patted Jonathon's back. "I love you too." He let Jonathon go and took a few steps back. "I want you to know that I won't stand in your way. You and Hope, I mean. You both have my blessing." I saw the glint of tears in his eyes, and an indescribable ache rose from somewhere inside me. I couldn't think of anything to say, so I just stared at him.

"Thanks, Ebbie. That means a great deal to me. To us." Jonathon reached for me, putting his arm around my shoulders. Ebbie's eyes bored into mine, and then without another word, he turned and walked away.

Jonathon squeezed me tightly before letting me go. He

began to cough again. "I'm so relieved," he said hoarsely. "I . . ."

I reached up and put my fingers on his lips. "Don't try to talk. You need to rest your voice. Why don't you go home and get some sleep? We'll talk more when you feel better."

He tried to say something else but was stopped by another bout of coughing. Noah came up next to him

"I'm going to drive you home," he said to Jonathon. "You can get your truck tomorrow. Right now you need to rest."

Jonathon nodded at him, not daring to try to speak again. Before he had a chance to get away, Bethany Mendenhall came rushing up to him, wrapping her arms around him. Something a pastor's wife wouldn't normally do.

"Thank you, Jonathon. There aren't words to thank you enough. You saved my husband's life. I will always treasure your bravery."

Jonathon nodded again, his face red, but I couldn't tell if he was flushed because of embarrassment, or coughing, or if he'd been slightly scorched from the heat of the fire. After Bethany left, Noah grabbed his arm and led him off toward his truck.

I scanned the area, looking for Ebbie. He was standing several yards away, leaning against a tree, watching the fire. I wondered who had really saved our pastor's life. Jonathon, who'd brought him out of the inferno, or Ebbie, who'd helped him to breathe again. Jonathon was receiving all the attention while Ebbie had quietly stepped aside.

I turned this over in my mind while I watched the fire department put out the last of the fire, the rain continuing to pour down. Our big beautiful church was a charred shell. And for some reason, I felt the same way inside.

CHAPTER 17

"*So you saw the man in the red truck* and about an hour later the church was on fire?" Noah asked again for the third time. I had the feeling he was having a hard time believing that in a few short hours, so much wickedness had found its way into our midst.

"Could the church have been struck by lightning?" I asked.

"I didn't hear any thunder," Lizzie said.

Noah shook his head. "One of the men from the fire department said the fire started from the inside. He found something thrown through a window in the back of the church. He called it a Molotov cocktail. Sounds like the same thing used to start the fire at our house."

"I heard they were used to start church fires in other towns too," I said.

We were sitting around a table in the dining room. Levi, who had been working at Noah's, was with us. "I'm so grateful our pastor survived," he said. "But it's hard for me to believe our church is gone."

Noah nodded, but no one else responded. The loss was

almost overwhelming. For some reason, we were all hungry after we came back to the restaurant, so Lizzie made sandwiches and poured us each a glass of cold milk. Charity had gone back to bed, but it had taken her a while to fall asleep. The fire had frightened her, but if she'd known it had been set deliberately, she would probably have been terrified. That's exactly how I felt.

"It had to be the guy we saw," Lizzie said. "Although I don't understand why he'd drive through the middle of town as if he wanted us to see him. It seems strange to me."

"I agree. And why not set the fire and leave town right away? Why wait for an hour? Where was he all that time?"

"Maybe he drove through town and then hung around because he wanted us to know it was him," Lizzie said. "He's probably proud of what he did. Maybe setting our house on fire wasn't enough for him. He wanted to see something bigger burn to the ground."

Noah grabbed her hand. "Regardless of this man's motives, we've got to remember that we've only lost a building. We're the church, and we're all still here. Like Levi said, we should just be grateful Pastor Mendenhall is still with us."

"Thanks to Jonathon," Lizzie said. She looked at me. "He's a brave man, Hope. Someone to be proud of."

Noah started to say something, but Lizzie held up her hand. "Yes, I know. We're not supposed to be proud, but I don't mean it that way. You know exactly what I'm saying."

"That's not what I was going to say," Noah interjected, "but you're right." He looked at me, a funny look on his face. "How did the man in the red truck get into town in the first place, Hope? Wasn't Jonathon supposed to be watching the road tonight?"

"No. It was Roger's night. Jonathon said he was going to your house to work."

Noah frowned. "He never showed up."

"Well, maybe I misunderstood. When the fire started he was in town."

Noah shook his head. "I can't figure out how this guy got into downtown Kingdom without alerting someone. If Roger was stationed at the crossroad, wouldn't he have seen him?"

I shrugged. "I'm sure there's a reasonable explanation." I didn't feel it was right to criticize Roger or Jonathon about the obvious failure of their plan, since they were watching the road out of the goodness of their hearts and their concern for our community. But frankly, the situation bothered me too. Where *was* Roger? What had gone wrong?

"We've got to call your father in the morning," Lizzie said, changing the subject. "Too much has happened. He'll be angry if we don't."

"I know."

"Yes, he needs to know about the church," Noah agreed. He reached for his sandwich and took a big bite. "And about the guy in the red truck."

Lizzie grunted. "That's not all of it. There's the fact that Hope was shot by Sophie Wittenbauer."

Noah's mouth fell open and he almost dropped his sandwich. "What? Shot? What are you talking about?"

I frowned at Lizzie.

She shrugged. "Sorry, sweetie, but there's just too much going on. Everything needs to come out in the open."

Although I didn't want to get Sophie in trouble, Lizzie was right. I took a deep breath and told Noah the whole story.

253

"In other words," I said when I was finished, "Papa left me alone for one night, and I got shot at, stalked by a killer, and watched our church burn down. I have a feeling he'll never let me out of his sight again." I sighed and took a bite of my sandwich. Lizzie's tuna salad was delicious, but for some reason, all I could taste was smoke.

Noah shook his head slowly. "This really presents a quandary. Sophie's actions prove the point the elders have been making. Trying to defend ourselves can lead to dangerous consequences. Someone could have been seriously injured or killed this evening. But then we've got someone coming into town and setting a fire that almost cost our pastor his life." He stood to his feet, his food forgotten. "What are we going to do?"

"You know what we decided, Brother," Levi said.

I'd almost forgotten that Levi was also an elder. He hadn't been around much since his mother had remarried. Noah was no longer living at home, so helping to merge their family farm with their new father-in-law's had fallen on Levi's shoulders. I knew he missed spending time at the church. And now it was nothing but a pile of ashes.

"When I thought Charity's life might be at risk, I went for a rifle," Lizzie said pointedly. "And I'm not sorry for it. When push comes to shove, I'm going to look after my daughter."

Noah's turned his attention to his wife. "She's *our* daughter, Lizzie. You're not in this by yourself."

Lizzie dropped her eyes. "You're right. I'm sorry."

"You're awfully quiet, Hope," Noah said. "What are you thinking?"

I stared at my sandwich, wondering if I could even finish it.

"I was just thinking about something Ebbie said. We should pray and trust God to defend us." I raised my head and met his gaze. "Why aren't we doing that?"

Noah stared back at me, not saying anything. Finally he said, "I guess I don't know how to answer your question, Hope." He looked at Levi. "Why *aren't* we doing that?" he asked.

Levi smiled sadly. "We've prayed for God's help and deliverance, but we're not acting as if we truly believe He'll provide it."

Noah walked over to the front window and stared out into the street. "Our time has been spent debating how to turn the other cheek, but we haven't talked about faith. About trusting God to be our true protector."

Lizzie wiped away a tear. "I guess I've been so busy trying to take care of Charity, I've forgotten that God is her Father and loves her even more than I do."

"I'm going to call a meeting with the elders and Pastor Mendenhall tomorrow," Noah said quietly. "And we're going to pray again. Instead of trying to figure out ways to defend ourselves, we're going to believe that God is exactly who He says He is." He turned around and gave me a small smile. "Thank you, Hope. I'm sorry you had to remind us that God is the Great Protector."

"Yes, Sister Hope," Levi said. "You've directed our attention back to where it should be."

"Ebbie's been saying it all along," I said softly. "And no one would listen to him. Especially me."

I caught Lizzie studying me with an odd expression, but she didn't say anything.

"I'll make certain he's listened to this time," Noah said. He turned back toward the window. "I feel ashamed of myself for not taking this stand before now."

"People talk about faith," Lizzie said, "but they only want to practice it when there's not much at stake."

No one responded to her statement. Probably because there wasn't much to say.

"I must get home," Levi said to Noah. "I hate telling our mother about the fire. She'll be so upset."

Noah walked over and put his hand on Levi's shoulder. "If anyone can deliver this news with discretion and grace, it's you, Brother."

Levi stood up, a full head taller than his brother. He smiled at us. "We'll all get through this. Kingdom is a special place, and you're all very special people. Together we'll come out stronger."

Levi's words gave me hope. He had a way of bringing encouragement to people and stirring up their faith. It was the reason Pastor Mendenhall looked to him to stand in his place when he had to be away from his pulpit.

We all said good-bye to Levi as he left to go home.

"Let's go to bed, Lizzie," Noah said. "I'm exhausted. The sun will be up way too soon. Why don't you put a sign in the window and let people know we'll be closed in the morning? That way, you can sleep in."

Lizzie stood up slowly. "No. Everyone will come to see the church and figure out what to do. They'll need a familiar place to sit and talk. To comfort each other and make plans. I'll be open as usual. The town needs us to be available for them."

Noah didn't argue. He just smiled and walked over to her,

holding out his hand. She took it and looked at me. "Are you coming to bed, Hope?"

"In a little while. I'd like to sit up by myself for just a bit. Is that okay?"

"Do you think it's safe for her to stay down here alone?" Lizzie asked her husband.

"I'm sure she'll be fine," he said. "No one's going to set a fire and then come right back to the scene of their crime. He has to know that we're all on high alert, looking out for strangers." He smiled at me. "Just turn off the light when you're done."

Lizzie and Noah started toward the stairs, but suddenly Lizzie stopped and turned to stare at me. "Will you check the front door, Hope? In all the commotion I can't remember if I locked it."

I waved my hand at her. "I'd be happy to. Don't worry about it."

"Thanks."

As they climbed the stairs I got up and checked the door. Sure enough, Lizzie had forgotten to pull the bolt. I wondered if other Kingdom residents would start locking their doors. The world we'd tried so hard to keep out of our town had come in with a vengeance.

I stepped outside and looked down the street. The fire truck was just pulling away. A few residents were gathered in front of the ruins of our church, as if they still couldn't believe what they were seeing. I walked out onto the porch and sat down on the steps. The rain had lessened to a very light sprinkle. It was only a few hours until sunrise, but today promised to be one of great sadness in Kingdom. A verse in

Psalms came into my mind. *This is the day which the Lord hath made; we will rejoice and be glad in it.*

"Give us the faith to rejoice, Lord," I whispered. "Help us to be thankful that you saved our pastor and that no one else was hurt. Protect us, Father. Take care of us, and help us to trust in you instead of ourselves." I started to say amen, but something else popped into my mind. I had to wrestle with my flesh for a few seconds before I could say it out loud. "I forgive these men, Lord," I said finally. "They need you. I pray their hearts of stone will become hearts of flesh, tender toward you. Help them, Lord. Forgive them."

Sometimes it was hard to forgive, but holding anger in my soul toward the men would only make the wound they'd caused last longer. Their hate had caused enough pain. I wouldn't allow them to move in and build an altar in my heart.

I watched as the people gathered around the smoldering ruins began to drift away and head home. When the last one was out of sight, I got up and went back inside the restaurant, carefully locking the door before going upstairs to bed. Would Kingdom ever feel the same again?

CHAPTER 18

Lizzie got up early to open the restaurant but didn't wake me, even though I'd asked her to. I'd wanted to help her, but as I lay in bed, I had to admit to being glad I'd gotten a little extra time to sleep. My whole body felt tired, and my head ached. The noise coming from downstairs made it clear the restaurant was exceptionally busy, so I rolled over and pulled myself into an upright position. I was sitting there with my head down when I heard someone speak.

"Mama said you probably need this."

I snapped my head up and found Charity standing inside the doorway of the bedroom holding a cup of what I hoped was coffee.

"How did she know I was awake?" I asked, amazed at the timing.

Charity grinned. "She didn't. I've been here a couple of times already."

I laughed and held out my hands for the cup. Charity walked slowly across the floor, watching the hot liquid carefully.

"How did you make it up the stairs without spilling it?"

She wrinkled her little nose and shook her head, her soft black curls bouncing. "Don't tell Mama, but I spilled just a little bit on one of the steps. The carpet soaked it up so you can't tell."

I reached out and took the cup from her hands. "I won't tell, and thank you very much. There's nothing I want more right now than a cup of coffee."

She nodded. "I better go back downstairs. Mama told me not to bother you."

"You're not bothering me."

"She said you'd say that, but I wasn't to pay any attention."

That made me laugh. Then something struck me. "Charity, why aren't you in school?"

"School was called off today because of the fire. Everybody's at the church, cleaning up the mess. Mama's feeding them." She had a solemn look on her face. "She's giving away our food," she said in a low serious tone. "We might go broke."

"I guarantee you won't go broke," I said with a smile. "Your mama and daddy would never let that happen."

She frowned at me, her expression dead serious. "Ebbie Miller said that when we give to people God blesses us back. Do you believe that?"

"Yes. Yes, I believe that. The Bible says that when we give it is given back to us pressed down, shaken together, and running over."

She looked puzzled. "So if Mama gives lots of free pancakes we'll get more pancakes back?"

"Well, maybe not pancakes, but God will bless your food."

"Why does He do that?"

I chuckled. "You're really taxing my sleepy brain this morning, Charity. First of all, He loves us and wants to provide for us. But also, if you show Him that you won't be selfish with what He gives you, He'll give you more because He knows He can trust you to help other people. Do you understand?"

Her face lit up in a smile that warmed my heart. "Yes, I think so. You're the first person who explained it so it made sense." She paused for a moment. "Except Ebbie." As she turned to leave, she suddenly stopped and looked back at me. "Can I tell you something, Hope?"

I took a sip of coffee, savoring the wonderful rich flavor. Lizzie made the best coffee I'd ever tasted. "Yes, of course you can, Charity."

"You are very beautiful. Like a fairy princess. Like Sleeping Beauty or Rapunzel. You should wear your hair like that all the time." She smiled once more and then ran out of the room, leaving me a little self-conscious but flattered all the same. No one had ever told me I looked like a fairy princess. Of course, since I didn't really know what a fairy princess looked like, it wasn't too hard to dismiss the compliment.

I stood up and grabbed my satchel where I'd put my brush, hairpins, and ribbons. I walked over to the dresser and stood in front of the mirror. I brushed my hair, which hung halfway down my back. My mother's hair had been almost white like mine, and her eyes were violet too, although mine were darker than hers. Instead of immediately wrapping my hair up in its customary bun, I brushed it out until it shone like silk and lay draped across my shoulders. Was I really beautiful? Jonathon had said the same thing. I'd never seen myself that way.

The image of the blond woman I'd seen in the fabric shop came back to me, and I wondered for a moment if I would look like her with modern clothes and makeup. As soon as the thought came into my mind, I dismissed it. There was no desire in my heart to live in the world. My life was in Kingdom, and I felt no call to be anywhere else.

I pulled my hair up and twisted it into a bun. Then I tied it with ribbon and stuck pins in it without looking in the mirror again. My prayer covering lay on the dresser, but when I picked it up, it smelled like smoke. Thankfully, I'd packed another one. I'd planned to wear a fresh dress today, but after yesterday's events, I had no choice but to wear the same dress I'd worn last night. It smelled of smoke as well, but there was nothing I could do.

After adjusting my apron, I pulled on my leggings and shoes, feeling silly for letting a child's comments stir up my vanity. No wonder Papa kept only a small, imperfect mirror in the house. He was probably afraid it would make me vain. I'd been taught that true beauty is something that exists on the inside, not the outside.

After downing the rest of my coffee, I headed down the stairs. As I'd imagined, the dining room was full. Callie was running around, getting orders. I grabbed her by the arm.

"Let me help," I said. "What can I do?"

She smiled gratefully. "Oh, Hope, thank you. Almost everyone is in town, helping at the church. I'm overwhelmed. Lizzie's cooking up a storm in the kitchen."

"Do you want me to take orders?"

She shook her head. "If you could clear and clean tables and pour coffee, I can keep up with the orders. Everything's free today since the town is coming together to clean up the church site and start planning for a new building."

"My goodness, things are moving quickly."

"The elders are meeting in Aaron's store, trying to decide what to do next." A look crossed Callie's delicate features, like a cloud passing the sun.

"Is something wrong, Callie?"

She held up a finger toward one table, signifying that she would be with them in a moment. "I hope you won't see this as gossip, but the story is all over town. Jonathon Wiese stormed into the meeting, demanding the elders start posting guards at the road into town. He accused them of offering us up like sacrificial lambs to be slaughtered. He almost came to blows with Ebbie Miller." She looked quickly around the room. "Dorcas Wittenbauer was walking past the store and heard everything."

If there'd been an empty chair close by, I would have sat down. My knees went weak, and Callie reached out to grab me.

"Hope, are you all right? I'm sorry, I didn't realize . . ."

I shook my head. "It's not your fault, Callie. I think it's all the excitement from yesterday. It's just too much to take in."

"Maybe you should go back upstairs and lie down," she said carefully. "I don't think you're in any shape to be on your feet all day."

I straightened myself up and threw back my shoulders. "No, I'm fine. We're all under pressure." I reached over and hugged her. "We need to stay together, as a town and as a church." I pointed toward John and Frances Lapp, who were looking rather antsy. "You'd better see to the Lapps while I get these tables cleaned off."

I turned away from her, hoping she wouldn't see that I was still upset. Jonathon and Ebbie almost coming to blows? What in the world had happened? Just yesterday they'd made up, and Jonathon had expressed doubt in his plan to protect Kingdom. Papa would never allow me to date Jonathon now. Not when he was at odds with the church. Papa! I'd forgotten that Lizzie had said we should call him. Had she done it already? I hurried into the kitchen to get a tub for the dirty dishes. Lizzie stood at the grill, flipping pancakes, her face shiny with sweat.

"Well, good morning, sunshine," she said with a smile. "Charity tells me you loved getting coffee delivered to you this morning."

"Yes, thank you," I said hurriedly. "Did anyone call Papa this morning?"

She nodded. "Noah called the motel. Samuel's on his way back."

"I know it was the right thing to do, but I hate to think his trip was ruined," I said, rinsing out one of the big plastic tubs Lizzie used to carry dirty dishes from the tables to the kitchen.

"Samuel told Noah that he and Herman had concluded their business in Junction City, so it turned out all right after all."

"Oh, thank goodness," I said with relief.

For the first time, Lizzie noticed the tub in my hands. "Hey, just what do you think you're doing?"

I explained my conversation with Callie, and over Lizzie's protestations, I headed into the dining room to pick up the dirty dishes that cluttered tables where new customers sat waiting for service. After clearing a second table, I looked up to see Matthew and Anna Engel, Lizzie's parents, watching me. I smiled and went over to greet them.

"How good to see you."

"It is good to see you too," Anna said. "But I wish these were different circumstances."

"I agree. I'm afraid it will take a lot of work to rebuild our church."

Matthew nodded. "When I finish breakfast, I will go over and help clear the debris." He looked out the window. "I know it is just a building, but those walls were witness to many wonderful moments."

Hearing Matthew speak in positive tones about the church was gratifying, since almost a year ago he'd walked away from his position as an elder due to his belief that the church was straying from its original mission.

"Does Charity know you're here?" I asked.

Anna shook her head. "We didn't want to bother Lizzie. I would like to help if you can use me."

"Oh, thank you, Anna, but I think we've got it under control now. Let me clear your table, and I'll send Callie over to get your order."

"Are you sure? We don't want to add to your burden."

"You two are never a burden." I smiled at her, noting the sweet smile she gave me in return. Anna was a gentle, loving soul who'd been instrumental in softening the heart of her husband.

After clearing their table and wiping it down, I took the dishes to the kitchen, rinsed them and the tub, grabbed clean silverware, and took it back to them. By the time I got there, Callie was already taking their order.

I'd been working about an hour when the door to the restaurant opened and Ebbie walked in. He sat down at a nearby table. We were almost caught up, and I noticed Callie start toward him. I tapped her on the shoulder before she could make her way across the room.

"Callie, do you mind if I take Ebbie's order?"

"Of course not. And take your time, Hope. You're due a break anyway. Thanks for your help."

I nodded at her and walked slowly toward Ebbie's table. He'd removed his hat, his usually messy hair as wild as ever. He looked surprised to see me.

"Hello, Ebbie. Are you helping over at the church?"

"No, not yet, but I'm headed over there after I eat. I just left the elders' meeting."

"I heard you met at Aaron's."

He eyed me suspiciously. "Oh? And what else did you hear?"

I slid into the chair next to him. "Well, I heard Jonathon was there."

"Are you pumping me for information, Hope?"

I met his gaze without flinching. "Yes, I am. What happened, Ebbie? I heard you and Jonathon almost got into a fight. That doesn't sound like you."

His eyebrows shot up in surprise. "It doesn't sound like me? But you think it sounds like Jonathon?"

"I didn't say that."

"You implied it."

"Hush," I hissed. "Tell me what happened."

"I'd tell you it wasn't any of your business, but it wouldn't help, would it?"

"No, not really."

He shook his head. "First of all, you shouldn't listen to gossip. Jonathon and I certainly did *not* come to blows."

"I was told you *almost* got in a fight."

"No, not even remotely. Jonathon asked to speak to the elders, he was permitted to do so, he spoke his piece, and that's all there was to it."

"And what was his piece?"

"I think you'll have to ask Jonathon that question. I'm not going repeat something said in confidence." He ran his hand through his hair, adding to its disarray. "I will only tell you that he stated his views and we all listened. Then he left. No fistfights. No yelling. No arguments." He frowned at me. "Who told you we were fighting? As far as I know, only the elders and Jonathon were in that meeting."

There was no way I could tell him that Dorcas was the source of the rumor. She was famous for spreading false stories, and it was obvious I shouldn't have given credibility to anything she'd said. "Someone walking past the store overhead you talking," I said innocently.

He looked amused. "Was this person someone you would call reliable, Hope?"

I bit my lip and shook my head.

His warm laughter made me even more embarrassed.

"Okay," I admitted, "I shouldn't have paid any attention. It's silly. I was just concerned."

"Well, everything's fine."

"I guess so. I'm still surprised about Jonathon. I thought he'd changed his mind after—" I caught myself and quickly shut my mouth. I'd almost told him about Sophie.

He sighed loudly. "You mean after Sophie almost shot you?"

My jaw dropped. "How . . . how did you . . . I mean how . . ."

"How did I find out?"

I nodded.

"Sophie told me."

I was shocked to say the least. "I didn't think Sophie talked to anyone except Jonathon."

He shook his head. "She worships Jonathon. She talks to me."

"I'm sorry. I don't understand."

Ebbie fingered his hat, which was on the table next to him. "Sophie's parents are very neglectful. That isn't a secret. Everyone knows it. I've been visiting them. Trying to show them how much their daughter needs their attention."

"That's wonderful, Ebbie. I had no idea."

He smiled. "I'm an elder in the church, Hope. It's my job to support and counsel our members. It's really not that surprising, is it?"

I thought that over for a minute. "Yes, it is. A lot of folks in Kingdom are put off by the Wittenbauers. They're . . . well, odd to say the least."

"So they don't deserve the love of God?"

I felt myself flush. "I didn't say that, Ebenezer Miller, and you know it." I lowered my voice and glared at him. "It's just that sometimes people who are different are a little . . . I don't know . . . scary, I guess." I pounded my fist lightly on the table. "I'm not saying this right. I sound prideful, and I'm not."

His expression softened. "I know you're not prideful,

Hope. Believe me. God has given all of us different callings. Different gifts. I truly believe my calling is to love the unlovely."

I laughed softly, my anger gone. "Well, the Wittenbauers are about as unlovely as they come. It was Dorcas who spread the rumor about you and Jonathon."

He chuckled. "I should have known. Dorcas and Elmer know people don't like them. It makes them feel disconnected from everyone. I think that's why they act the way they do. They're just hungry for attention."

"Maybe they need to be more concerned about their daughter than what their neighbors think," I said pointedly.

"You're right. That's what we're working on, although we certainly haven't made as much progress as I'd like."

I studied him for a moment. "Did you tell the other elders what Sophie did?"

"No, of course not. What Sophie told me was in confidence. Anything said to an elder during counseling is kept private. The only reason I told you was because you already knew. And because I trust you."

I was stunned. "You . . . you trust me? After what I did to you?"

He grunted. "What did you do, Hope? You fell in love with someone else. It wasn't on purpose, yet you were willing to marry me anyway. You were determined to keep your word. You had no intention of hurting me." He shrugged. "So yes, I trust you. Completely. Always have. Always will." His dark brown eyes peered into mine. "You see, I know you, Hope. I know your heart."

I didn't know what to say. His words gave me a sense

of release from the huge burden of guilt I'd been carrying around, yet at the same time, for some reason I couldn't understand, inside I felt miserable.

"Thank you," I said finally. "I appreciate your faith in me, even though I'm not sure I deserve it. You're a very kind and gracious man."

"Well, thank you, but it isn't kindness. I'm simply accepting the truth. You love Jonathon, and that's all that matters. If God has brought you and Jonathon together, it's not my place to interfere in His plan. I'm content to wait until God sends someone who will love me the same way."

I nodded, wanting to say something else, yet I had no idea what it was. It was a confusing sensation to say the least. I reminded myself that I'd put this part of my life in God's hands, and I had no plan to break that commitment.

"Let's get back to the meeting, Ebbie," I said. "What are we going to do? These men have broached our borders now. Pastor Mendenhall could have been killed."

"All I know is that we can't become vigilantes," he said, raising his voice a notch. "We spent the morning in prayer, asking God for wisdom. And we forgave the people who have come against us."

"Is that it?"

He frowned at me. "No, but I think that's the most important part, don't you?"

As I looked at him, I noticed that his eyes seemed to have depths I'd never explored. "Ebbie, did you pray for protection?"

"Yes, for the entire town."

"And do you believe God has heard your prayer?"

His mouth twitched just a little, and I wondered why.

"I believe what I read in His Holy Word. That He is our refuge, our shelter from the storm."

"If we really believe that—"

"Why do we scurry around trying to take care of ourselves?"

I nodded. "Noah, Lizzie, and I talked about that after the fire. We pray for protection, and then we try to defend our own lives and possessions. As if we don't believe God will answer our prayers."

His expression softened. "Hope, you've asked an honest question. One that some people never ask. And it might explain why I don't think we should be running around with guns."

I raised my eyebrows, indicating he should continue.

"First of all, I believe in the Mennonite teaching of nonviolence. Jesus left us in this world to bring peace and reconciliation. How can we do that by inflicting pain or death on one another? Even when we are trying to protect those we love? Jesus didn't resist evil with violence."

"Are you talking about His crucifixion?" I asked. "I have to agree with Jonathon on this point. Jesus was fulfilling His calling. He accepted the cross willingly. I don't believe we're called to suffer the kind of persecution we're experiencing now, nor do I believe it was God's will for Avery to die on the road to Kingdom."

"I agree with you about Avery, but you must remember that the Lord told us we would suffer persecution. They persecuted Him, and they will persecute us. However, we must not allow that persecution to void the promises God has given us. We must use our shield of faith to quench the fiery darts of the enemy. Persecution will come, Hope, but God hasn't left us helpless. I'm afraid too many of our brothers and sisters leave their shields down either through unbelief or by trying to substitute the plans of men for the supernatural promises of God."

He frowned and drummed his fingers on the tabletop. "When I say Jesus didn't resist evil, I'm not referring to his sacrifice on the cross. I agree with you and Jonathon about that." He took a deep breath and gazed at me intently. It was obvious he'd put a lot of thought into what he was getting ready to say. "Do you recall the story of Peter cutting off the ear of a servant when the soldiers came to arrest Jesus?"

"Yes. Jesus rebuked Peter and healed the servant's ear."

Ebbie smiled. "Why?"

"Because it was His nature."

"Exactly. Jesus didn't have to do that. The servant must have been manhandling Him or Peter wouldn't have gone up against the man. In essence, the servant was a bad man. Still, Jesus didn't react with anger. He reacted with compassion. It isn't wrong to resist evil, Hope. But it is wrong to resist evil with evil."

"I've heard this over and over," I said. "Pastor Mendenhall said the same thing at Avery's funeral. We're not supposed to resist violence with violence. But everyone seems to have a different opinion of what we *are* supposed to do."

He thought for a moment. "Do you also remember the story in the fourth chapter of Luke, when Jesus went to Nazareth and taught in the synagogue?"

"I'm not sure."

"Jesus' words stirred up anger among those who were listening to Him. The Bible says they were so upset they dragged him to the top of a hill and tried to throw Him off a cliff." Ebbie had a look of wonder on His face.

"Somehow He passed right through them," I said, remembering the passage he referred to.

He nodded.

"So what are you trying to say?"

He sighed. "I can't say I understand it all, Hope. But Jesus resisted the crowd's attempt to harm Him without resorting to violence. I believe He passed through the mob because He knew God's protection was something He could count on. To Him, it wasn't some pie-in-the-sky concept. It was real.

"We have a choice. Do we try to protect ourselves, or do we walk through the crowd because we believe God is actually with us?" He smiled. "Please trust me when I say that I'm not suggesting we act foolishly. We should be as wise as serpents and harmless as doves."

"Which means?"

He leaned back and folded his arms across his chest. "Which means that we're asking everyone to stay off the main road for now, and if they have to travel, not to go alone. Staying together is imperative. Safety in numbers."

"But no special patrols?"

He shook his head. "Jonathon informed us that he and Roger Carson would continue to guard our boundaries no matter what decision we made. We're not sanctioning it, but we understand that Jonathon's just trying to help. His heart's in the right place. He's a godly man who cares very much about this town."

"I'm glad you're not mad at each other anymore."

Ebbie chuckled. "I was never mad at him. Just concerned that carrying guns might cause trouble."

"And it did," I acknowledged.

"Yes, it did. And Jonathon agrees. No more guns on patrol."

"I'm not sure Roger will go along with that. He doesn't see things quite the way we do."

Ebbie shrugged. "Jonathon is going to talk to him about it. Unfortunately, when a door is already open, it can be tough to close it again."

"Do you carry a rifle, Ebbie?" It had suddenly occurred to me that even though almost every man in town carried a hunting rifle from time to time, I'd never seen Ebbie with one.

"No. I hate guns, Hope."

"Do you hunt?"

He sighed. "I'm sure you'll think even less of me now, but no, I don't. My father took me hunting when I was a boy. I pointed a rifle at a deer, but I couldn't pull the trigger. I just couldn't. So my father brought him down. I'll never forget watching that poor animal suffer and die." He shook his head. "Ever since that day, I haven't liked guns. Even the sound of them."

"So after that incident you never picked up another gun?"

He smiled. "Actually, I did once. Father was out in the fields one day, and my mother had an accident in the kitchen. She dropped a skillet of hot grease and it splashed on her, burning her rather severely. She was in such pain, she wouldn't let me leave her, but I needed my father to come and take her to the doctor in Washington. So I got out one of the rifles, took it outside, and fired it into the air. Father came running. In the end, I found a useful purpose for a gun. Getting help when you need it."

I studied him for a moment. Finally I said, "Just so you know, I don't think less of you for not carrying a rifle. And I don't blame you one bit for not liking to hunt. I hate it too. Frankly, I don't see how anyone can shoot an innocent animal and find enjoyment in it."

Ebbie chuckled. "Yes, but you're a woman. It's okay for you to feel that way. Men who don't like to hunt? Not really acceptable in our community."

"I don't care. I respect you even more now, Ebbie. I really do."

His eyes widened with surprise. "Well, thank you. That means a lot to me."

I nodded. "Ebbie, something is bothering me about last night. Did Jonathon explain how the man in the red truck got into town?"

"No, and we didn't ask him. I know he feels guilty about it, and he shouldn't. We never asked him to put himself or Roger in that position in the first place. It was something they took upon themselves." Ebbie shook his head. "But I think that's why he so was insistent about going back out to patrol. He feels responsible for allowing that man into Kingdom and indirectly responsible for the fire at the church."

"That's ridiculous. It's not his fault."

Ebbie sighed. "I know that and you know that, but it might take a little longer to convince Jonathon. He seems to carry too much responsibility on his shoulders."

I stared past him, out the front window. "Those people

came into our town, Ebbie. It was different when they were only out on the road. I feel so—"

"Violated?" he asked.

I nodded, trying to blink away the tears that came into my eyes.

"I know. I feel the same way. But . . ."

He stopped talking, and I was certain it was because of the look on my face. Sheriff Ford stood in the doorway, looking like he'd come to arrest the entire town. He scanned the room. All conversation came to an abrupt halt, and Ebbie cranked his chair around so he could clearly view the sheriff. I was glad to see that he was alone this time. Tom wasn't with him.

"Can we help you, Sheriff?" Ebbie asked, since no one else seemed to be willing to step up and confront the lawman.

"Fire chief called to tell me you people had a fire of suspicious origin. I gotta check it out. You all know who burned down your little church?"

"We assume it was the same person who killed Avery Menninger," Ebbie said. "A red truck was spotted driving down Main Street last night. Looked a lot like the one that forced Miss Kauffman off the road the other day and confronted her and Noah Housler not far from the turnoff toward our town."

"You got any proof of that?" The sheriff stared at Ebbie as if the question were a challenge. To his credit, Ebbie didn't flinch.

"Of course we have no proof," he said evenly. "But someone set the church on fire, and it certainly wasn't anyone in Kingdom."

Ford's eyebrows shot up. "You interview everyone in town, son? You gotta badge or somethin' I don't know about?"

"No, Sheriff. But why would one of us burn down our own church? That doesn't make much sense, does it?"

He glared at Ebbie. "You tryin' to tell me that nobody in this town has a beef with your religious leaders? You folks would be the first people in history to accomplish that."

Ebbie took a deep breath before answering Ford. It was obvious the sheriff was trying to bait him. "We don't always agree, Sheriff. But we don't express our opinions through arson."

Ford shrugged. "No proof anyone but you all was in town last night. And since you can't point to anyone as a suspect, I'm gonna assume either your fire wasn't suspicious at all, or one of your own residents took exception to somethin'. If you get any evidence that points another way, whoever has a phone give me a call."

He cast one more exasperated expression our way, shook his head, and left. The door slammed loudly behind him, signaling more than just his exit. Obviously the sheriff had no intention of looking into who'd started the fire. He got into his car, gunned his engine, and sped out of town, once again startling the horses.

"Well, he sure isn't going to be any help," Lizzie said. She'd come out of the kitchen and was standing in the back.

Someone in the crowd spoke up. "Did you think he would be?"

No one responded since the answer was obvious. A few seconds later, a buzz of conversation broke out in the room. The topic of conversation wasn't hard to guess.

"He appears even more agitated than usual," I told Ebbie. "I know he doesn't like us, but at least he seemed willing to look into Avery's death."

Ebbie nodded. "You're right. He's a hard man to read."

Lizzie came over and sat down at the table with Ebbie and me. "So how do you think the fire started?" she asked.

I shrugged. "It had to be the same people who set those other church fires. And tried to burn down your house. Whoever was driving the red truck."

"I suppose so," she said slowly, "but the whole thing seems strange somehow." She shook her head. "The guys from the fire department were certain the fire was intentionally set?"

"That's what I was told," Ebbie said, "and I don't have any reason to doubt it. No one in Kingdom knows anything about Molotov cocktails."

"I do," I said without thinking. When he looked at me oddly, I smiled. "Don't worry. It wasn't me. I was with you, Lizzie. Remember?"

She frowned. "I'd forgotten that you mentioned Molotov cocktails before. You said you knew they'd been used to burn other churches in the county."

"But where did you hear about them?" Ebbie asked.

"Jonathon told me. He talked to someone at a church in Haddam. The fire in their church was started that way."

I watched as Ebbie and Lizzie looked at each other. "Oh my goodness," I said. "Don't be ridiculous. Jonathon would never do such a thing. Besides, he risked his own life to save our pastor."

"Of course he didn't set the fire," Ebbie said. "Jonathon's not capable of anything like that."

Lizzie was quiet, and I stared at her with concern. "Lizzie, surely you don't believe . . ."

She sighed and cut me off. "Jonathon said something odd when Bethany told him Pastor Mendenhall was in the church. He said the pastor wasn't supposed to be there."

"For crying out loud," I said. "He only meant that Daniel should have been at home that late at night. You're casting aspersions at the wrong person."

She held her hands up in a gesture of surrender. "You're right. I'm sorry. I just don't know what to believe anymore. I'm beginning to suspect everyone. Unfortunately, I'm not the only one. All kinds of rumors are circulating through town. This situation is causing confusion and discord."

"We can only pray it will soon come to an end," Ebbie said. He rubbed his hands together. "You know, I was starving when I came in here, and I still haven't eaten. If one of you lovely ladies wouldn't mind—"

"Oh, Ebbie," I said. "I came over here to take your order, but then the sheriff walked in."

He chuckled. "It's okay. But I'm already too skinny. Let's put some good food in this body so I can go over to the church and get to work."

"Get this young man whatever he wants," Lizzie said to me with a smile. "Guess I'd better get busy too."

She said good-bye and headed toward the kitchen.

"I haven't see Charity or Beau," Ebbie said. "Surely Charity's not cleaning up rubble."

I laughed. "Hardly. School was called off today, so she's hanging out in the kitchen."

"And Beau?"

"He's with Noah. No matter how many times Noah told him to stay, he kept trying to follow him out the door. Noah finally gave up and took Beau with him. That dog has an overwhelming desire to help people."

"Just like Avery," Ebbie said quietly.

"Just like Avery," I repeated. "I miss him so much."

"So do I," he said, looking away. I patted Ebbie's shoulder to let him know I understood his emotion. Then I wrote down his order of pancakes and sausage and was almost to the kitchen when Papa came limping into the restaurant, his face pale. It took a few minutes to calm him down and explain that I was all right. He finally joined Ebbie at his table, and I ordered the same breakfast for him as I'd turned in for Ebbie. Papa kept rubbing his legs. The air was still moist from the rain, which seemed to aggravate his arthritis.

As I worked the rest of the morning, clearing tables and doing whatever I could to help out, I kept seeing the look on Lizzie's face when I told her Jonathon knew how to make Molotov cocktails. It was absurd to think he was involved in the fire, but questions kept popping into my head. Who bombed our church? If it was the man in the red truck, why hadn't anyone seen him actually start the fire? As far as I could tell, he'd never gotten out of his truck.

There was one other thought I couldn't wrap my head around. The man left quite a while before the fire started. If I understood the concept of a Molotov cocktail, the fire would blaze up quickly. It wouldn't smolder for a long time, would it? Maybe he drove out of town and came back, but that really didn't make much sense.

And how could Roger have missed seeing him when he came into town and again when he left? Once was an accident, but a second time seemed highly unlikely.

Lizzie had said that something about the fire seemed strange. Even though I was afraid to voice my agreement, she had a valid point. An extremely uncomfortable feeling burrowed itself into my mind and stayed there the rest of the day.

CHAPTER 19

The town pulled together to remove all the debris from the church property. Men working at the site bunked outside, not only so they could start work early in the morning, but also because everyone wanted to make sure Kingdom was safe from further intrusion. It took only two days for them to clear most of the area where our church had stood for so many years.

Plans were completed for a new structure, but it involved some strenuous debate because everyone seemed to have an opinion about what was needed. The elders made the final decisions, and three days after the fire, the framing for the church began. Lumber piled up and supplies poured in.

No one left town alone, and only those with trucks or cars traveled the main roads. Even then, at least one other vehicle followed them. I hadn't talked much to Ebbie since that first morning after the fire, but he came in several times to eat while he worked at the church site. I stayed with Lizzie so I could help out in the restaurant.

The quilt shop was closed, as was almost every other

283

business in town. For now, restoring our church was the number one priority. Leah started school up again, but trying to get the children to concentrate on their studies was difficult at best, which made getting them through the last of their school work difficult. But Leah met the challenge with commitment and determination.

Jonathon worked as hard as everyone else, and we finally found some time to share lunch. "Lizzie can't keep feeding everyone for free," he said as we munched on chicken salad sandwiches.

I smiled at him. "Folks have been bringing all kinds of food by to help out. She's got more supplies than she knows what to do with. The restaurant will be fine. Besides, she plans to start charging again tomorrow night."

He laughed. "Maybe I'd better have a couple of sandwiches then."

"I think you're too honest for that."

"Well, thank you. I appreciate the affirmation. At this point any positive comments about my character are welcome."

Beau, who had curled up on the floor next to me, moved his head, resting it on my foot. "What are you talking about?"

Jonathon sighed and put down his cup of coffee. "A few people in town seem to feel that my efforts to protect Kingdom sparked the attack on the church. That I only succeeded in drawing attention to our town."

"But . . . but you saved Pastor Mendenhall's life!" I shook my head in disbelief. "I don't understand . . ."

"In their eyes, if I hadn't inflamed the wrong people, our church would never have been singled out." He shrugged. "I don't want to make it sound like the whole town feels this way. Most folks tell me they appreciate what I'm trying to do."

I wanted to ask exactly who was blaming him for the fire but decided against it. Knowing would only make it harder to keep a good attitude. "Jonathon, it just isn't true," I assured him. "You didn't do anything to *inflame* anyone, and neither did Avery or Noah. Nor did any of the churches or people who were attacked in other towns. You have nothing to feel guilty about. The only people to blame are the instigators of these crimes."

His blue eyes met mine. "Thank you, Hope. I wish I could be sure you're right."

I reached across the table and took his hand. "Look, I've listened to everyone's opinion as to what we should or shouldn't do. I may not have all the answers, but one thing I do know: You're doing your best to protect us. So is Ebbie, and so are the other elders. Lizzie got a rifle the other night when she thought her daughter might be in danger, even though she'd usually never pick up a weapon.

"What I'm trying to say is that this is a difficult situation. I doubt that anyone is completely right or completely wrong. All your decisions have been about helping Kingdom and keeping us safe. Your motives are right, and I know God understands that. I think the thing that concerns Him most is our attitude toward our brothers and sisters. Especially those we disagree with.

"And I've come to realize that life is about taking steps, not cowering in fear. I've been hiding behind my father, not wanting to make a mistake, afraid to fail, but life doesn't work that way. We can only do our best with the information we have. That doesn't mean we're right. And it doesn't mean we're wrong. It means we're growing. In the end, we've got to trust that if we veer off the course God has for us, He'll point us back in the right direction. But that's His job. Not anyone else's."

Jonathon put his other hand over mine. "Wow, that's incredible, Hope. And you're right. I'm sure I've been too harsh in judging our elders. They're trying to be faithful to what they believe." He took a deep breath and let it out slowly. "You know, in the end, this situation, as unpleasant and awful as it's been, has forced all of us to examine our beliefs a little more closely. I guess faith isn't worth much until it's tested."

"I believe that's true." I gently pulled my hand away. "So what happens now?"

"Roger, Mary, and I are still watching the road at night. For now anyway. As I said before, I'm not carrying a gun, loaded or empty."

"So what if you see someone headed for Kingdom who looks suspicious?"

"Well, the elders asked us not to confront any strangers by ourselves. Instead, we're supposed find Levi, Noah, Lutz Zimmerman, and Ebbie. They all live close to the main road. The elders will deal with any outsiders."

I frowned at him. "That will take some time."

Jonathon nodded. "I worry about that too, but for now, it's the only plan we have." He leaned forward a little and lowered his voice. "I locked up my rifle in a toolbox in the back of my truck. No one can get to it except me. At least it's there if I need it."

I didn't say anything, since I'd just declared that people

on both sides of the debate shouldn't judge each other, but Jonathon's admission made me feel uneasy. All I could do was pray he'd never be put in a position where he felt using his gun was necessary.

"What about Roger? Didn't you say he's still taking his rifle with him on patrol?"

Jonathon rubbed his hands together. "I said I wasn't sure, but I believe he is." He shook his head. "I can't tell him what to do, Hope. He's not Mennonite. I trust him though. I really do. He's a good person."

"Look, I hesitate to say this. I know we talked about not holding the past against Roger . . ."

"Go ahead."

"I'm just not sure about him. I mean, he used to really hate anyone who lived in Kingdom. Now he's protecting us? It bothers me, Jonathon. And it doesn't have anything to do with forgiveness. How do we know he's really changed? How do we know he isn't involved somehow in what's going on? Of anyone I've ever known, Roger has shown more animosity toward us than anyone else."

"He married a Kingdom girl, Hope. And he and Mary are trying to heal the relationship with her parents. Isn't it obvious that he's changed? He may not be Mennonite, but he and Mary attend church. As far as I know, he loves God and would never do anything to hurt us."

"Yes, he married Mary Yoder, a girl who left Kingdom behind. Basically, she disowned us. And just because she wants to see her parents, that doesn't necessarily mean that Roger accepts us as a town."

Jonathon didn't say anything, just stared at me. Did he

have doubts about Roger too? "Look, I'm not accusing him of anything, nor am I judging him. Like I said, that's up to God, but at the same time, I believe we need to ask questions if something bothers us. *Someone* set the church on fire. It might not be anyone we know, but looking a little closer to home might be wise as well."

"What about Mary? Do you feel uncomfortable around her too?"

I thought back to the beautiful cross Mary wore around her neck. "I . . . I don't know. Not really." I waved my hand at him. "Maybe I'm just overreacting."

Jonathon smiled. "If you're going to form an opinion about everyone by their childhood, you'd better lock me up right now. According to my parents, I was a handful."

I laughed. "You're still a handful."

"Thanks a lot."

He gobbled the last bite of his sandwich. "I'd better get back to work. If I can get away for a bit, I'm going to try for a quick nap before I patrol tonight. Not sure it will happen though. We've all got schedules at the church site, and woe to anyone who doesn't stay on track. Mennonites can disagree about doctrine, but when it comes to building something, we're as organized as ants."

I almost choked on my sandwich.

Jonathon looked concerned. "Are you all right?"

I coughed a couple of times while nodding. Stupid ants. Would they always remind me of Ebbie? How silly was that?

Jonathon wiped his mouth and stood up. "When things settle down, we need to talk about our future."

"Yes, I know." He turned to leave, but I called him back.

"Jonathon," I said softly, "how did the driver of the red truck get into town Tuesday night?"

He shrugged. "Roger fell asleep in his truck. After working all day, he was just too tired to stay awake. He feels awful about it."

"What about when the man drove out of town? Was Roger asleep then too?"

"Roger says he slept until he was awakened by Noah and the other men heading into town after Ebbie alerted them to the situation."

Jonathon's answer certainly didn't quell my concerns about Roger. It only made me more suspicious. "Can I ask why you were in town that night? I thought you said you were going back to Noah's house to work."

"That was my plan, but I had a flat tire. By the time I ate dinner, found a spare and put it on the truck, it was so late I decided not to go after all. I was outside our house when I smelled smoke and decided to drive back to town." He frowned at me. "Why are you asking, Hope? Is something wrong?"

"No. Not at all. I just wondered why you were so close, that's all."

"I'd like to believe it was God. He knew our pastor would need help."

"Yes. I'm sure you're right."

He said good-bye and left.

I finished my coffee and thought about what Jonathon had said. Maybe Roger really did fall asleep. However, it was certainly convenient timing. I hated feeling so suspicious, but I couldn't shake the feeling that there were too many odd twists of fate working in the situation. And why had Jonathon seemed so surprised when he found out Pastor Mendenhall was working late in the church?

But the question that worried me most was how strangers could enter our town, bomb our church, and slip out without anyone seeing them. There was only one way into downtown Kingdom, and it was almost impossible for anyone to drive down Main Street without drawing some attention. Of course, it was late, and since almost everyone lived away from town, I suppose it could happen. And it was raining, so any resident who might have noticed the truck was safely tucked inside, keeping dry.

I still couldn't get past the time difference between the man in the red truck leaving town and the discovery of the fire. Why not start the fire before he left the first time? Could the bomber be someone else? Someone we hadn't considered? Was I missing something, or were all of us failing to pose questions that should be asked?

I tried to forget my concerns while I helped Lizzie the rest of the afternoon. By three thirty the dining room was empty. Lizzie wasn't sure if tonight would be a regular night since the men who'd been camping out at the church grounds were going home until the supplies that had been ordered were delivered. Since it would be a couple of days before they arrived, it gave everyone a much needed break and a chance to spend some time with their families.

Charity came bouncing in the door about three forty-five, a big smile on her face. School was over until the fall, and she had gotten a hundred percent on her last math worksheet, even with the distraction caused by the fire. Lizzie was ecstatic, and Beau jumped up to greet Charity as if celebrating her achievement. But as usual, his tail stayed down. I was beginning to believe that Avery was the only person who could ignite that kind of joy in the small dog.

I wasn't the only one waiting for the little border collie to become himself again. I'd caught Papa looking closely at Beau's tail, trying to see if it was injured in some way, just as I had. But his examination didn't reveal any kind of physical disability either. Beau's lack of tail wagging was becoming a topic of conversation in Kingdom. Everyone seemed to be waiting for some kind of breakthrough.

Callie came into the restaurant about four thirty, just in case we got busy, and Lizzie prepared her usual fare. A few minutes before five, the doors opened and people began to file in. Working together all week seemed to have bonded them more tightly together. Before long the restaurant was full. Even though our gathering wasn't over a pleasant situation, the atmosphere was joyous. As I looked around the room at these lovely, warm-hearted people, I felt honored to be one of them.

We weren't able to close the doors until after eight thirty. It didn't take long to clean up, since Noah was there to help. Papa offered to carry plates to the kitchen in spite of his legs hurting. But Noah found a way to reject his offer without making Papa feel bad. By a little after nine, the dining room was spotless and the last dish had been washed.

"I feel funny leaving you two here alone," I said to Noah and Lizzie. "Will you be safe?"

Noah smiled. "We'll be fine. After what happened, I don't want Lizzie and Charity here by themselves at night until these people have been caught. Besides, I don't have time to work at the house right now anyway. Rebuilding the church comes first."

"But what if they try to burn your house again?" I asked.

"I'm pretty confident no one will risk doing something like that after what they did to our church," Noah said. "But Jonathon and Roger have volunteered to keep a close watch on it since the house sits so close to the turnoff."

"Wouldn't they be pretty stupid to come back to town?" Lizzie asked.

He nodded. "I doubt they'll come anywhere near us for a while, but I can't take a risk. I won't leave you here alone, Lizzie. I just won't."

"Why don't Hope and I remain here too?" Papa said. "We've got cots at the shop."

Noah slapped Papa on the back. "We really appreciate the offer, Samuel, but I don't think that's necessary. Aaron also volunteered to stay in town at night until things settle down. He intends to leave the store lights on so the street doesn't look so deserted."

"I still think it would be a good idea for us to stay," I said. "If anyone does make it past our borders, maybe a show of strength will force them to turn around and leave. The idea of you, Lizzie, and Charity here by yourselves doesn't sit right with me."

"Well, remember that the road is being watched," Noah said, sounding doubtful. "You two would certainly be more comfortable at home."

"The driver of the red truck got past them the other night," I replied. "I'm sorry, but that really worries me. And what if

Jonathon or Roger do see strangers headed into Kingdom? By the time they find additional help the way the elders have asked them to, these men could easily throw another Mol . . . Mol . . ."

"Molotov cocktail," Noah said, smiling. "It's up to you. Stay if you want, but we're not asking you to."

"Then it's settled," Papa said.

"What's settled?" Ebbie asked from where he was standing in the doorway. My heart fluttered when I saw him. He'd obviously cleaned up after working all day. He looked so handsome, and for once his hair was combed. I was pretty sure it wouldn't stay in place long. Funny thing was, I'd begun to like his chaotic locks. Lizzie told me that out in the world, men actually paid a lot of money to have their hair styled just like Ebbie's. I found it funny, but somehow knowing that made him look even better.

"What are you doing here?" Noah asked.

"I'm going to stay in town tonight," he said. "I don't want you three here by yourselves."

Lizzie burst out laughing. "I guess I should have stayed open. You people just won't go home!"

"Well, not for a while anyway," Ebbie said. "For some reason, I feel I'm supposed to be here. So here I am."

"I'm afraid the floor is a little hard," Noah said. "We've got blankets . . ."

Ebbie waved his hand at Noah. "No need. I brought a sleeping bag and a pillow."

"Hope, why don't you stay in the spare bedroom?" Lizzie said. "I'm sure it will be more comfortable than your cot."

I started to protest, but Papa interrupted. "I think that is a splendid idea."

"But I don't want you to be alone downstairs," I said.

"He won't be alone," Ebbie said. "Samuel and I will bunk together in the dining room. That way we can keep an eye on the street."

"Thank you, Ebbie," Papa said with a smile. "That sounds like a good idea, as long as Noah and Lizzie don't mind all this company."

"We'd love to have every single one of you stay with us," Lizzie said, chuckling. "You're all such good friends. We appreciate your thoughtfulness more than we can say."

"If I'm going to sleep here again tonight, I want to get a few things from the shop," I said. "Beau needs his blanket, and I'd like to get my quilt so I can work on it when we're not busy. I'll get the cot and a blanket for you too, Papa."

"I am afraid it is too much for you to carry, Daughter. I will come with you."

"Let me go, Samuel," Ebbie said. "You rest your legs."

"I would appreciate that, Brother Miller," Papa said.

Papa wasn't the kind of man to let another man do things for him, so either his legs hurt more than usual or he wanted Ebbie and me together. I suspected the latter but hoped that wasn't the case.

"Thanks, Ebbie, but I don't need any help," I said. "The cot is light, and everything else will fit into one bag."

"I don't believe you should be outside alone," he said firmly. "I'm coming. No arguments."

"All right, but the shop is so close, I'm sure there's no danger."

"Hope, quit arguing," Papa said, frowning. "Either Ebbie goes with you or I do."

I sighed. "All right. I guess I could use some help carrying everything back." I smiled at Ebbie. "Thanks for the offer. I appreciate it." We'd started toward the front door when Lizzie called out my name.

"Hope, wait a minute. Take this flashlight with you. It's getting dark outside."

I thanked her and grabbed the light. Suddenly, I remembered something. "Is Leah in town? It might be best if she didn't stay in her apartment alone tonight."

"She won't be," Noah said. "She's staying with Lizzie's parents for a few days. Then she's traveling to Topeka to see her family. You don't need to worry about her." He looked up at the clock on the wall. "I'm supposed to drive her over to Matthew and Anna's."

"I thought Leah had a car," Papa said.

"She does," Noah replied, "but Levi is tuning it up before she drives all the way to Topeka."

"I had no idea Levi was a mechanic," I said.

Noah grinned. "Seems funny that someone so quiet, who loves spending every moment he can at the church, can make any motor he touches run like new. My brother has the kind of mind that can figure out how almost everything works. He started fixing our tractor engines when he was only ten. It's a gift, I guess."

"Enough about Levi," Lizzie said. "You need to get going. Leah's probably waiting for you."

Noah smiled at his wife. "I feel a lot better leaving for a while knowing you'll have protection."

Lizzie snapped her fingers. "Wait a minute," she said. "I've got an apple pie for you to take with you. Mother loves them."

Noah rubbed his chin. "Hmm. I may have to stay a little bit longer than I planned to help them with that pie."

Lizzie grinned. "I'd better send two pies then. You think one slice is a quarter of a pie."

"You mean it isn't?" he asked innocently.

Ebbie and I laughed while Lizzie rolled her eyes.

"I suppose those are the only two pies you have," Papa grumbled.

"You know me better than that, Samuel," Lizzie said teasingly. "There's plenty more. As soon as I get Noah on his way, I'll bring you pie and coffee. How about that?"

"I suppose that would suit me just fine." Papa winked at me.

I went over and hugged him around the neck. "By the way," I whispered in his ear, "I know what you're up to, and it won't work. Ebbie and I are only friends. So stop it."

I let him go, and he gave me his most innocent look. Shaking my head, I grabbed the large flashlight Lizzie handed me. Once Ebbie and I got outside, we were happy to have it. The small porch light outside the restaurant didn't glow very brightly, and although Aaron had the lights on in the general store, they didn't do much to illuminate my side of the street. For some reason, he hadn't turned on the streetlight yet. I kept the flashlight's beam shining in front of us as we made our way down the sidewalk.

Walking late at night in Kingdom was usually peaceful because the streets were deserted. In the spring, the scent of honeysuckle permeated the air, but sadly, tonight a burnt odor lingered from the fire. It wasn't just the smell of destruction that hung over our town; there was also a pall of innocence lost. We were vulnerable. Kingdom's founders had sought refuge from the world, but the world had entered anyway. Ebbie was quiet as we made our way to the quilt shop, and I wondered if he was thinking the same thing.

He opened the door when we reached the shop. Like most businesses in Kingdom, our front door was almost never locked. In fact, even though there actually was a lock on the door, I had no idea where the key was. I swung the beam from my flashlight toward the counter where our oil lamp sat. Laying the flashlight down, I reached under the counter for matches. Suddenly I heard an odd noise behind me and turned to see Ebbie lying on the floor. Before I could react, someone grabbed me. A hand went over my mouth while an arm encircled my waist. I tried to cry out.

"Shut up right now." The man's voice was full of anger. "You give me a hard time and you'll be sorry."

My mind couldn't accept what was happening. Moments before I'd questioned whether Kingdom was still a refuge from the world. Now I knew the answer.

CHAPTER 20

Although it was hard to see anything in the dark room, I could make out Ebbie's body lying motionless. Was he dead? I couldn't help him. I couldn't move.

"We're walkin' out the back door together," the voice said with a snarl. "If you fight me or make any noise, I'll snap your neck. You got it, girlie?"

Unable to speak, I nodded. The man grabbed the flashlight and began pushing me toward the back of the shop. The thought flashed through my mind that if we left the store, my fate would be sealed. As he kicked open the rear door, I bit his hand as hard as I could. His grip relaxed as he yowled with pain. I took the opportunity to push away from him and run. But before I could get far, he seized me from behind and I fell to the floor. He grabbed my wrists and sat on top of me.

The flashlight, which had dropped to the floor beside me, provided enough light for me to see my attacker. It was Tom Ford, the sheriff's son. He lowered his face down close to mine, and I could detect the stench of stale cigarettes and something else. Liquor. A girl I'd known in school had a father who drank, and his breath had smelled the same way.

"You try that once more, and I'll kill you before you have a chance to regret it. Understand?"

He let go of one of my wrists and slapped me hard across the mouth. I could taste blood. Fear kept me from being able to speak so I nodded to let him know I wouldn't try to fight him again.

"Stop bawlin'. No one is here to feel sorry for you." He grabbed my wrist and stared at me. "I saw you lookin' at me the other day. You probably wonder what real men are like, don't you? You don't got nothin' around here except them wimpy pretty boys. Tonight you're gonna find out what you been missin'."

"No," I said, finally finding my voice. "Please. Please don't do this."

"Why don't you cry out to that God of yours?" Tom said, his face inches from mine. "See if He'll help you. I bet He won't. No one's here. No one listenin' to you at all." He cackled, and his laugh made my blood run cold. "If there was a God, He'd strike me dead, and He isn't, is He? You people need a big dose of reality, and tonight you're gonna get yours."

He pulled me to my feet and took a gun out of his pocket, aiming it right at me. Then he yanked off my prayer covering. "Take your hair down," he ordered.

With trembling fingers I removed the pins and ribbon that held my bun in place. Then I shook my hair out.

"That looks better." He swung me around and stuck the barrel of the gun in my back. "Now get goin'. We're not waitin' around here so one of your Mennie friends can come to your rescue." He sniggered. "'Course, they won't help you none. They're too busy hidin' behind all that goody-goody religious junk. You're on your own, girlie." He picked up the flashlight and shoved it at me. "You keep that light in front of us. Drop it, and I'll drop you."

I held the flashlight tightly, the beam shaking in my trembling hands. Then he pushed me out the back door and toward the trees that surrounded our town. We were almost to the tree line when I saw his truck. It was familiar. Red, with a dent in the passenger side door.

"You . . . you tried to run me down on the road."

"Sorry about that," he said, keeping his voice low. "If I'd seen how good lookin' you was that first day, I would have tried harder not to ruin the merchandise. I saw it was you the other day though. You and some Mennie man. If it weren't for my daddy comin' to your rescue, me and my friend Todd woulda had you then. I didn't like havin' to wait, but it was worth it. You won't get away this time."

"Did . . . did you kill Avery?" I had no desire to make him angry, but I had to know.

He actually hesitated a moment. "Didn't mean to kill that old man. We was just playin' with him." The slight tinge of regret in his voice disappeared with his next statement. "Stupid old guy shoulda just stayed on the road. We wasn't gonna run into him. He ran himself off the road. It was his own dumb fault."

I could have pointed out that Avery had no way to know that, just as I hadn't when I'd faced Tom's truck barreling right for me. But my words would have been lost on him.

"You were in Kingdom the other night," I said. It wasn't presented as a question, but just a statement of fact. I knew it was him.

He hooted as if I'd just said the funniest thing he'd ever heard. "I was lookin' for you. Didn't plan to take you though. Not then. Had to check on somethin' and see if I could get into town without too much trouble. Trial run, I guess. Easy as pie. After that, I knew I could come back whenever I wanted. Wasn't sure where to find you tonight, but my daddy said you worked in the quilt store so I headed here. Nice of you to keep it unlocked for me. Even more considerate of you to walk right in like you did."

I didn't feel like talking to him, but for some reason I couldn't shut up. My emotions were swinging out of control. "If . . . if you were just looking for me, why did you set our church on fire?"

He guffawed. I was beginning to realize that Tom Ford was either insane or on some kind of drugs. His eyes were wild and his physical actions jerky and uncontrolled. "I'd like to take credit for that, but it weren't me or my friends. Only fire we started was at that Mennie house on the edge of town."

I wasn't really listening to him, since there was no way I could believe a word he said. However, if I could keep him talking, maybe I could stall him long enough that someone would find us. Before it was too late for Ebbie. And for me. I dug my heels in, unwilling to reach the truck. If he got me inside, all would be lost.

"H-how did you get into town tonight?" I asked, my voice sounding small and shaky. I hated it, but my entire body was trembling, and I couldn't control it. "We have people watching the road."

He laughed, his tone cold and harsh. "It was a little harder than the other night. I had a plan to distract your little friend sittin' out there, but he helped me by fallin' asleep. Great protection you people got." He snorted. "Tonight took a little more effort. That Mennie won't be watchin' nothin' for a long, long time."

"Oh no. Jonathon. Did you . . . did you . . ."

"Kill him? Don't know. Don't care."

We were almost to the truck when the fear that had enveloped me began to dissipate, and I heard Ebbie's voice speaking clearly in my mind. *"Do we try to protect ourselves, or do we walk through the crowd because we believe God is actually with us?"* I began to say the only thing that came to me. "'No weapon that is formed against thee shall prosper. No weapon that is formed against thee shall prosper. No—'"

"Stop it," Tom hissed. "Stop callin' on your made-up God. You do that again and I'll—"

"You'll what?"

Tom whirled around, keeping his grip on me. I swung the flashlight toward the voice. Ebbie stood there, staring at us. A thin stream of blood ran down the side of his face.

Tom swore loudly. "I thought I took care of you, Mennie boy. Doesn't matter though, does it? What are you gonna do about it? You got a gun or anything?"

Ebbie shook his head, not taking his eyes off me. "I don't have a gun, but I won't let you take her away."

"And just what do you intend to do about it?"

Ebbie's eyes bored into mine for a moment. Then he

turned and glanced quickly behind him, toward the back of the restaurant. When he swung his gaze back to us, I saw something in his expression that made my heart drop to my feet. I suddenly remembered the story he'd told me about his mother being burned by hot grease, and in that moment, I knew exactly what he was planning to do. If he could get Tom to fire his gun, someone might come here and help me. But Tom wouldn't fire into the air the way Ebbie had when he'd tried to get help for his mother. Tom would shoot Ebbie.

"No!" I cried out. "No, Ebbie. Please."

"I love you, Hope. With all my heart. I always have, and I always will."

"No!" I tried to fight, tried to get away, but Tom's grip only tightened on me. He took the gun from my back and aimed it at Ebbie. Obviously, he hadn't figured out what Ebbie already had. All I could do was whisper "'No weapon that is formed against thee shall prosper.'"

"I don't think I'd do that if I were you."

I swung the flashlight to the right of Ebbie. I'd been so busy watching him that I hadn't seen Jonathon advance toward us. He'd been beaten badly. One eye was closed, and the other was swollen. He had blood on his cheek, and his left arm lay useless against his side. In his good hand he held his rifle, and it was leveled right at Tom. I felt the young man tense and the arm he held across my neck tightened, making it hard for me to breathe, let alone quote Scripture. All I could do was repeat the familiar verse over and over in my mind.

"A Mennie with a gun?" he said. "You gonna shoot me with that, Mennie boy? I thought you pansies don't like hurtin' people. Seems you're breakin' all them religious rules you made up."

"I don't know about that," Jonathon said, his voice thick with pain. "But I will not let you shoot my friend. And I won't let you hurt Hope."

"No, Jonathon," Ebbie said. "This isn't the way. Put the rifle down."

"Yeah, put the rifle down, Jonathon. Besides, if you try to shoot me, you're gonna kill this pretty little lady." Tom laughed. "Don't look to me like either one of you has a chance of stoppin' me."

"You don't understand something," Jonathon said, his voice flat and emotionless. "My rifle isn't for looks or because I think it makes me look like a man. I can shoot the wings off a fly if I want to, and I can take you down without touching Hope. Easy shot. Let her go, or I'll show you exactly what I mean."

I felt Tom's grip loosen a little. Then it tightened again. "Maybe I don't understand what a crack shot you are, Mennie, but I do understand somethin' else." He swung the gun back up and put it next to my head. "You shoot me and my finger will twitch. You might get me all right, but you're gonna kill her deader than a doornail. Now toss your rifle on the ground. Now!"

If Jonathon gave up his gun, Tom was either going to throw me into his truck and take off, or Ebbie was coming after me in an attempt to get help. Tom would certainly shoot him. Maybe both of them. My eyes locked on to Jonathon's, and I could see in his face that he knew how serious our situation was. Almost imperceptibly, his focus slid down to the big heavy flashlight I had pointed toward him. When he gave me an almost indiscernible nod, I knew what he wanted me to do.

Although fear tried to put me back under its power, I prayed for courage and drew on every ounce of strength I had inside me. Without allowing myself to think about it, I swung the flashlight up and hit Tom in the face. When his hold on me released, I fell to the ground. Then I aimed the light right into his eyes, trying to blind him. Everything seemed to be moving in slow motion. I saw Tom point his gun at Jonathon, and I screamed. At the same time, Ebbie yelled and ran toward me.

Suddenly, a shot rang out. It frightened me so much, I dropped the flashlight. Someone cried out, and I screamed again. Who had Tom shot? I watched as Ebbie fell a few feet away from me. I reached for the flashlight, shining it at Tom as if it would protect us from his next bullet. The look on his face was a mixture of surprise and alarm. Then without warning, the gun fell from his hand, landing right next to me. He dropped to the ground and grabbed his shoulder. Blood poured out of a large wound.

All I could hear was an odd sound that seemed to go on and on. A wailing. It took several seconds before I realized it was coming from me. I scrambled to my feet. Ebbie! I ran over to him, falling on my knees next to his body.

"Ebbie? Ebbie?"

I heard a mumbling sound as he pushed himself up to his knees. "I-I'm okay. I stumbled over a rock."

"You weren't shot?"

"No. Jonathon shot Tom."

I swung the light toward Jonathon, who was standing in

the same spot, an odd look on his face. He shook his head. "It wasn't me. I didn't have time to pull the trigger."

"That's 'cause it was me."

The three of us looked behind us. Sheriff Ford stood there with his gun drawn, a terrible look on his face. "I wasn't sure until tonight that my boy was part of all the stuff happenin' in the county, although I suspected it."

He turned his head to look at me. "I knew he was the one who threatened you and that other guy on the road because I was followin' him. That's the real reason I showed up when I did. But when I confronted him he told me it was the only time he'd ever done somethin' like that. That he had nothin' to do with the rest of it. I wanted to believe him. I tried.

"But after the fire, I started worryin' again. That's why I followed him tonight. He's not the only one who's been up to no good. His rotten friends are behind a lot of it. Them boys is all goin' to prison, I promise you that."

"But . . . you just shot your own son," I said. "How could you—"

"He was gonna kill you," the sheriff said simply. "I had no choice. It had to stop. I couldn't let it go on anymore.

"It's my fault, you know. I taught him to despise God 'cause I was mad at Him for takin' my wife away. I went to church, and I tried to do everything right. Then she ups and runs off with our preacher."

He took a deep, shaky breath. "I pounded my hate into Tom for years. It was wrong. I just didn't realize." His voice broke. "I just didn't realize," he said again.

Tom moaned in pain, and I moved away from him. Sheriff

Ford came over and picked up Tom's gun, flinging it a few feet away. He knelt down to check on his son.

"You're gonna be okay, Tommy," he said. "Just a shoulder wound. Had to make sure you dropped your gun."

Tom seemed to be in too much pain to answer. The sheriff stood to his feet and faced us. I kept the flashlight focused on him.

"That's why you seemed reluctant to investigate the attacks," Jonathon said. "You were afraid Tom was involved."

The sheriff nodded. "I wish you'd quit shinin' that flashlight in my face, young lady. You're blindin' me. I'll turn on my headlights so we can see."

I noticed for the first time that Sheriff Ford's cheeks were wet with tears. I quickly clicked off the light. Within a few seconds, we were bathed in the glow of the sheriff's headlights. As Ebbie had suspected, the sound of a gunshot had gotten the attention of everyone in town. Papa and Lizzie appeared in the clearing, followed by Aaron. The sheriff got on his radio and called someone.

Papa hobbled over to me. "Are you all right, Hope? Did he hurt you?"

I shook my head and reached out for him. As Papa's arms went around me, I began to weep, and I couldn't stop.

CHAPTER 21

The next day I slept almost twelve hours. Jonathon and Tom were transported by ambulance to Washington. The paramedics treated Ebbie at the scene.

Along with lots of cuts and bruises, Jonathon suffered a broken arm and three cracked ribs, but he was going to be fine. Tom was recovering from his bullet wound and would be transported to jail once the doctor decided he was ready.

Sunday the church gathered together on the lawn in front of the spot where our building had once stood. Pastor Mendenhall talked about how the enemy had come into our town like a flood, but God had raised a standard against him. He spoke about forgiveness, healing, and peace. We prayed for the men who had terrorized our county. All of Tom's friends had been rounded up and put in jail. Sheriff Ford had turned in his badge and was being investigated for participating in the attacks as an accessory. We prayed for the sheriff too.

Papa and I visited Jonathon in the hospital. Although Papa still didn't see eye-to-eye with him in some areas, he recognized Jonathon's brave attempt to rescue me. He'd driven into town, almost passing out more than once. When he heard me scream, he'd raced to protect me instead of getting the help he needed.

Ebbie, who had been willing to give his life for mine, disappeared. When I asked about him, Pastor Mendenhall explained that Ebbie needed a few days away for fasting and prayer. Pastor assured me Ebbie was fine, he just wanted to spend some time with God. I understood that. God and I had some sessions together as well.

After a lot of prayer and contemplation, I came to the conclusion that two men I cared about had made different choices. One chose a gun and the other didn't. Both men were brave. Both men were willing to put themselves in danger for me. I loved them both for it, and I was unwilling to judge if one was right and one was wrong. I believed with my whole heart that God understood both choices and that His judgment was full of mercy, love, and grace.

But I did come to one definite decision. After spending time thanking God for his protection, I received the direction I'd been praying for. I finally knew what God wanted me to do. While Jonathon recovered and Ebbie prayed, I sat in the quilt shop and completed the wedding quilt. In the final square I added the name of the man I intended to marry. When it was finished, I folded it and put it in a box, planning to present it to the person whose name I'd stitched into the final square. I'd just put the box under the counter when Papa came in. He'd been over at the saddle and tack store with Herman.

"Daughter, Pastor Mendenhall is on his way here. He's asked to speak to us."

I nodded. Although I wasn't sure what our pastor wanted to say, I imagined he was checking to make sure Papa and I were all right, since we'd both been through a very traumatic experience. Of course, Pastor Mendenhall had too. It had taken him a few days of rest to recover from the smoke he'd inhaled in the fire.

The door opened and the pastor came inside the shop. "Hello, Hope," he said, smiling. "Your father told you I need to talk to both of you for a few minutes?"

"Yes, Pastor."

"Why don't we sit down." Papa pointed toward the table and chairs in the corner near the front door.

"Thank you. I'm still a little shaky on my feet. Sitting for a while sounds wonderful."

"Can I get you some lemonade?" I asked.

He shook his head. "No thank you, Hope, but I appreciate it."

We gathered around the table, and Papa and I waited for our pastor's words of consolation. But what came out of his mouth was something we couldn't possibly have prepared ourselves for.

"When I got up this morning, I found a letter shoved under my door at home," he began. He reached into an inside pocket and took out an envelope, which he put on the table in front of him. "I am not going to read it to you because there are a few things inside I feel I should keep to myself. However, the author of the letter asked me to deliver her message to certain people. That is what I'm doing right now."

"What do you mean, Pastor?" I said. "Who wrote this letter?"

Pastor Mendenhall touched the envelope with his long fingers. "Sophie Wittenbauer."

I frowned at him. "I'm sorry. I don't understand."

He smiled at me. "After I explain you still might not understand, but she has some things to say that are important for all of us to know. Even if we cannot comprehend how they could be true."

Papa and I glanced at each other. For the life of me, I couldn't figure out what our beloved pastor was talking about.

"I apologize," he said. "I am being very cryptic, and I do not mean to be."

"Why does Sophie need someone to talk for her?" Papa asked. "Where is she?"

"She is gone. Sophie has left Kingdom, and I am not sure she will ever return."

"She's gone?" I said. "Where did she go?"

"That I do not know." He sighed and shook his head. "Our church was not burned down by Tom Ford or any of his . . . companions. It was Sophie who set the fire."

I gasped. "What? What are you talking about?"

"Sophie was afraid that Jonathon was going to dissolve their association. More than anything in this world, she wanted to feel as if she belonged to something. She got it in her head that if the church caught on fire, we would blame the same people who burned the other churches. She was right, of course. To her way of thinking, if we really believed we were in danger, then the patrols would continue and Jonathon would remain in her life." He sighed deeply. "She did this in league with Tom Ford. That young man put the idea in her head."

My mind had gone numb. "Tom Ford? I don't understand."

"Tom and Sophie knew each other from school. When Tom saw her in town the day his father brought him here, he knew he could use her to get what he wanted. You. He used her anger at you, and her attraction to Jonathon, and she fell right into the trap. Tom realized she needed to feel important—a part of something. So he convinced her that he needed her. That she was special to him."

"But . . ." I couldn't come up with a coherent sentence. In my mind I saw Sophie talking to Tom through the window of the sheriff's car. Then I thought I saw her again at the fire, hiding from me as I came down the street.

"I know it is hard to believe," Pastor Mendenhall said.

"Wait a minute," Papa interjected. "How could Sophie and Tom meet to make plans? Tom did not have free access into Kingdom."

Pastor shook his head. "No, but nothing kept Sophie from walking across the fields and meeting him out on the road. There may be only one way to drive or ride into Kingdom, but anyone can walk here if they cut through farmland."

"So Sophie set the fire," I said. "It's so hard to believe."

"Yes, Tom taught her how to do it."

I frowned. "But Tom hurt Jonathon. Sophie would never have allowed that."

Pastor sighed. "Sophie's letter does not explain everything, I am afraid, but I think that the original idea was for Sophie to distract Jonathon or Roger whenever Tom wanted to get into town. Unfortunately—"

"Jonathon forbade Sophie to patrol with him," I finished.

He nodded. "She had no idea Tom planned to come into

town the night he came for you. As you say, she would have never let Tom attack Jonathon. He could have been killed."

How could this be true? Sophie had risked the pastor's life and the lives of others because she wanted some attention? Because she wanted to be near Jonathon? Anger flushed through me. "I can't believe it. Of all the selfish, self-centered things to do—"

"I know, I know," Pastor Mendenhall said. "The realization that people had been seriously hurt and could have been killed finally made her realize she needed help. She seems to be especially distraught that Jonathon was injured so badly."

"I thought there was something wrong about that fire," I said slowly. "The timing seemed wrong. You know, Tom told me he didn't set the church fire."

Pastor nodded. "He was telling the truth." He looked at us kindly. "I know you are having a hard time accepting this. Sophie knew we would. That is why she chose to go away."

"You could have died, Pastor," I said, unable to keep the frustration out of my voice. "Ebbie could have died. And Jonathon. And me."

"Yes, that is true. Thanks be to God for keeping us all safe."

"Do Sophie's parents know?" Papa asked.

"Yes. I went there first." He shook his head. "Sophie's life has not been easy. Her mother and father are not . . . loving. They seem almost glad to be rid of her." He paused, and I could see his great compassion for the girl who had almost taken his life through her own carelessness. My emotions swung between sympathy and rage.

"Will they call the police? Sophie's only seventeen."

"No, Hope. They will not. Sophie will turn eighteen in a

matter of days." He folded his hands together, almost as if he were getting ready to pray. "I thought very seriously about contacting the authorities myself, but I have decided to give Sophie a chance to change her life."

Papa cleared his throat. "But how will she get along, Pastor? She has no money."

"Actually, she does. She went to someone before she left and told them the truth. This person gave her money and helped her to get out of town." He smiled. "This may sound strange, but I believe Sophie will land on her feet. As I said, there are other things in this letter that I do not feel comfortable sharing. But if she follows through with her intentions, she will be fine."

There was no need for me to ask who had given Sophie the money she needed. I knew the answer. Lizzie had helped her just as I had helped Lizzie all those years ago. I wondered if one day Sophie would find the road back to Kingdom just as Lizzie had.

"As I said, I had my doubts about the fire," I repeated, trying to take in the reality of Pastor Mendenhall's revelations, "but the idea that Sophie was involved never crossed my mind."

"Sophie had unhealthy feelings for Jonathon," Pastor Mendenhall continued. "But in the end, she recognized that what she felt for him was not from the Lord. She was afraid that if she did not leave our midst, those urges would continue. In truth, I think her decision was very courageous."

I stared at him, wondering how he could call Sophie's actions brave. She'd left our town with the task of rebuilding our church and our shattered emotions. As if reading my mind, he reached over and patted my hand.

"Losing our building has brought us together," he said, his eyes twinkling. "Sometimes, overcoming adversity can make people stronger. I predict that will happen in this instance. Besides, I believe we are reconstructing more than just a building. We are the real church, you know. As we work together, I believe God will use this experience to finally heal the fractures of the past. A new church. A new spirit."

I loved the analogy and told him so. "Have you told Jonathon about Sophie yet?" I asked.

He shook his head and sighed. "No, and I am not looking forward to it. Jonathon is the kind of person who will try to take the blame for Sophie's choices. I am praying that I can help him to see clearly that none of this was his fault. He is a virtuous man. A man of passion. Unfortunately, sometimes passion clouds our thinking." He chuckled. "Jonathon reminds me of the apostle Peter. He was impatient and full of zeal too."

"Pastor, may I ask why you came to talk to us personally?" I still wasn't sure why he was sharing Sophie's letter with us, because Sophie disliked me so intensely.

"First of all, I have no intention of addressing this from the pulpit. I feel that talking one on one to our members might keep them from reacting with anger. But more importantly, I came to you because Sophie asked me to."

My jaw dropped open. "But . . . but I don't understand. Sophie hated me. Why would she ask you to speak to me?"

He picked up the envelope on the table and pulled out the letter inside. "There is one part of Sophie's letter I feel comfortable reading to you."

He unfolded what looked to be about five or six pages. When he got to the page he wanted, he folded the rest and put them back into the envelope. Then he took his glasses out of his pocket and balanced them on the end of his nose. He peered at me over the top of the lenses. "If you do not mind, I will paraphrase some of what Sophie wrote. She was ashamed of her weakness with the English language and was determined to better her education after she left Kingdom. I would feel more comfortable reading her words as if they were written correctly."

I nodded my agreement.

He cleared his throat and began to read:

"If you would speak to Hope Kauffman for me, I would appreciate it. She is one of the reasons I found the courage to leave Kingdom. I know she thinks I do not like her, but she is wrong. All I ever wanted was to be just like her. Hope is smart and skilled, able to run a business and have friends. She is loved by everyone. I may never be able to live up to her example, but I intend to try. Maybe if I was more like Hope, Jonathon would have cared for me. Will you please tell her that I am sorry for the way I treated her? All I can do is pray that someday she will forgive me. She has no idea what it is like to wonder what life would be like if you could be someone else, and I have spent my whole life wanting to be Hope. Please let her know that I wish her and Jonathon the best. I know they will be very happy."

I wiped tears from my eyes. All this time Sophie had been comparing herself to me? If only I'd reached out to her in friendship. Jonathon had been right. I should have tried again.

"Do her words bring you any comfort, Daughter?" Papa studied me with concern.

"Some, Papa," I said, sniffing. "I just wish I'd tried harder to be her friend. Maybe none of this would have happened."

Pastor Mendenhall grunted. "No, Hope. Sophie chose her own path. I do not believe you could have made a difference."

I sighed. "But I will always wish I'd tried harder."

"The road behind us only leads us the wrong way, Hope," Pastor Mendenhall said softly. "It's time everyone in Kingdom start looking to the future." He put the page he'd read with the others in the envelope. "I am glad I shared this letter with you." He slid the envelope back into his pocket and stood to his feet. "I must be on my way now. There are others I must visit."

When I stood up, the pastor reached for my hands. I held them out and he clasped them. "Pray for her, Hope. Keep Sophie in your heart and in your prayers. She is one of ours, and I believe she will come home to us someday."

"I will certainly pray for her, Pastor," I said.

He shook hands with Papa and left. His meeting with us had left me feeling a little drained.

"I hope everyone will be as forgiving as our pastor," Papa said as we stood at the front door and watched Pastor Mendenhall walk across the street. "I am fearful that some folks will not understand."

"I believe our prayers will help."

"I am sorry to engage you in another serious conversation, Hope," Papa said. "But after speaking with Herman, there is something I must say to you."

The seriousness in his tone made my heart sink. What now? Were the days in my beloved quilt shop coming to an end sooner than I'd anticipated? "What is it, Papa?"

He sat back down at the table, and I joined him. "The past few days have helped me clarify my thoughts in several areas," he said slowly. "First of all, I realize how close I came to losing you." He reached out and took my hand. "But as I pondered that, I also became aware that God took care of you, and in the end, you are not really mine to lose. God has given you a life, and that life belongs to Him." He squeezed my hand and blinked back tears.

"I will always be your loving daughter, Papa. No matter what."

He smiled. "I know that you love me, Hope. I have tried to keep you close to me because I was afraid. Afraid of losing you like I lost your mother. Unfortunately, my actions were out of fear, not out of faith. It was wrong. You are a mature young woman. Old enough to make your own choices."

"What are you saying, Papa?"

"I am going to run the saddle and tack store," he replied, "but you will run the quilt shop yourself. If you want to."

"Oh, Papa, it would mean so much to me. I love this place. I feel so close to Mama here."

He let go of my hand and patted my cheek. "I do too. You will do a wonderful job. I have no doubt about it. And if you ever need help, I will be right across the street."

I leaned over and hugged him. "I will always need my Papa."

"And I will always need my sweet Hope," he whispered.

I sat back, took a tissue from a nearby box, and dabbed

at my wet eyes. "You said you found clarity in several areas, Papa. Was there something else?"

He sighed deeply. "Yes. When you were in danger, I wasn't there. I thank God for protecting you, but I saw that there were two other men willing to put themselves in harm's way to keep you safe when I couldn't." He ran his hands over his legs. "These old legs weren't in any shape to run to your aid. As strange as it sounds, knowing two good men stood in my place helped me to see that you don't need me to take care of you anymore."

"But Papa . . ."

He shook his head. "No, Daughter. Not only do I speak the truth, but it brings peace to my mind. One day you will marry, and that man should be the one who stands first in line as your defender."

"Papa, you said *two* good men. Are you saying that you've changed your mind about Jonathon?"

He smiled. "Once I realized I had to release you to live your own life, I was able to see him through your eyes instead of through my judgmental way of thinking. I have not changed my beliefs, Hope. I still stand by our doctrine of peace to all men. But I realize now that sometimes standing firm in what we believe takes more than words. It may require everything we have—everything we hold dear."

"Yes, I know," I said quietly. "I've always admired you because you won't back down from what you think is right. Even when others disagree or when circumstances and emotions make it look like you might be wrong. Real faith is believing God no matter what." I shook my head. "I've seen real courage expressed in the past few days, Papa, by people like you standing unbroken in faith. And I've seen the deliverance of God. I know He will stand by His promises, and I am determined to trust Him with all of my life, not just part of it."

My father nodded. "I believe that too, Daughter. Sometimes walking through the fire burns away the useless things in our lives and refines what is left." He got up and came over to me, wrapping his arms around me. "And what I see in you is gold, my darling daughter. Pure gold."

"Thank you, Papa," I whispered. When he released me, I went to the window and gazed out at our town. "I've also come to understand that we will all make choices in our walk with God. Some choices will be right. Some may be wrong. God doesn't ask us to understand everything. He just asks us to keep our hearts right. In the end, I believe we will be judged only by what we knew and how we responded to it. The things we didn't understand won't matter."

"I know what I believe. I believe I have a very wise daughter."

"Thank you, Papa." I turned to look at him. "I finished my wedding quilt, and I intend to give it to someone. Do you want to see the final square?"

Papa gazed at me for a moment, and then he shook his head. "I know whatever name is sewn into the last square is the right one. The man you intend to give the quilt to should see it before I do."

I stood up and took the box from under the counter. "Will you watch the shop for a while?"

"I would be happy to do that, Daughter." He smiled. "Go with God, my Hope. I will be praying for you."

I put the box under my arm and left. After securing it

under the carriage seat and waiting for Beau to jump up next to me, I flicked the reins, urging Daisy into the street. Summer was approaching, and the afternoons were growing warmer. Thankfully, a nice breeze cooled the air and kept the ride pleasant.

Finally I reached my destination. I was tying Daisy up to a fence post when I saw him. He was walking from the barn and noticed me watching him. After hesitating a moment, he came over to where I waited. Beau left my side and ran up next to him. He bent down to pet Beau before joining me at the fence.

"It's good to see you, Hope," he said slowly, looking surprised. "But why are you here?"

"I brought you something." I went back to the buggy and took the box out from under the seat. I walked over and handed it to him.

"What is it?"

I smiled. "It's a wedding quilt. I started it months ago, but I finally completed it today. You probably know that usually the names of the bride and groom are stitched into the final square. I thought you might like to see how I finished it."

He opened the box and took out the quilt, turning it over until he found the last square. He ran his fingers over the names. "I . . . I don't understand."

"I don't completely understand it either," I said, "but until recently I've never had to really look at myself—or at what I believe. What this town has gone through has helped me to understand some things. Like what faith is and what's important. Who I am and what God wants for me. I've learned that all I have to do is be the person God created me to be.

With my strengths and even with my weaknesses." I sighed. "Papa has always tried to protect me, and in many ways he ran my life. The truth is, I let him do it. It was easier that way. I didn't have to think for myself or make any decisions that were uncomfortable for me."

"What's changed?"

I sighed and looked past him at the green wheat blowing gently in the breeze. "I've watched people, good people, struggle in their walk with God. Although I couldn't figure out exactly who was right and who was wrong, I saw real bravery. Real conviction. In the end I realized that none of us has all the answers, and that's okay. God doesn't expect perfection. He just wants us to trust Him. We each have a road to follow. My road may not be another's, but if we truly love Him, He'll lead us to the special place He's prepared for us. I'm ready to trust my instincts and believe God is guiding my steps. I don't have to know everything, and I don't have to be right all the time. I just have to take that next step of faith."

"And what does that have to do with us?"

I gazed into his deep brown eyes. "You were willing to lay down your life for me. When you did that, I saw Jesus in you. And I knew. I knew you were the man I wanted to spend the rest of my life with."

Ebbie shook his head. "Standing by my beliefs could have cost you your life."

"I know that. You love me, Ebbie. Really love me. Yet you would have sacrificed yourself—and even me—to stay true to what you believe God wanted. He's truly first in your heart. That's the kind of man I can give my life to. The kind of man I can trust to make our lives pleasing to Him. That is, if you'll have me."

His eyes narrowed as he studied me. "What about Jonathon?"

"He's a good man who also did what he thought was right. This isn't about one of you being better than the other. It never was a contest. This is about finally realizing that you are the man God has for me, and I am the woman He has for you. After you broke up with me I tried to forget about us, but my heart wouldn't let you go. I know now that it was because God himself had placed you there."

His eyes flushed with tears. "I feel the same way. But when I thought you were in love with Jonathon—"

"You released me, and you took the blame for our breakup. You would rather paint yourself in a negative light than have the fault fall back on me. I should have realized right then that you loved me with the kind of unselfish love only God could inspire." I gazed deeply into his eyes. "When you look at me now, Ebbie, what do you see?"

A single tear rolled down his cheek as he nodded. "I see the kind of love that will last a lifetime."

"Any doubts?"

He frowned. "I may still talk about things you aren't interested in."

I laughed. "For some reason, I've become very interested in all kinds of topics. Especially ants. Such fascinating creatures. Did you know that ants actually have two stomachs?"

The corners of Ebbie's mouth twitched. "And where did you learn that?"

"I asked Leah for a book from the school library."

His quick smile warmed me inside. "Are you sure about this, Hope? I can't go through another broken engagement. I don't think my heart could stand it."

I held out my hand, and he took it. "No more broken engagements, Ebbie." I ruffled his hair with my other hand.

"You're messing up my hair."

"I know, but I like it that way."

"Have you spoken to Jonathon?"

"Yes. We talked in the hospital. He was hurt but gracious. More than anything, he wanted what was best for me. What would make me happy. In the end, he wished us both well."

Ebbie took a deep breath and handed me the quilt. Was he rejecting my proposal? Before I could ask his intentions, he got down on one knee and reached once again for my hand. "Hope, I love you. I have loved you ever since I first laid eyes on you. There is no one in this world for me but you. If you marry me, I will always keep God first in our lives, and I will love you forever. Hope Kauffman, will you marry me?"

"Yes, Ebbie Miller. I will marry you. And I will thank God every day that you are my husband."

I took my hand from his and put the quilt back in its box. Then we stood to our feet, and Ebbie kissed me gently. His kiss felt so right. So natural. When he let me go, we laughed at each other's tears.

He suddenly grabbed me and turned me around. "Hope, look," he said, his voice heavy with emotion.

I followed his gaze. Beau stared up sappily at us, his tail wagging so fast I could barely see it.

I leaned my head against Ebbie's shoulder. "It's a sign."

He nodded and kissed the top of my head. Then he reached

down and patted Beau. "God has given us beauty for ashes, the oil of joy for mourning, and the garment of praise for the spirit of heaviness."

My heart soared at his words, and I thanked God that I had finally found myself by looking into the deep brown eyes of a man with unkempt hair, a spirit that refused to be broken, and the kind of love in his heart that would bind us together with God for the rest of our lives.

Discussion Questions

1. At the beginning of *Unbreakable*, Jonathon Wiese expressed doctrinal views that differed from some of the other members of Kingdom Mennonite Church. Did you understand how he felt? Did you agree or disagree with him?

2. In the media there have been several reports of people vandalizing churches and religious graveyards. This kind of persecution seems to be increasing. What do you think fuels these kinds of attacks? How should people of faith respond?

3. Noah refused to help Jonathon and Roger guard the road to Kingdom. Did you agree with him? Why or why not?

4. Lizzie had a hard time trusting Roger because of the way he treated her and other Kingdom children when they were in school. Was she right to be wary of him,

or should she have simply accepted him without question? What would you have done?

5. Samuel was so opposed to Jonathon's views that he treated him with suspicion even after Jonathon rescued Hope from an attack on the road. Do you think Samuel treated Jonathon unjustly?

6. Should Ebbie have broken his engagement to Hope, or should he have fought for her?

7. Were you able to feel compassion for Sophie Wittenbauer, or did you dislike her for her selfish choices?

8. What about Sheriff Ford? Could you understand his bitterness toward the church after his wife ran away with his pastor? Have you witnessed anything like this in your own church? How can we avoid these hurtful incidents?

9. If the citizens of Kingdom had been more willing to fight back, would it have saved Avery's life? Should they have been more proactive?

10. How do you feel about the Mennonite belief in nonviolence? Do you understand the reasons they hold fast to this doctrine? Did reading *Unbreakable* change your mind?

11. What did you think about the different ways Jonathon and Ebbie chose to defend Hope's life?

12. Did Hope choose the right man to marry? Why or why not?

Acknowledgments

As always, my thanks to Judy Unruh, Alexanderwohl Church Historian in Goessel, Kansas. *Unbreakable* took us into new territory. Your encouraging words about my attempts to portray the struggle Mennonites face as they stand "unbreakable" in their nonviolent beliefs meant more to me than I can say. Thanks for hanging in with me through this literary journey. You're such a blessing.

To my dear friends Gus and Penny Dorado: Thank you for being there for me, answering my questions, and giving me a recipe for Amish ice cream!

To the "Girliebeans" who have lifted me up and encouraged me more times than I can count: I love you all. Thank you so much for being there.

To Raela Schoenherr and Sharon Asmus: You're my heroes. I thank God for you both.

To the employees of Bethany House and Baker Publishing: You've shown me through your support and encouragement that this isn't a one-woman show. It's a team effort. I'm so honored to be a part of such a great team.

Most important, I offer up humble thanks to my loving Father, who carefully orders my steps and keeps me from straying off the path He's planned for me. All I want is to honor Him.

Nancy Mehl is the author of thirteen books and received the ACFW Mystery Book of the Year Award in 2009. She has a background in social work and is a member of ACFW. She writes from her home in Wichita, Kansas, where she lives with her husband, Norman, and their puggle, Watson.

If you enjoyed *Unbreakable,* you may also like...

Lizzie Engel left her Mennonite hometown, her family, and her faith, vowing never to return. But false accusations, a stalker, and a string of anonymous threatening letters have left her with no other option but to run again—back to Kingdom, her hometown.

Inescapable by Nancy Mehl • ROAD TO KINGDOM # 1
nancymehl.com

In the picturesque Amana Colonies, family secrets, hidden passions, and the bonds of friendship run deeper than outsiders know. In each book of her Amana series, Judith Miller explores the life of a different young woman as she comes of age—and finds love—in this quiet community.

DAUGHTERS OF AMANA by Judith Miller
Somewhere to Belong, More Than Words, A Bond Never Broken

HOME TO AMANA by Judith Miller
A Hidden Truth, A Simple Change
judithmccoymiller.com